Praise for

WRECK

"*Wreck* wrecked me. Kirstin Cronn-Mills has a singular way of getting inside characters heads and making their stories come to life. This book will make you cry."

—Bill Konigsberg, award-winning
author of *The Music of What Happens*

"A provocative, unflinching, and emotionally-complex deep dive into mortality and loss while Tobin and her father grapple with almost unfathomable decisions. A wrenching and empathetic look at the tumultuous waters and seemingly bottomless grief that can interrupt an otherwise placid life."

—Amanda MacGregor, *Teen Librarian Toolbox*

"This book has heart and empathy as vast and deep as the Great Lake on which it's set."

—Geoff Herbach, award-winning
author of *Stupid Fast* and *Hooper*

"Kirstin Cronn-Mills has written an elegiac novel about friendship, family, and yes, terminal illness. She asks readers to walk alongside Tobin and her father as they navigate the grief, pain, and white-hot rage of a life ending too soon. *Wreck* isn't just good—it's utterly beautiful."

—Bryan Bliss, author of *We'll Fly Away*

"A realistic take on ALS, caregiving, loss, and loyalty, with an appealing main character."

—*Kirkus Reviews*

WRECK

WRECK

KIRSTIN CRONN-MILLS

Sky Pony Press
New York

This book is for you, Keith Arnold Cronn (1943–2011).
I miss and love you every day.

This book is also for you, Grover,
after all this time. And always.

WRECK

NOVEMBER 10

I make the rock cairn at the edge of the water. I picked them specially—flat, stackable—from farther up the shore. These rocks don't exist in my backyard. Here it's just sand.

Today is the anniversary of the wreck of the *Edmund Fitzgerald*, an iron ore freighter that left from here and sank a day later, killing all twenty-nine people on board. Dad would have remembered it like he always did, by playing the famous Gordon Lightfoot song as many times as I am old—eighteen this year. I don't know if other people in Duluth, or other people who live along Lake Superior, remember this day. But he always did.

So I'm remembering him remembering his favorite ship as he played his favorite song.

The cairn shifts a little as I place the top rock, but it holds. Five in the stack. One for him, one for me, one for Ike. One for the future. One for the past.

I had no idea that pieces of my memories would just . . . drift away. Like the ashes he became. They float off, and you know you'll never get them back.

Silly little things. Which side of the door he left his running shoes on. Which days he wanted peanut butter on his toast, and which days he wanted rhubarb jam. Stuff I didn't pay much attention to in the first place—but I should have.

Those things drift out from the shore, and all that's left is the big stuff. The color of his hair (blondie-brown, a bit of white by the end). The color of his eyes (gorgeous blue, the same shade his lake sometimes is). How he looked when he bounced out the door, on his way to save people. How tired he was when he came home. How he smiled when I told him about my day.

I have the important parts. But the ashes—the daily details—wash away.

It hurts.

Dad's Big Book of Advice #1
(in no particular order)
When you're upset, just imagine a T. rex
trying to make a bed.

BEFORE
MARCH 15

The words jump off the page at me: SCHOLARSHIP APPLICATION.

It's the last ten minutes of the day. I've been staring at it in every class.

SCHOLARSHIP APPLICATION.

To my dream college, the Colorado School of Visual Arts. To which I am already admitted. To which, if I don't get a scholarship or find a sugar daddy, or get struck by an act of God, I'm not going to get to go.

I brought the admissions letter to show Mrs. King, my guidance counselor. She hugged me, which is probably off-limits, but it's not every day you get into the college you wanted.

Now all I have to do is make a portfolio. Which isn't tough—yes, it's tough to make a *good* portfolio, one that's organized into a coherent narrative—but it's not tough to make a lot of photographs. I do that all the time. But the portfolio has to be our origin story. Which I suppose everyone has, but mine is just . . . boring? Dumb? Average?

I was born in Duluth on September 22 seventeen and a half years ago. I'm an only child because my parents didn't get along, according to my mom. According to my dad, I'm an only child because you should stop when you've achieved perfection. I've got friends, but I'm also a loner who likes to be quiet and watch the world. I live on a tiny sliver of land sticking out into Lake Superior, and I go to an unremarkable high school. I like the color dark blue, starry nights on the beach, and dreaming about living someplace that's not so damn cold. I have no superpowers except the ability to take photos, and even those aren't very good most of the time.

I have zero idea how to translate these facts into photographs.

My phone buzzes right as I'm walking to my locker. I throw the miscellaneous school crap into my locker after I fold up my application and stick it in my back pocket. Then I head toward the bus stop, pulling out my phone.

Come to the hospital after school.

I go to a different bus stop. It's such a pain in the ass to only have one car.

Nobody wants to get a text that says *come to the hospital after school*. But maybe it's less scary if your dad is a paramedic.

My dad's origin story is much less boring than mine.

He was born in Duluth, Minnesota, as the fifteenth-ish generation descended from the voyageur Daniel Olivier and his badass wife, Mariette, both in the fur trapping party of the guy who founded Duluth: Daniel Greysolon, Sieur du Lhut. My dad grew up knowing his family had lived in the area for 340 years, give or take, which is longer than the United States has existed. He got through high school as the class clown and had a million girlfriends, because he wrote them all poems. Then he got a hotshot scholarship to study English at Columbia, so he moved to New York City, finished college, published two books, then couldn't get editors to like any more. He got sick of the big city, moved back to Duluth, and put his boundless energy into running marathons and helping others. On the day he finished paramedic training, he met a cute girl five years younger than he was. They got married and had a baby, then she moved to Paris for work and never came home. He kept writing in notebooks that stacked up under the stairs. His superpower is peeling people off roads and tree trunks, as well as out of wrecked cars. He took care of the little girl the mom left behind, who grew into a quiet-but-sassy, cautious, boring, artistic teenager who tries not to be crabby.

He's gonna tell me that it will be impossible to make a living with my work. Look what happened to him. And I'm going to tell him that I at least get to try, just like he did.

I get off the bus and head to the emergency department, expecting my dad to meet me at the door. His rig is parked there, but I don't see him. So I start with Alice, the receptionist. She and my dad used to date when I was in elementary school. She's pretty, with big eyes and gray streaks in her dark hair.

"Hey, Alice."

She looks up and smiles when she sees it's me. She was always nice. "Hey, Tobin. Whatcha doin' here?"

"Got a text from my dad. Know where he is?"

"Uh, nope. Just got here." She looks behind me toward the door. "He's not with his rig?"

"Doesn't seem to be."

A nurse in dark-blue scrubs with a very serious face comes out to hand her a folder. Alice turns to him. "Have you seen Stephen Oliver?"

The nurse points inside. "He's in here." Then he goes back into the emergency department.

"Hmm." Alice looks at her computer, and a cloud crosses her face. "He's in room twenty-two, just around the corner and to the right."

"He's helping someone in room twenty-two?"

She writes down "22" on a slip of paper. "No." She reads the screen. "He's a patient."

I take the paper from her as my scalp bursts into tingles. "Thanks."

"I'm sure he's fine—or he will be, anyway." She smiles. "He's your happy-go-lucky dad. Nice to see you, Tobin."

"Yeah, uh . . . you, too." I practically run around the corner.

My dad is the one who fixes people who are hurt. Not the one who's hurt.

My aunt Allison sees me first, because Dad's messing with his phone. "Hi, sweetheart." She reaches for me, but she can see I really don't want to be hugged. "Thanks for coming."

"What happened?" I try for a smile, but my tingly scalp is now leaping off my head.

Dad can see I'm trying to be cool but failing. "Just a broken wrist, honey. Nothing more than that."

Allison reaches out to stop him, but Dad evades her and gets off the bed. When he reaches me, I let him hug me with one arm, and I hug him with both my arms, tighter than I mean to. He groans because I bump his left arm with the broken wrist, but I hug him even tighter.

I do not like this picture, but I take in the details, because that's what I do. He does not belong on a gurney, in the middle of medical supplies and equipment. He's the helper, not the guy being helped.

He tries to smooth things over. "I fell down a flight of stairs at work, right around two. School was almost out, and I didn't want to bother you until you were free. Better now?" He pulls back to look at my face, and I can see the concern in his eyes, even with the pain. "It's not horrible. I won't need surgery."

"Get back on the bed. I can't imagine the doctor will like it if you're running around."

Allison reaches out for him again. "It wouldn't be helpful if you fell, especially before your cast is on."

"You two are pains in the butt." But Dad goes to the bed and climbs back up. It's obvious he's hurting. A lot.

A small dark-haired woman about Allison's age, also wearing dark-blue scrubs, comes in with a metal rolling table. On it are a bunch of packages that look like they contain bandages. "Cast time, dude." She bustles around and gathers a few more things before she brings the table over to Dad's bedside. "With what's coming up, we need to keep this sucker superstrong."

"What's coming up?" My scalp starts tingling again.

"Molly, not now." Dad's eyes shoot her some daggers, which I don't miss.

She looks at me, then at Dad. "How's the discomfort? We've got lots of room in your pain management, if you're hurting." She bustles in the awkward silence, taking rolls of casting material out of their packages. "Rate it from one to ten."

"Obviously you two know each other?" I glare at Dad.

"Tobin, this is Molly. She was an emergency department nurse, but now she's in orthopedics. We used to work together a lot. Molly, this is my daughter, Tobin. And to answer your question, the pain's a five, except when Tobin bumps me." He smiles, but I don't.

"A pleasure to meet you, Tobin." Molly also smiles in my direction, though she's busy with what's in her basin. "Your dad's one of the best paramedics out there. Shame it's not going to be the same."

"What's not the same?" Now my whole body's tingling.

Allison stands up and takes Molly by the elbow. "How about you come with me for a second?" She propels Molly out of the room, shutting the curtain as she goes. Like curtains keep out a lot.

"What does she mean, it's not going to be the same?" I fix Dad with a look.

Dad sighs. "We can talk after this, Tobin, okay? It's a long conversation, and it doesn't make sense to start it now. How about a dad joke?"

"No thanks." My insides are twisting like snakes.

He grins, trying to get me to smile back. "Too late. Two guys walked into a bar. The third one ducked." He laughs at himself.

"Ha ha ha." I give him a look. He quiets down. I don't say anything more, just look out the window. You can see a sliver of lake from here, between a couple buildings. Lake Superior is the centerpiece of this town—Duluth, Minnesota, wouldn't be anything without it.

What's not the same?

The words become a border around each object I look at, like some novelty photo frame in a gift store window: WHATSNOTTHESAME. Bent into a square around Molly's basin for whatever liquid she needs to make the cast work. Curved into an oval around scissors and instruments on the second shelf of the cart. Angled into a rectangle around the colored bins on the wall, labeled with anything else an ED room might need.

"Tobin?"

Teenagers keep secrets, not parents. But I don't have any—no older boyfriends, no weed in the closet, not even midnight candy bars under my bed. Seventeen years old and boring as dirt.

If I move a single hair, I will lose it.

"Honey, look at me. We'll work it out, all right?"

"We'll see." I keep my eyes fixed on that single sliver of lake. I am not good at this. My dad is the one who mends other people and cares about them. Not the one who needs to be mended and cared for.

The curtain clatters open again and it's my dad's ambulance partner, Rich. His face is smiling, but his eyes aren't.

"Medic 3464! What's the dealio? I hear there was a crash and burn. Better you than the whole rig." Rich is a big guy with a big heart and a big mouth who's never been quiet a day in his life. He was the best at throwing kids into the lake during barbecues on the dunes behind our house. The number of their rig is 3464.

Dad sighs. "No big deal, Medic 3464. Puts me off my game for a few days."

"But you'll be back when the cast comes off, right?" Rich pats my dad's foot like Dad might be losing it soon.

Dad glances at me, and Rich follows the glance. Then Dad answers. "Things are still up in the air."

"Oh. Okay." Rich closes off his face. "You know I'm here if you need me." And he disappears.

Allison and Molly come back in, and both of them immediately start chatting: hasn't the sun been nice, we'll have some strong April storms, when will they get Highway 2 into Wisconsin repaired, and on and on and on.

I don't say a word. To anyone. My dad joins in the chatter, keeping his eye on me and grimacing when Molly handles his wrist with a little too much force. Allison watches me, too.

I grab my camera out of my backpack, just for a place to put all the freakout I feel inside me.

His fingers jutting out from the cast.

Molly's hands on his cast-up wrist.

His feet, with shoes, on the bed.

A close-up of one foot. They all stare at me as I take that one.

Molly makes the cast too tight the first time, so Dad's hand turns purple and she has to cut off the whole thing and start again. By the time it's all over, nobody's in a good mood. Dad says his pain is up to a seven. I'm hungry. Allison can't stop tapping her foot. Finally, after the doctor discharges him— after a lengthy conversation about an accident victim Dad brought in last week—it's 7:30 and we can get out of there.

Allison drives us home in our car after we go to Walgreens for Dad's pain pills. She walked to the hospital from Canal Park, and she says she'll walk home, which isn't hard, because she lives about eight blocks from us. She escorts Dad up the front stairs, holding his elbow so he doesn't stumble. He's pretty high, actually. I'm behind, feeling really glad I put a roast in the slow cooker before school.

She gets us settled in at the table and turns to me. "You haven't said a word."

I look at her. I'm good at quiet stares. Always have been.

She sighs. "Call me if you need anything, all right? All of this will make sense soon." She turns to my dad. "You should have told her before now."

"How I parent Tobin is none of your business, Allison." He's kind of slurring his words, but he means it. She's judgy about the littlest things sometimes. Five years ago, when my dad made me buy my own tampons and pads, Allison was not happy. He took me to the store and explained it all, and I chose what I wanted. She lost her mind. Said it was an important moment to share with a woman. Whatev. When you deal with bodies for a living, my dad said, menstruation is a piece of cake compared to a severed artery. Makes sense to me.

"You're botching it." She turns to me again. "I'm here for you, Tobin. No matter what. All right?" She's waiting for me to answer her.

I don't.

She sighs again. "Good night, you two." And she walks out.

I get the roast and veggies from the slow cooker. Our kitchen is huge enough to have the dining room table in it, so I set it while the food's cooling. My dad pours two glasses of milk, very carefully, with his unbroken hand and wrist, and leaves them at our places. For a tiny family, we're kind of traditional in our supper behavior.

He sits down in his spot. "What happened in school today?"

I put butter on my potatoes, even though they're already delicious, and stay quiet.

"Tobin?" His eyes are searching my face. "Please talk to me."

I don't say a word.

"Come on. Don't be like this." His eyes have tears in them, which seems extreme, but it's enough to melt me.

"Only if you're straight with me about what's going on."

"Deal. But not tonight." He chews a mouthful of roast. "What happened at school today?"

"What the hell do you mean, not tonight?"

"I mean not tonight. I feel like shit, and you're shook up, and tomorrow is soon enough." He gives me the glare that says it's final.

I return the look. I drill him with my eyes. But he holds steady. I finally have to look away.

"Let's start again. What happened in school today, Tobin?" He chews another bite, waiting for my answer.

I sigh. "I took pictures of some jerky guys from metal shop. And Rowan Hansen set a book on fire right after first period. It's the third time this month."

"Does he have a pyromania problem?"

"He's just bored."

"Why hasn't he gotten expelled?" Dad serves himself more roast. "This is great, Tobin. Thanks."

"He has been. Twice. This time he got kicked out for good. And you're welcome."

My dad grimaces. "Too bad for him. But what else happened today to *you*—not to your classmates?"

"I got my history test back with an A-plus and I got accepted to the Colorado School of Visual Arts." He doesn't have to know the letter came yesterday. He wasn't home when I went to bed, so today is close enough.

He drops his fork but picks it up fast. "You did? After all the back and forth and torturing me with your every thought about the right place, and how much money they all cost?" He's grinning.

"If I get an entrance portfolio submitted by September fifteenth, I have a chance at a full-ride scholarship."

He pats my hand with his cast-up fingers. "Even if I want you closer to home, who am I to argue with the chance for a full-ride scholarship?" When he picks up his fork, it clatters to the plate again. He captures it again and attacks his roast. "It's an excellent choice, daughter. Just outstanding. I'm proud of you." He grins around the food. "Tell me more about the entrance portfolio."

Not a single word about making a living with art and how that's a dumb choice.

Weird.

I watch him eat second helpings of carrots and potatoes and a third of meat, like it's the last time he's going to have food. "It needs to be our origin story."

He looks at me over his glass of milk while he drinks it dry, then he puts the glass down. "Origin story? Like how you got to be a superhero, that kind of origin story?" He spreads his arms out, cast-up wrist and all, providing a benediction over supper. "You are the Mutant G-Force Superhero of Good Food. You make supper appear with no effort at all."

"Sometimes I have my shit together."

He laughs. "More than sometimes."

The rest of the night is calm. I do homework. He falls asleep on the couch. I wake him up and help him to bed without hurting his wrist.

The cold and windy lake argues with itself outside our windows.

In the middle of the night, the question wakes me up. Not like it didn't keep me awake for an hour in the first place.

What's not the same?

He's got cancer.

We have to move away. *He* has to move away, and I have to stay.

I've got a brother or a sister somewhere, and they're coming to live with us.

His old books are being reprinted—the ones he wrote before I was born—and he's going on a book tour.

He's going to take me on a fabulous South American vacation.

He's going to become an accountant.

He's going to run across the entire United States as his very own personal marathon, and I have to quit school to be his support team.

I have no idea.

After I make a list of about twenty possibilities in my head, I'm sleepy.

I don't know what he's hiding, but we're all right, whatever it is.

I trust him.

Dad's Big Book of Advice #2
Never hesitate to become a pizza delivery person. People are always happy to see you.

MARCH 16

"Tobin, we need a poem *now*. Not tomorrow. And what's with this photo?"

Twin Ports Academy has the world's worst school newspaper. It's not even a newspaper. It's a newsletter, six xeroxed pages with a few photos. People read it because they're sick of looking at their phones. Stephanie Allen, editor of the *Twin Ports Weekly*, wants to talk about my weekly contributions. I am generally a nice person, but I'm not always a patient person, especially when she doesn't like what I give her. Which is every time I give her something.

I hold out the poem in front of me. "You're not going to like it."

My brain isn't working so great. All morning, off and on, it's been echoing: *What's not the same?*

Well, my poems are the same—they suck, as always. People think I can write poems because my dad did. LOL. Stephanie reads. I watch her face.

There once was a rock from Enger Park
who lined up with others in the dark.
When light came around,
no space to be found,
the rock flow had carried in Noah's ark.

She looks at me hard. "This is terrible. And you were supposed to photograph motion. Like a basketball game. Or even a gym class." She frowns.

"The Zen garden has flow in it. Look." I point. "They're moving." The rocks are flat black ovals, and they're stuck into the cement in ripple patterns, like water. "Who needs more photos of gym class?"

"People like gym photos because they know the people in them. Nobody cares about a bunch of rocks." She turns her chair so she can face the computer where she's laying out the *Weekly*. The *Weakly*.

"Give me twenty minutes." I wrap my camera strap around my neck and walk out of the room.

What's not the same?

Stephanie is the same. Still bitchy. Gym class will be the same. I'd bet money on it.

On my way back from capturing candids of my fellow uninterested juniors pretending to play volleyball, I pass my dad's shrine—that's what I call it, even though it's just a trophy case with his author photo, two books, and a newspaper article in it.

It's awkward.

According to the trophy case, Twin Ports Academy alum Stephen Oliver went to New York City and published a book of humorous poetry, mostly haikus, called *Seagull with French Fry*, and a goofy mystery novel called *Icy Depths*, about a woman who gets pushed off a sightseeing boat and freezes to death in Lake Superior and the dumb private eye who solves the case. The yellowed old *Twin Ports Weekly* article has this headline: FUNNY ALUM STEVE OLIVER TAKES HIS GOOFBALL SELF TO NYC. There are two dusty books in there—one with a weird-looking seagull on it, and one with a double-decker sightseeing boat on it. Both look kind of nineties and kind of sad.

I give the glass a thump, leaving a handprint, then blow it a kiss.

The trophy case is the same. Probably will be until the school falls down.

When I get back to the room, I hand Stephanie the camera, and she clicks through the shots.

"Not like this!" Stephanie scowls. "I wanted something that was happy. Carefree and positive."

"You said gym photos. It's not my fault they didn't smile."

She huffs at me—like actually blows-air-out-through-her-mouth huffs at me. "We don't have time to find a picture. If I could replace you, Tobin, I would."

I sigh. "If I could do anything else during this period, Stephanie, I totally would." I pick up my camera from where she chucked it on the desk and check to make sure it's not damaged. I don't have money to fix it right now.

Mrs. Longness comes in to see how we're doing with this week's issue.

"Do you have some action photos now?" Longness gestures to me to give her the camera, so I do. She clicks through the shots and laughs. "One of these will work." She smiles at me. "People must really love gym class."

Stephanie rolls her eyes.

I go out where Mrs. Longness came in.

My camera goes in its case and gets tucked into my locker, where I swipe my lunch from its perch on top of a stack of books. Then I swim with the crowd out the door toward our green space. It's only thirty-five degrees, but it's super sunny, so everyone's gotta be outside. You never get a picnic table, but it's still good to stand around. Not a single person is wearing a coat.

Twin Ports Academy is high on the side of the hill that slopes into the lake, so there's lots of city spread out underneath us. And Lake Superior—our claim to fame, my dad's BFF, *Gichi-gami* in Ojibwe, goddess and ruler of our little corner of the world—looks like an ocean from up here, because it fades into the sky.

The snow is mega-slushy now, and the sun makes it feel like it might become spring at some point. It's winter for at least nine months of the year in Duluth. Close to the edge of the pavement, I can see green grass where the snow has retreated.

While I lean on the south school wall, basking in the glow and snarfing my boring PB&J, I text Gracie. We've been friends since kindergarten, and our lunch periods overlap by ten minutes. She goes to Immaculate Heart, which is across town from Twin Ports Academy, and she has a crap-ton of homework at night, because her parents are expecting her to go Ivy League.

She also really loves hashtags. She says they're tiny little summaries of the conversation. Or tiny poems, if you do them right. She must be my dad's daughter.

Me: *New package from Paris is here. All yours.*

Her: *You know I love her gifts! #girlyFrenchstuff*

How's lunch?

Reading HP6. Gracie is a complete Harry Potter nerd. *#textmelater #HPforlyfe*

Gracie is the same, and that's a good thing.

I don't remember much about my mom. Her name is Meredith. I was five when she left for Paris. There are pictures of us as a family of three—she was a great photographer, and she bought me my first camera—but it feels like she was always four thousand miles away.

She's not a communicator, but she sends packages of stuff she hopes I'll like, lacy T-shirts and perfume and sweet little pillows you're supposed to put on your bed. Gracie is happy to take everything off my hands.

I throw the crusts of my sandwich on the ground for whatever seagull wants them—they're everywhere, and they don't just eat french fries—and slurp down my water as I walk around the corner. Sasha from my math class is sitting on top of the rock in front of our school, the one where you can see almost to Two Harbors, twenty miles away.

"Tobin! Want to climb up?" She pats a spot next to her.

"I'm good." Not a fan of heights. The hill is high enough as it is.

Sasha's buddy Enzo scrambles up next to her and plops his butt down, legs hanging off the side. "Tobin, how come you never hang out with us?" He starts kicking his feet, and I grab my phone and focus on them, trying to find some good shapes in the middle of the motion of the shadows.

I like to be alone sounds pretty rude. "I work a lot."

"Where do you work?" Enzo can see I'm looking at his feet, so he kicks them faster.

"Zenith City Trash Box." Which is really Zenith City Treasure Box. Allison owns it.

"Did you know she's got old *Playboys* and *Penthouses* in the back room?" He grins.

I snap a photo of his grin. "We threw them out after you and your buddies started stealing them." I start toward the door. The math homework I didn't finish last night is calling my name before next hour.

"Tobin!"

I turn around, and Sasha and Enzo have a new buddy on the top of their rock—Sid Smithson, a kid I grew up with. Gracie, Sid, and I were the only three kids in our section of Park Point. Then Gracie's family moved up by Enger Park when she was ten.

He's posed himself up there like a Greek god. "Take pictures of me!"

I click off a few more shots. "You can be the cover of the yearbook." He does look pretty cute.

Sid climbs back down as quickly as he got up there. "Want a ride to work after school?"

"Um. Sure. I guess." I try to give Sid a smile, but I know it comes out crooked. He's sort of out of context, even though I see him almost every day. Maybe because he's never offered me a ride before.

Sid is the same and not the same, simultaneously.

"Great! See you then." He disappears back behind the rock. I look up and see Sasha and Enzo laughing.

Sasha looks down at me. "He's only wanted to ask you out for a year. Boys." She gives Enzo a whack on his shoulder.

I roll my eyes. "We've known each other since we were little kids."

Sasha raises her eyebrows, daring me to contradict her. "Whatever you say, Tobin."

"Girls are impossible." Enzo climbs down from the rock, three steps behind in the conversation as he holds up a hand for Sasha to climb down, too. "Gaming is what matters."

Everybody goes to class.

I look at my photos while the teacher's taking roll, while I'm pretending I've got my math homework done. A couple shots of Enzo's feet aren't bad, so I email them to Stephanie, with another limerick:

There once were two feet, up high,
and beauty began to supply.
They moved with some grace,
their shadows apace,
clueless owner continuing, spry.

It sucks, too, but maybe Stephanie will like it better than one about rocks.

I see Sid walk by in the hall. He smiles and waves. I wave back, trying not to look weird.

Sid's a nerd like Gracie, though his jam is John Williams music instead of Harry Potter. That means film scores for movies like *Star Wars*, *Jaws*, and *Raiders of the Lost Ark*. He wants to be a conductor someday, and he plays the violin. If it's really quiet at night and our windows are open, I can sometimes hear him on his back porch, five houses down.

I text Gracie: *Do you think Sid likes me?*
Why wouldn't he like you? #ParkPointForever
Like I was a real girl.
LOLOLOLOLOLOLOLOL.

That's what I thought.

He's right there after school, by my elbow, before I even have a chance to think about it. "Can I still give you a ride?" Sid looks nervous.

"I'd be late if I had to take the bus." I had to talk with Mrs. Longness about Stephanie and her crabbiness. I'm lucky Mrs. Longness likes me.

Once I've got all my homework, I shut my locker and we walk out to the parking lot. Awkward silence. Sid and I haven't hung out in ages.

He leads me to his dark-green beat-to-crap Saturn. "Does Zenith City Treasure Box get any business in March?" He unlocks the door for me and goes around to the driver's side.

"It's pretty quiet for now."

"Do you actually like selling antiques?" Sid gives me a sideways look as he drives out of the lot, like junior girls who sell antiques are destined for lives as crazy cat ladies, and maybe we are. He's plugged his phone into his aux cord, and the opening song from the *Jurassic Park* soundtrack comes roaring—ha ha, that's a pun—out of his crappy speakers.

"Dinosaurs? Really? It's not just selling antiques, so you know. I dust and put things where Allison tells me." Sid laughs, and I roll my eyes. "It's pretty much working at McDonald's, minus the food and grease."

He points at me. "Yeah, but do you know how hard it is to clean up vomit from six tourists who were seasick on the same trip? Or take registrations from families of twenty who want to be on the two o'clock harbor cruise, but there's only ten places left? Try that for a while." He works at Vista Fleet, where his dad is a boat pilot. Nobody probably recognizes it, but it's a Vista Fleet boat on the cover of my dad's book. They do big business around here.

"I'll dust antiques."

"If your aunt ever needs someone else to work, let me know." His car slides partway down the hill toward Superior Street, almost into a parked car. "Spring ice sucks."

Then we're on Lake Street, and almost to Trash Box. Things look pretty traditional for the middle of March—one or two people on the street walking around, but shopkeepers are working in their windows, setting up displays to lure in the visitors who'll show up in a few weeks.

He pulls up and I hop out fast, before it gets too weird. "Thanks, Sid." I smile through the window at him.

"Can we do it again sometime?" He looks like a kid. He was always getting Band-Aids for me and Gracie when we fell down or getting water for all of us when we were hot and sweaty. He was perpetually sweet and kind, for whatever reason an eight-year-old has for that, and he looks exactly like that kid right now. Same but not the same.

"Um, yeah. Sure." I smile again and walk fast enough to end the conversation, but not so fast I look like I'm escaping.

As I put my backpack behind the counter, my eyes catch the flyer on the wall that says VOYAGEURS AND TRADERS— MINNESOTA'S FUR-ST WHITE PEOPLE! My great-uncle Paul does that presentation every year at the Tall Ships Festival in August. It says "first white people" because there were Ojibwe and Dakota people here long before French fur traders arrived, duh. Paul's a total history buff, and he may know more about Duluth and the area than the Minnesota Historical Society does. And no, we don't normally have tall ships in Lake Superior—the kind with masts and sails that look they're from *Pirates of the Caribbean*—but somebody somewhere decided they were tired of ore boats and cargo ships 24/7/365. So now we have a Minnesota history/ American history/colonizer history weekend in August, complete with pirate ships.

Paul also knows a crap-ton about our family. According to him and family legend, one of the trapping camps Daniel Olivier worked for was where our house is right now, which is how we were able to purchase the land. A family member built the house we live in during the late 1800s, and there was a cabin on the land for 150 years before that. If Dad hadn't inherited it, we couldn't afford to live there any other way. There are million-dollar mansions all around us.

Paul also says, based on Mariette's journals—he had to have them translated from French—that Daniel and Mariette worked hard to have a good relationship with both the Dakota and the Ojibwe in this area, which is more than lots of white invaders can say. Mariette wrote about trades and friendships, and all the times the women saved her butt. She was from Quebec, Paul said, and she was given to Greysolon's party because she was being punished for petty thievery. He said she was terrified, and she knew nothing about how to live in the woods. Daniel was kind to her, and they fell in love, and now I'm here, almost 350 years later.

I hope my ancestors were kind to the people they found here. I like to pretend it would make us less invasive, which it can't. But you'd be an idiot not to be kind to the people who know how to survive the winters. I would carry their water for the rest of my life if they could teach me how to avoid frostbite.

I go back to the front counter to see if Allison's left me a list. Sure enough, it's on the counter.

TODAY FOR TOBIN TO DO:
1. *Dust figurines and dishes*
2. *Clean bathroom*
3. *Sweep in the back room*

Yes, ma'am.

The figurines and dishes are in a couple short aisles on the far edge of the store. Allison has a rotation of dusting, which is good, because it would take hours to dust the whole damn store, and I'd sneeze myself to death. She makes me use a feather duster, too, which I then beat on the wall outside in the alley after I'm done. More sneezing. Last summer a guy from the restaurant next door actually came outside to see if I was okay.

Allison doesn't say anything to me today, aside from a basic greeting and instructions. She gets like that sometimes. She just looks at me. I look back.

What's not the same? It's floating around my brain.

Allison is very much the same.

When I go into the back room, I take in the ten-foot-high chalk drawing of a rubber duck. She's the same, too—big and yellow and peaceful. There's a haiku beside her.

My dad made the drawing and the haiku a few years ago, and since the store belonged to my grandparents before it was Allison's, he told her she couldn't take it down or she'd piss off their dead parents.

Mama Duck is another creature who always goes to the Tall Ships Festival, at least since I can remember. She's six stories high and she's pulled by a tugboat, gliding along with her mysterious smile, looking at the crowds from her comfortable spot on the lake. My dad is fascinated with her, probably because she's his polar opposite. Physically, he's one of the least calm people I know.

Six stories of Zen
make their way to the water:
Mona Lisa duck.

I have no idea why someone decided to add a six-story rubber duck to a Tall Ships festival, but it doesn't matter. She's pretty cool. And when she's lit up at night, she reminds me of the Stay Puft Marshmallow Man from the first *Ghostbusters* movie.

"Hello, Mama Duck."

She smiles a little bit, though it's obvious she's tired of being captured on this wall. She'd clearly rather be out on the water.

Allison, who's just come into the back room, bursts into tears.

"What the flipping hell?" That was unexpected.

"Nothing." And she races for the door into the alley.

"Okay then."

I sweep the back room, around piles of books and boxes of china and old rolled-up carpets and antique dressers. Allison comes back from the alley, sniffling and heading for the box of Kleenex she keeps behind the counter. I don't even ask.

On my way back to the front with the dustpan and broom, I spot a box of action figures on a shelf, tucked next to some other toys. A box of *my* action figures.

I dig into the tangle of arms, legs, and heads. My dad's tiny Lando Calrissian, from the first Star Wars movies, is in there, and his bigger Professor X is there, in his wheelchair, along with my Mystique, complete with skull-head belt. Both of them are X-Men. There are also two Reys—one the size of Mystique and one the size of Lando—from the reboot of Star Wars a few years ago. I have no idea why I had two Reys—I had just become a teenager when that movie came out. Dad probably gave them to me, hoping I'd go back to being a little girl.

There's a bunch more, too, some of which I don't know because they're from my dad's era. He gave them to me when I was about eight, then I added even more. When I was a kid, they were a hundred times better than Barbies, because Barbies were boring girls who went shopping. These people had adventures.

"Allison, where did these come from?" I take the box off the shelf and bring it into the store.

"Your dad brought them in last week." She blows her nose again. Her eyes are red.

"They're off the market."

She sighs. "That's the most you've said since the hospital."

I don't reply, just put the box with my backpack and go to clean the bathroom.

What's not the same?

My dad bringing stuff to the store.

Allison crying.

He tripped and fell last week, too, when he was walking toward the lake.

I saw him.

A weight settles into my stomach.

I don't know if I want to know or not.

I mean, I do.

But of course I don't.

I leave at 5:30, in silence, snapping photos as I go. The sky is gorgeous. Tourists would pay a shit-ton for a photo of pink air as seen through the aerial lift bridge. Maybe Allison would let me sell some prints. In five minutes, I'm over the bridge and on my way home, carrying my action figures.

The lift bridge is one of the main reasons people visit Duluth. The part of the bridge you drive and walk on moves up into the bridge supports, so big ships can come into the bay to load and unload stuff. After the lake itself, it's probably the thing people like to visit most. Sure, it's neat to watch the road go way over your head, and yeah, big cargo ships are cool, but it's an enormous pain in the ass when you're trying to get home or into town and a ship's going through.

Park Point is wide enough for one street down the middle of the land, with one row of houses and businesses on the south side of the street. On the north, there's a little more land—the houses are sometimes two deep before you get to the trees and ginormous sand dunes that come before the beach and the lake. On the south side of the land, there's the bay for ships to use, and then it's Wisconsin on the other side of the bay. On the north side, it's the lake, which looks like an ocean.

Even though our house is one of the crappiest out here, it's still worth $387,000, according to the assessor of St. Louis County, State of Minnesota. And even thirteen blocks away, you can still hear the ships when they blow their horns as they cross under the bridge. Floating giants with deep voices.

What's not the same? What's not the same? My feet beat it out as I walk.

When I come in, Dad's there, and the table's already set.

"What are you doing home?"

He raises his left arm with the cast. "Remember?"

"Oh yeah. Right." I've tried so hard to figure out what he's going to tell me that I forgot about his wrist. "What's for supper?"

"Leftover pot roast. That okay with you?"

"That's why we have leftovers, isn't it?" I smile, and he smiles, and that helps the knot in my stomach.

When we're almost finished, I remember what I brought home. "Please tell me why the hell there was a shoebox of action figures that belong to me at Trash Box. Allison said you brought them down."

"Don't call it Trash Box." He always says that.

"It doesn't change the fact that I found my box of action figures on the shelf. I repeat: What the hell?"

He swallows. "Just cleaning closets. Figured you didn't want them anymore."

Had he asked me if I'd wanted them a week ago, I would have told him no. "You should ask before you give away something of mine, you know." I give him a look over the top of my milk glass and take a swig.

"My bad." His eyes tell me he's sincere. He thought I wouldn't care. "I was just ... cleaning. So you'd have less to do ... someday."

"Less to do?"

He looks at the floor.

I keep myself calm. "Tell me what's not the same."

My dad takes a long gulp of his milk. "Time for a dad joke, Voyageur."

He calls me Voyageur sometimes because my middle name is the same as Daniel Olivier's wife, Mariette, and because I never, ever, used to stay where I was put when I was little. He says I was lucky I didn't voyage my way into drowning or getting run over before I made it to three.

"No thank you."

"Did you hear that the administration confiscated a rubber band pistol from a student at Twin Ports Academy? It was a weapon of math disruption." He smiles, with a look that shows how much he wants me to smile back.

"That wasn't horrid." I return the grin, even though it's hard, and my guts are screaming WHAT'S NOT THE SAME WHAT'S NOT THE SAME WHAT'S NOT THE SAME.

"Thank you for enjoying it. And it's beyond time to tell you all this." He sighs. "To be blunt, I am the patron saint of the totally fucked."

"That's the painkillers talking." He doesn't say things like that.

He gets up from the table, goes to his desk in the corner—the one where he pays bills and signs serious papers—and reaches into the middle desk drawer. When he comes back, he lays a booklet in front of me. The cover says *What to Do when Your Parent has ALS*.

Nope. Not the same.

"This is why I fell up the front steps two weeks ago, and why I fell down yesterday. Why I can't hold on to a fork sometimes." He reaches out for my hands, and I let him take them, though it's hard to hold hands with someone in a wrist cast.

"Why you fell last week when you were walking toward the lake?" I see it again in my head.

He nods. "Remember the ice bucket challenge? Sometimes it's called Lou Gehrig's disease. A person's muscles eventually stop working. Remember Mrs. Nealy down the street?"

Mrs. Nealy. When I was a tiny girl, she used to come with me over the dune to visit the lake, and then we'd go to the neighborhood grocery to get a Coke. But then she couldn't walk, and then she couldn't talk or breathe, and then she died. When she was trapped in her wheelchair, not able to say a word, I could see in her eyes how badly she wanted to be like the rest of us, up and doing things, living in the real world, but she was stuck. Doomed. She seemed ancient to me, but she might have been in her fifties or sixties when she died. Not that old.

"You have the same thing Mrs. Nealy did?"

He closes his eyes.

NOT THE SAME.

"Your body's going to quit on you, and you're going to die?"

He coughs, looks at the floor, then at me. He's crying, but he's not making a sound. Tears are just flowing silently down his face, splatting on his shirt as he holds my hands, one tight and one awkward.

Nothing will ever be the same again.

I'd swear someone's blowing whistles in my ears.

"We'll get through this together, okay? I'm still here. For as long as I can be here, I'm here."

He says this with the same smile he's always had, the one that made me laugh when I landed on my ass the first time I tried my in-line skates and scraped my leg from butt cheek to back of my knee. The smile that says he's not too pissed, like the time I burned the macaroni in the microwave, when I forgot to add water to it, and then sprayed the microwave with perfume to try and cover it up, and our house smelled like a torched Victoria's Secret for days. The I-know-you're-trying smile. The I-know-this-is-tough smile. The smile that tells me all is well.

Told me all was well. Not anymore.

"Say something, Tobin. Anything at all." He's staring into my eyes, almost into my heart.

Words are chunked and broken in my throat. All the good things I could say, like "I love you, Dad," and "You're the best dad ever," are mixed in with the words I said when I hated him, even for two seconds. I could have been a better daughter so many times.

My eyes go to the photo on the wall between the kitchen and the living room. My mom took it. I'm about three, in my dad's lap, and we're laughing. Our hair is blowing in an invisible breeze, and you can see our beach dunes behind us. We're looking out into the lake, dad and girl, the unit we've always been.

I bolt for the sink and puke.

When I turn on the water to rinse everything down, I realize he's there with me, hand on my back.

"It's a gut punch, isn't it?"

"That's one way to put it." I wipe my mouth and get a glass of water. "How long have you known?"

"Since early February."

Before I answer, I gulp the rest of the water in my glass, for strength.

Then I let him have it. At full volume.

"Why are you so," I spit the word at him, "*casual* about it? I can't believe Molly and Allison knew, and I didn't. Oh my god, you suck. This SUCKS." If I could breathe fire, I would. "How am I going to handle all the shit you handle? How am I going to handle ANYTHING?" I feel like I'm gonna puke again, but there's nothing left in there.

He tries to pull me into a hug, but I shrug away. He teeters, but grabs the counter, face white. "You can't do that, okay? It's easy for me to tip over."

The room is whirling. "How did you figure it out?"

He pulls himself steady. "When I had trouble in the Twin Cities Marathon, back in October, Marshall told me to get myself checked out." Marshall's the guy he normally runs marathons with. "They give you lots of tests, and they have to rule things out, so we weren't really sure until six weeks ago. Then . . ." He pauses and the tears start flowing again. "Then I didn't know what to say. Or how to say it. So I just . . . didn't say anything at all."

He looks lost, like he's in the middle of the woods with no flashlight. He reaches out for my shoulder, to touch it, but I shrug away.

"I love you, Tobin. We'll get through this."

My voice is a hiss. "You could have told me when you fell the first time. Or the next time. Any time in the last month you could have told me."

"Tobin . . ."

"I asked you if you were okay, and you said yes. *You lied to me.*" We don't lie to each other.

I slam out the back door, out to the lake, and leave him standing in the kitchen.

When I walk over the dunes, I'm out of sight of the house, and it's dark, with no moon, so he can't see me to come and find me. The sky is clear and full of stars, and the lake is whispering her night song of waves. Where we live, she's not loud unless it's windy or stormy. No big rocks for waves to crash on. Here, she seems peaceful and calm, though she's still icy dangerous. Here, she specializes in illusions.

I google ALS for the next ten minutes. By the time I'm a frozen popsicle—sitting by Lake Superior on March 16 is a recipe for human popsicles—I'm confident the next two to five years are going to be the worst ones of my life, and the last of his. So I scream into the lake until I'm hoarse. Nobody hears me because it's cold. Nobody has their windows open.

Not ever fucking the same again.

What am I going to do when I can't see him running up the street toward me, sweaty and happy? Or wading in the lake in August, big grin on his face, or surfing on the waves in his wet suit in May, icicles hanging from his elbows? He used to swing me through the air at the water's edge, big arcs where my toes would graze the waves, and he'd laugh right along with me. What about Medic 3464, and Rich, and not sleeping for thirty-six hours because he was pulling thirteen people out of nine different car wrecks on the Fourth of July weekend when there were too many drunks on the road?

What about his wavy blond hair? His hands, which have a million calluses on them from lifting stretchers and equipment? His laugh? His dumb dad jokes?

What about his notebooks?

What will I do when he can't walk anymore? Or talk? Or eat? Or breathe?

Who will help me fix my house when I'm old enough to buy one? Who will fix *this* house? What about the car? Who's going to approve my future husband? Hold my first child?

I scream. It's so loud and long. But the wind carries the sound away.

I do it again. And again. And again.

Then I cry until I can't catch my breath.

If you add up all the times I was a shitty daughter, then add in the fact that he won't see me graduate from college, maybe not even high school, and he sure won't see me get married or have kids or be forty-nine, which is how old he is right now, and square that number by a Lake Superior–sized anger, then divide by an eternity of freezing cold, white-hot sadness, you'd have my insides right now.

When I go back in, I can't find him, which sends me into a panic, but the car is still here. Then I go upstairs and see his bedroom door is closed. I hear his soft snuffle of a snore. Like nothing's wrong. Like that sound won't be gone before I'm twenty-two. Or twenty, for that matter, because that's only three years from now.

There's a note in the bathroom.

Pain meds make me tired. Wake me up if you want to. Let's chat tomorrow. Love you so much. Dad

I can't feel my face when I brush my teeth. And no matter how many blankets, socks, pajama pants, and sweatshirts I put on, I can't get warm.

<u>March 17, 1:42 a.m.</u>

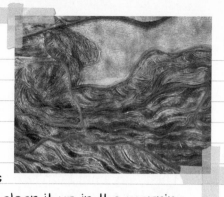

The heart is the strongest muscle in the body, and I'm finished with mine.

In my dream, I rip my heart straight out of my chest. Blood goes everywhere. I decide to clean it up in the morning.

Then I walk, strong and clear, down the stairs, out the door, over the dunes. There's a kayak. I paddle it out, miles from shore, until I'm sick with exhaustion. Lake Superior is the deepest Great Lake, and I know I'm not in the middle, but I'm far enough out for it to be almost...

...infinite.

With no fanfare, I pitch my heart over the side, wait and wait and wait until it thunks on the silty bottom. Fish swim over, nudging its hard, icy edges from its slow watery descent. Lake Superior is also the coldest Great Lake. My heart never stood a chance. It will become frozen debris, down on the dark bottom. No one can disturb it. No one can find it.

I paddle my dream kayak back to shore, pull it on the sand dune, and glide back inside the house, ghost body with no girl inside. I cannot get warm.

Dad's Big Book of Advice #3
Learn to change a tire.
What if you're the only one in the car?

DURING
MARCH 17

When I wake up, the sun's gushing in the window, which means it's late. Maybe not as late as I think, but late. I check my phone: 7:49. School starts at 8:15.

"DAD!" I shriek it when I fly to the bathroom to pee and brush my teeth. "ARE YOU STILL HERE?"

I hear a chuckle from the kitchen. "Decided to start your day, did you?"

I slam the door.

No shower today. It's 8:02 when I'm done, and I barrel out of the bathroom toward the kitchen.

"Can you give me a ride, please? I don't have time to take the bus this morning." I say it as politely as I can. Three and a half hours of sleep is not enough, minus waking up to write about the dream.

His eyes aren't smiling, but his mouth is. "Sure thing." He grabs his keys from the desk, stumbles a little, catches himself on the edge of the table, and stops to settle it all back in place.

I grab a banana and a cookie. "Let's go."

Once I'm settled in the car, the events of last night rush at me. I look out the window so Dad can't see my face.

"I thought we didn't lie to each other."

He sighs. "I'm sorry. We don't. I was just ... trying to absorb it myself."

I don't look at him.

He's still here, still driving me to school. But there's a gray haze over us, a big blanket of

NOTHING WILL EVER BE THE SAME

and

I AM GOING TO BE AN ORPHAN NOW

and

WHAT THE HELL DO I DO

and

IF I HAVE TO LIVE WITH ALLISON, I WILL LOSE MY SHIT.

We're almost there, almost up the hill, when he finally says it. "When you get home, can we talk? I'm so sorry, Tobin." He winces as he guides the steering wheel with his bad wrist.

"You should drive with your other hand."

He winces again, but then we're there. "We need to keep talking. And planning."

"I'll take the bus to Trash Box after school. Later." And I slam my way out of the car, not looking back, hand over the left side of my chest.

No heartbeat. Good. The dream worked.

I'm halfway up the steps of the school when I realize I forgot my camera. Without its comforting weight deep in my backpack, I feel like I'm going to float away.

This day can suck it.

Gracie texts: *Want to hang out later?*

Sick. I can't think of anything else to say. *Not today.* :(

OK. Love you. Feel better quick. xxoo #healingvibes #ifithelps

How do I tell people like Gracie?

The hours are blurry and edgy, all at the same time. I am sharp and rude and snap at Mrs. Longness when she wants to talk about photos for graduation. Nice me has also been dropped over the side of the dream kayak.

After school, I slam my locker hard and turn around to find Sid. His face is clouded.

"I hear you haven't had a very good day today."

"Who told you that?" The last thing I need is for people to talk about me. "I didn't get much sleep last night. I'm crabby." I'll have some apology texts to send tomorrow as well as an email to Mrs. Longness.

"Want a ride to Trash Box?"

"As long as we don't have to talk."

"Just a ride." He holds out his hand to me. "This way, crabby girl."

"I'm not interested in holding your hand, thank you."

It comes out ruder than I mean it to, and Sid's face shows me. "Sorry. Just . . . not in the mood. No disrespect."

"All okay." He walks ahead of me.

Today's soundtrack is *Raiders of the Lost Ark*, I think.

"Is this a young Harrison Ford running around in his fedora?" It's one of my dad's favorite movies, which is the only reason I know.

"It's not my favorite, but it's good. Adventurous. Not enough strings in the opening theme, but good brass. And the strings get more involved as the song goes along."

"Lots of horns in there." I can't think of anything else to say. Then we're there. "Sid, you are really kind to give me a ride. Thanks."

Before I can jump out, he puts his hand on my arm. "You look so sad."

I put my hand over the spot where my heart should be. Still nothing. "It's a long story, and I've got to work." I bolt out the door as fast as I can.

"I'll text you." He says it before I can slam the door. And he will. Because he's a nice guy. Sid's niceness is the same.

The bell dings when I open the door, and I wait for Allison to jump me. She'll want to talk. But she's not there. At least, she's not up front. And that's really good.

My list is right where it always is.

TODAY FOR TOBIN TO DO.
    1. *Sort magazines—keep architectural and home/garden.*
    2. *Talk to me about how I can help.*

Number 2 is a hell no.

I start on the stack of magazines that she's left on front of the counter—there might be a hundred of them. It's kind of soothing. I'd swear I closed my eyes for just a second, classical music floating through the store and soothing my jagged edges, but I wake up when the magazines fall out of my hands.

"Shit!"

"Hey now, Tobin. Enough of that." A quiet voice with a smile in it comes from behind me.

I whirl around, and it's my uncle Paul. He lives above the store, just like he has since 1984 or something.

"Um, yeah. Not very with it today."

He has a gentle face, and he's looking at me now with an expression you might use to tame a feral cat. "Things all right, Tobin? Most people don't fall asleep standing up."

"How did you . . . how long have you been in here?"

"Not long." He smiles, very kindly. "Long enough to see you fall asleep standing up." A rear stairway in the back room goes up to his place, but when he comes and goes, we don't always see him. "Allison ran to your house for a moment, so she asked me to watch for you. And I was in the back, look-ing through some new treasures, and wasn't paying attention." Paul moves toward the back room door. "I'll be heading up now. Let me know if you need me. I know this is a long road coming up."

My head snaps up. "She told you?"

He nods. "Your dad did. This is the time for a village, Tobin, and I'm one of your villagers. Can't do much any-more, but I can watch a store. I can tell you not to swear when you drop your magazines."

"How come everybody knew but me?" My anger is fast.

"Your dad didn't want you to worry. No parent wants to burden their kid." His eyes are concerned. "I'm always here, even when you're pissed."

"Yeah, well . . . thanks."

He's hard to stay mad at. I give him a quick peck on the cheek, then shove the throw away magazines in one heap with my foot so I can stack the saleable ones on the counter in a neat pile.

If I had a heart, Paul would make it feel better. He's like that. He's the same.

"Tobin?" As soon as the back door slams behind her, Allison is calling for me.

"Right here. Organizing magazines. Chatting with Paul."

Paul lifts his hand to me, and I return the wave. He disappears into the back, and I hear he and Allison say a couple words, though they're talking too low for me to make out the words.

Allison comes out to the store. "How are you feeling, Tobin?"

She doesn't even pause for me to answer, just envelops me in a hug that makes me accidentally knock a glass bowl off a shelf when she pins my arm to my side. I feel it go and brace for the crash.

But she doesn't move. She just keeps hugging me and petting my hair. Awkward. "It's gonna be tough for a long time. But we're all in this together. I'm here to help with everything." One more pet of my hair and she lets go. The sound of the breaking glass finally registers in her brain. "Oh dear. Guess we need to clean that up. Luckily it's not worth much."

"I'll get it. My fault." I move to find the broom, which is usually behind the counter.

"Tobin?"

Allison wants me to talk, cry, or do something more than get the broom and dustpan. In a flash, I see my heart at the bottom of Superior. It's a black, frozen blob. You can't even tell it's a heart.

"Not today."

"You have to talk about this."

"No, actually, I don't." And I walk by her, back to where the glass is in chunks on the floor. At least the thin, gross carpet kept it from shattering into a million pieces.

My dad is asleep on the couch when I come in. I don't bother him.

He has scattered notebooks all over the table. Ones that have lived in boxes under our stairs for as long as I can remember. Ones I have been forbidden to look at. Ones my dad said he'd turn into his next book.

I pick one up and peek inside. Poems.

After I've baked a frozen pizza, I stand and stare. Stephen Oliver isn't a sleep-on-the-couch kind of human.

I nudge him on the foot. "Dad. Time for supper."

Nothing.

"Dad?"

He's dead.

"DAD!"

The shriek wakes him up. "Huh? What? What's wrong, Tobin?" He literally—literally—jumps from horizontal to standing in the span of two seconds. He wobbles, but he stays up. "What's the emergency?"

I burst out laughing, which annoys him. He looks at his watch. "Is it really six-thirty? I laid down at four."

"Supper's ready. Come on." All of a sudden, I feel thumping in my chest. That display of paramedic bravado was so like him.

It turns out to be a bad idea, a beating heart in my body again. Dad keeps trying to joke and be funny, and he asks me about my day, which I barely remember because I'm so tired, but feelings crash over me in alternate waves of love and fear. All I can do is think about how terrible he looked, asleep on the couch. Pale. Thinner than normal, and he's already a thin guy.

I want to brand him on my mind, so I don't forget this mostly-healthy dad, this happy-right-now dad. This sort-of-the-same dad.

Once I get the leftovers put away, Dad motions me back to the table.

"I need to do homework. Lots of it."

He gives me the fish eye. "You don't do homework on Friday night. And I haven't told you my best joke for today. I looked up a bunch while you were at school."

"One more. But that's it." I try to look stern.

"Did you know that the fattest knight of the Round Table was Sir Cumference? He acquired his size from eating too much pi." And he loses it. *Loses it.* He can't stop laughing, and his laughter makes me laugh.

"Okay, that wasn't horrible."

"Do you know why nobody could hear the pterodactyl in the bathroom?" He's still chuckling.

"No idea. Why?"

"Because the P was silent!" And he's off again, in gales of laughter.

I move toward the stairs. "I've got to work on my origin story for the scholarship, so I really am going to do homework tonight instead of tomorrow and Sunday."

He shakes his head, still smiling. "No, you're not. You just don't want to talk to me."

"Really, and then I was going to go to bed."

"Really you aren't going anywhere." He's stern, and he points to the chair. "Sit down."

The doorbell rings, which never happens. The only people who come here are people who knock and walk right in.

Dad stands and moves slowly toward the front door. There are voices in the living room, but my eyelids are doing that thing again, so I sit and put my head down on the table. They'll wake me when they need me.

Which is right now.

"Tobin!" Dad kicks my chair, which is a little more like him. "Wake up and see who's here."

I pull my head off the table with a giant effort to see a really big guy who looks familiar. Once I manage to focus my brain, I realize it's Ike Navarro. Ike is Rich's son—my dad's rig partner Rich—and the last I knew, he was in Afghanistan.

"Hi, uh, Ike. Hi. A little tired, sorry."

He smiles like it's perfectly okay that people put their heads on the table and sleep there. "I hear the last twenty-four hours have been a bit stressful."

Dad clears his throat. "Ike is my new PCA."

"PCA?" I have no idea what that stands for.

"Personal care assistant. Person to help your dad out." Ike answers for him.

My brain goes *tilt*, like the tiredest pinball machine in the world, and everything freezes inside again.

Dad tries for cheerful. "I don't really need Ike now, but I will. You have school and getting ready for college, and Ike was a medic in the army. I figured it would be better if we had someone we knew. Someone we like." He flashes Ike a grin, and Ike flashes one in return. When he does that, Ike looks just like Rich.

"I see." I'm surprised I can't see my breath, I'm so frosty.

Ike tries to make it light. "Nothing radical's going to happen right now. I just came over to say hey. I don't think I've seen you since you were twelve or so."

A memory surfaces: We're in my back yard. I'm probably twelve or thirteen, and Gracie and I are looking sideways at Ike, who's a graduated senior on his way to boot camp. We think he's dreamy. The Ike in my kitchen is still damn good-looking, with his amazingly lovely brown skin, jet-black hair, and deep dark eyes, but he's ... weary. A little bit beat up. Like sadness is permanently attached to him.

The chair scrapes as I push it back. "I'll leave you gentlemen to the details, if you'll excuse me. I'm really, really tired."

"But you haven't heard my best Stephen Hawking jokes yet." Ike smiles at me. "Stephen Hawking survived longer with ALS than any other person on the planet, so he's our guide now." His eyes are twinkling.

My dad's intrigued. "Like What Would Stephen Hawking Do? WWSHD?"

Ike smiles. "Exactly. When you're in a jam, you just ask the question, and the answer will appear."

"Hmm." My dad's processing this idea.

Ike holds out his hand to Dad. "Can I see your wrist? How's it doing so far?"

While they chat, my eyes stray to the wall next to the refrigerator, where we have a big bulletin board with my dad's race stuff on it. Old bib numbers, finisher medals, race maps. He's been running marathons for about twenty years, so the board can't hold everything, but it's still crowded, with both recent and old stuff.

There's nothing under the huge push pin with the white label attached, saying SEND ME IN SO I CAN RUN. No more registration forms. I wondered where they were.

Not the same.

Tilt.

I stand. "Good night, Ike. Nice to see you again. Good night, Dad." I can't contemplate Stephen Hawking, Dad's wrist, or the absence of registration forms right now.

"Can't we talk a little more?" My dad is desperate. Ike can tell it's not a good time.

"I just . . . need to sleep." I walk out, leaving them to stare after me.

"Nice to see you, too, Tobin." Ike's voice holds a note of apology.

Up the stairs, hit the bathroom to brush my teeth and pee, hit the closet for an extra quilt, then I wrap myself in five blankets and lose myself in oblivion.

I wake up from a dream about action figures. Rey was pushing Professor X in his wheelchair. I hop out of bed in my frigid room, grab the shoebox, and put it on my desk, so I'll see it. Then I race back to bed, because I'm shivering and my toes are going to break off if I stay outside the covers much longer.

When I was a kid, I used to pose them in all sorts of ways out on the sand dunes, so they could blast the crap out of everything in sight and build houses out of leaves and sticks. Then they'd conquer rock piles and swim in the lake. They were one big Star Wars X-Men fam.

The secret to my scholarship is probably in that box.

I add another quilt and go back to sleep. In my next dream, Lando is having flying races with Iron Man, and my dad is down below them, screaming "Help her! Help her!"

This time I wake up with wet cheeks.

Dad's Big Book of Advice #4
Never go to bed angry. Stay up and work it out.

SATURDAY

I stay in bed.

SUNDAY

My dad won't let me stay in bed.

I sit at the kitchen table, do homework, and refuse to look at him.

MONDAY

I get home, and there are seven men working in my yard. Building a ramp. *Not that he needs it right now*, Ike says, *but he will. Better that it's ready.*

I am never going to be ready.

THURSDAY

This very old, very orange car comes up the street toward me as I lurch over the lift bridge. Gracie, in her '92 Dodge Neon we call Tangerine, probably looking for me so she can yell at me for blowing off her texts for three days.

She pulls up to the curb and gets out. Her face is a mix of pissed and worried.

"Tobin Mariette Oliver, what the hell is your problem? You've ignored me or sent me back one-word replies for the last three days. Spill it." She crosses her arms and glares, like I'm supposed to be intimidated. Normally I'd laugh in her face.

"My dad has ALS. He's dying. Actively. Right now."

Her mouth drops open.

"I'm a little preoccupied. Gotta go." And I start walking again.

"*Tobin!*" She slams the door and runs after me, grabbing my arm and turning me around. "Like Mrs. Nealy? *Why didn't you tell me?*"

"How do I put that information next to all your Harry Potter references?"

"If you'd told me what was going on, I wouldn't have been making Harry Potter references." She's hurt. "Why didn't you say anything?"

I look at the sidewalk, the sky, anywhere but at her. "It's just not something you can say."

"It *is* something you can 'just say' to your best friend." She grabs my face and turns it to her. "This is serious shit, and I'm here for you." All of a sudden, she's hugging me, and my frozen, bottom-of-the-lake heart is beating again, and I am almost almost almost crying, but I hang on to it. I hold in the howl.

When she lets go, she motions to the Tangerine. "Get in. I'll take you home."

So I do. We don't say much, but she makes me promise to text her later. She tells me she'll keep my news a secret until I'm ready to share it.

Against my better judgment, I let her hug me one more time.

Walking up our stairs, next to our brand-new ramp, I pull my heart out of my body and chuck it a good ten miles, over my house and deep into the lake again.

Clunk. Instant popsicle.

When I open the door, Ike and my father are disco-ing around the living room to some nineties pop tune. They're both singing "Groove is in the heaaaaaaaaaaaaaaaaaart . . ."

My dad is mostly being the guy he used to be, except he looks more fragile. Ike's seriously busting a move. It's quite the sight.

In the middle of a turn, my dad sees me standing there. "Groove is in the heart, Tobin! Come on!" Not like he was a huge dancer, but he boogies over and tries to grab my hand.

I don't move. I'm glad I just threw my heart back in.

"Tobin, you can relax for two minutes. I promise. Come on!" He tries to swing me around, and I don't go.

But the song is contagious. Ike's egging me on, doing stuff I can't even name.

My dad starts doing the Twist, sort of, and it's hilarious. I chuckle. He sees me, and he smiles, reaching out for my hand one more time. And my feet move before I tell them not to.

I start to get into it, and my dad and I Twist together for a second, then I'm showing off some dance moves I've perfected in the *Twin Ports Weakly* classroom. We all just groove around the living room until the song ends.

It's normal. Ish. Same-ish.

When the song's over, my dad claps Ike on the back. "That was genius. Thank you. Do you have any Gordon Lightfoot on your phone?"

Ike laughs. "I specialize in late twentieth-century dance music, not seventies easy listening." He's a bit out of breath.

My dad's breathing is easy, since he's still got a marathon runner's lung capacity, but he sits down on the couch like he's run one. "Tobin, will you bring me my phone?"

"Where is it?"

"On the table."

I fetch it, and he pulls up his Gord's Gold 4 Infinity playlist. This isn't the first time he's made me listen to it.

"All right, you young whippersnappers. Time for some true musical genius. Everyone sit down and be quiet. Second track, Ike." He hands Ike the phone, then points to him, then to the couch, on the other end from where he's sitting. I sit in the chair and close my eyes. I know what's coming.

Sure enough, "The Wreck of the Edmund Fitzgerald" pours out of Ike's speaker. My dad sings along softly. I have no idea what Ike's doing, because I've got my eyes closed, but I'm betting he's trying not to laugh.

My dad has pretty good taste in most art forms—current and vintage—but he has an unnatural love for Gordon Lightfoot, thanks to this song. On November 9, 1975, my tiny dad was coming home from school, to this house, in fact, and was stopped by the lift bridge. The *Edmund Fitzgerald* steamed right in front of his face, and he remembers his mom helping him sound out the long name. When it sank the next day near Sault Ste. Marie, Ontario (and Sault Ste. Marie, Michigan, because they're twin ports, just like Duluth and Superior, Wisconsin), my dad took it hard. Way harder than you'd think a little kid might. Of course, everybody was talking about it, since the ship left from here. When the song came out the next year, he listened to it so much that Allison still refuses to hear a note of it. And that song led to his love of Gordon Lightfoot.

When the song is over, I open my eyes, and I'm right—Ike's trying not to laugh. He looks almost exactly like Rich in this moment. "Care to explain the Gordon Lightfoot love?"

My dad sighs. "It's a long story, full of heartache, intrigue, and even more seventies music. Another day."

Now Ike really does laugh. "I don't mind Gordon Lightfoot. But does Tobin?"

I roll my eyes.

Dad rolls his eyes back at me. "She's more than familiar with my Gordon Lightfoot adoration, and she begs to differ. But she puts up with me. We can't really boogie to it, but we could slow dance, if you want, Ike." He grins.

Ike grins back. "As long as you don't make me lead."

"Deal." Dad moves his leg up and down, almost testing it. "I want to keep my muscles going until the very second they can't."

I frown. "You've got more muscles than most people. It'll be a while."

Ike nods. "Dance parties as often as we can. There's research that says exercise might slow down the disease progression." He pats his gut. "I need to move myself. Too much mazapan."

"What's that?" I've never heard of such a thing.

"The sweetest, most delicious Mexican candy you've ever had. It's just peanuts and powdered sugar, but it's incredible."

"Sounds kinda dull."

"I'll bring you some. You'll be sorry you ever said that." Ike smiles at me.

My dad sticks his legs out in front of him and stares at them. "This is ... surreal." He closes his eyes. "I've been an athlete since I was little."

We have photos of Dad competing in 5Ks when he was in elementary school and surfing up by Two Harbors in a little tiny wet suit. My grandma was lucky the lake didn't eat him.

Ike reaches over and slaps his knee. "As long as we can, we keep moving."

Dad studies his left leg, like he's never seen it, like it hasn't been dangling off his torso for forty-nine years.

Ike hooks his phone back up, and the playlist of dance tunes starts again. But that moment has passed. I feel the ice creep back into my chest.

"Know what I want?" My dad suddenly sounds strong. Definite.

"A glass of water? Gonna get one for me, too." Ike gets up off the couch and heads toward the kitchen.

"A party." Dad looks at me. "A fiftieth birthday party. I've never had a big one, so the time is now."

My mind is suddenly full of cakes and people and streamers and a guy in a wheelchair. "I have no clue how to make that happen."

"But we'll figure it out, won't we, Tobin?" Ike brings my dad a glass of water. Dad gulps it down like he hasn't had any for days while we have a mind meld. My eyes say, *I cannot do this. I'm a kid and I'm clueless.* Ike's eyes say, *Relax and we'll work it out.*

Dad's getting excited. "I want it at the Beach House, too." That's a shelter house east of here, on the lake, with a party room along with the usual lifeguard stuff. "All sorts of people and lots of food and cake. No presents. Just a big party."

"You got it, boss." Ike looks at me like I'm falling down on the job. *Say something,* his eyes ask me.

"Okay, Dad." I frown.

Ike smiles, like he's got a secret. That secret better be party-planning skills.

Dad's Big Book of Advice #5
Nap ➔ instant reset button. Take one anytime you can.

APRIL 2
1 A.M.

There's a text from Gracie, from 11:49 p.m. Back when I was asleep.

Can you talk? Are you doing OK? #worriedaboutyou

I don't text back. Aside from the fact that she's probably asleep now, I never know what to say to "Are you doing okay?" Sure. I'm walking, talking, and breathing. I'm going to work and doing homework. Is my heart working? No. Am I petrified about the future? Yes. So does all that add up to okay? I have no idea.

My dad is sawing logs when I tiptoe past his room. I'm so lucky the stairs don't creak. He sleeps more than he did, but his sleep isn't good. Sometimes I hear him thrashing around. Sometimes he yells, so I get up to check, but he's still asleep.

There are very few street lights out our way, but our back steps are familiar enough. Tonight, the moon is half full, and it's making the lake glitter.

I start walking east. The light diamonds ripple while the water sounds soothe my anxiety.

The Beach House is maybe two miles from here. How soon do you have to start planning a birthday party?

Sid's light is on, so I sneak a little closer. When I do, I realize the window's open and he's playing in his room. It's pretty quiet, because it's so late, but he sounds like he's in the middle of an orchestra. He's not making any mistakes, either, because I can't tell where he stops and the recording starts.

I text him, even though I probably won't get a response: *You could be a professional, you know.*

All of a sudden, the music stops. My phone vibrates. *Where are you?*

Look out your window. When his head appears, I wave.

"What the hell, Tobin?" He sounds more pissed than pleased.

"You sound great."

"You shouldn't be standing down there listening to me." I can't see his face because of the light behind his head, but he sounds just like he did when we used to tell him that the *Jaws* shark was real and lived in the lake. He loved the music to *Jaws* when he was about ten.

"Why not? Someday you'll be playing for thousands."

"That day is not today. What are you doing here?"

"I couldn't sleep, so I was walking, and I heard you. So I listened."

"Stay there." And his head disappears from his window.

I wait for him, wishing I had grabbed a heavier jacket. And socks. My moccasins are lined with alpaca fur—all the rage at Twin Ports Academy, straight from the Mall of America, even though I had to bribe Gracie to bring a pair back to me—but even alpaca fur isn't enough right now.

"Sneaky you, Tobin."

I jump when he talks. "Not really. Just out walking."

He looks at the ground. "Are you going to be mad at Gracie if she told me what's going on with your dad?" He clears his throat. "I remember Mrs. Nealy, too." It's hard to hear him, because he's so quiet.

"I'm sorry I haven't texted you. I've been . . . hiding." I keep my voice down, too.

"You know we can help you if you need it." The moonlight is glinting off the edge of his glasses.

"No disrespect, but everybody says that. And I have no idea what kind of help I need."

"Well . . ." He thinks. "I can always come over and watch your dad, if you want. When he gets . . . further along. My mom used to do that for Mrs. Nealy, be there when her husband went to the store. Maybe your dad will like it better if I bring my violin?"

"He'd love it if you played all the Star Wars stuff. I hope it won't get to that point, where someone has to stay with him."

Once it's out of my mouth, I realize I'm an idiot.

Sid looks down again. "I think it always gets that bad—Mrs. Nealy bad."

My stomach lurches. "Can we not talk about this right now?"

"Okay." Sid looks at his watch. "You know it's 1:30, right? And we have school soon? Like in seven hours?"

"You weren't supposed to see that text and come out here."

"I saw my phone light up. C'mere." He grabs my hand and pulls me into a hug.

I've never been hugged by Sid Smithson before. He's not particularly meaty, but he's a good hugger. Just for a second, I let it be nice. But I pull away before I can feel my heart start to beat again. "Thanks for the offer."

"I'll play for him any day."

I wave, and Sid does the same, then he disappears around the corner of his house. I trudge back through the sand. Two houses before mine, in the one spot where there's a yard light, there's a kayak leaned up next to a garage, and it says PussyDestroyer69 on its side. I mentally put a frame of dick pics around it. Keepin' it classy on Park Point.

When I make it back inside, Dad's awake.

"Where were you?" I hear him call from his room when I come up the stairs.

"Grabbed a banana and sat on the back steps. Couldn't sleep." I stop in the doorway to his room. The only light is the glow from his Kindle screen.

"You've got school tomorrow."

"Going back to bed now."

He holds out his arms to me. "Hug?"

I squeeze once, quick, and bolt.

One middle-of-the-night hug with a guy at the beginning of his life. One with a man who's at the end of his.

My alarm and 7:30 come way, way, way too early.

Dad's Big Book of Advice #6
Real men squint, but smart people actually protect their eyes with sunglasses.

By the time we get to April 21, which is today, it's almost-but-not-quite pretending to be warm. We can pretend spring is coming, and that it might not snow again, but we all know that's not true. Today it's fifty-five degrees and sunny, and it's Saturday, so the nice weather isn't wasted on a school day.

I'm sitting on the dune in our backyard, trying to figure out how to pose the first few photos of my origin story. The box of action figures is next to me, and I've drawn a face on a pea pod, cribbed from the fridge and wrapped in a scrap of ribbon for Mystique to hold, like it's me. Mystique can be my mom. Professor Xavier, out of his wheelchair, can be my dad. Lando is Paul.

I tried taping cards together to make a house—better symbolism—but it's hard as hell to make a card house with the slippery kind of cards. So I swiped a cardboard box from the back of Trash Box and did some cutting and drawing. It's big, maybe a foot and a half tall. Mystique and Xavier are standing outside the card mansion, looking like they want to fight, since that's what action figures do, but they have this baby pea pod to take care of.

Of the twenty photos I take, maybe five are useful. But that's five more than I had.

Then I arrange one with Lando, Mystique, Pea Pod, and Professor X, like it's a portrait in a studio, but with beach grass and a sand dune as a background.

Little Rey will come in handy, because she can be the transition between Pea Pod and Big Rey, who's gonna be the now-me. Little Rey will learn to fight from Mystique and Lando, and she can sit at the feet of Professor X and get her mutant learning on.

I move the house so it's on top of the sand dune, so you can see Lake Superior in the background, and snap some shots.

I like it. A lot.

"Tobin! Where are you?"

I raise my hand up and wave it. The roll of the dunes can hide you pretty well.

"Can I come out there?" It's my dad, yelling from the house.

His voice doesn't sound quite like his.

I don't want him to come out here.

I see my heart on the bottom of the lake, and it's a big black ice cube. You can't even tell it's a heart if you don't know what it is. A fish noses it—a huge fish—but then swims away.

Right after my mom moved to Paris, which was also in April, we used to sit out here on the dune and stare at the lake and the ships when they came by. I alternated between sad five-year-old, angry five-year-old, and regular five-year-old, sometimes in the space of thirty seconds, and my dad would tell me stories about the lake, and fish, and seagulls, and whatever else he could think of to get my mind off things.

I remember him saying it was okay to be sad and angry, because feelings aren't facts. Feelings just are. Feel them and let them go, so you can deal with what's in front of you.

It was pretty heavy for a five-year-old, but evidently it stuck.

Here's my seventeen-year-old conclusion: feelings can suck it. Right now and forevermore.

When I've got a few more shots, I sit up and watch my dad walk out to me.

In the last two days, my dad's used a cane enough for it to really qualify as a full-time thing, and his progress is pretty slow. He sways and pitches like the ground is actively moving as he walks. His face is set in stone concentration, because he has to watch his feet as if they might escape.

He looks rickety. And he doesn't walk, exactly, anymore. He rickets.

At least the cast on his wrist is gone. He's down to a brace.

I grab the Star Wars X-Men Fam and their house and jog to him. "It's too far. Let's just go back to the house."

He motions me back to the dune. "I am not an invalid. Six months ago, I ran a marathon." He glares.

"Then give me a sec." I dash back to the house, fast as I can go, throw down my stuff, grab two fold-up chairs, and hustle back out to the dune, passing my dad before I get there, because he's not going any faster than he was before.

Dad laughs. "That's the first time I've seen you run since eighth grade."

"Probably even before that." I'm winded when I stop.

He makes it to me while I'm setting up the chairs on the highest dune in our backyard, facing the lake. The wind is still damn cold, and even though I've got on a couple layers of fleece, I'm shivering. Dad's got on a fleece pullover, a sweatshirt under that, gloves, and a hat. I get the impression it's harder to hold on to body heat. He wears his hat in the house sometimes.

By April, the lake doesn't look so much like it will eat you, but you'll still freeze to death in less than ten minutes if you go in.

He breaks the silence. "Time for a dad joke."

"Haven't heard one for a while."

"A ham sandwich walks into a bar and orders a beer. The bartender says, 'Sorry, we don't serve food here.'"

I chuckle. "Ham sandwich on a barstool."

He grins.

We sit and watch the lake ripple in the bright sun, trying not to be cold.

I fumble for a topic. "Do you want anything special at your birthday party?"

"A big cake in the shape of an ambulance." Dad looks hopeful.

"Maybe Allison can figure it out."

"Have you started planning with her?"

"Not yet." I haven't told her about the party.

"You know what else I want?" He's on a roll now. "Mama Duck."

"Six stories of Zen?"

He nods. "Yup. That's my Make-A-Wish."

I roll my eyes. "I'll work on that."

He chuckles. "You do that, Tobin." Then he clears his throat. "How you doin', honey? Really? No bullshit."

"Hanging in there." I keep my voice as normal as possible.

He puts his hand on my arm. Still strong, still comforting. "Honest, or are you trying to make me feel better?"

"There is no good answer to 'how are you?' when your dad is dying." It comes out in a rush.

"I see your point." He reaches in his pocket and pulls out a piece of paper. "Maybe this will help?"

Information for a support group. Family members of people with ALS. I fold it back up and hand it to him. "Nope."

"You can't just keep it all inside." Such a dad thing to say.

"I'd be the only teenager there, and it would suck." I touch my hand to the left side of my chest. Nothing. Good. "You're still here. I'm all right for a while."

He sighs. "It will be impossible to convince you otherwise, won't it?"

I'm not talking to anyone about what my guts do every night. Or the fact that I either can't sleep or want to sleep for twenty-four hours straight. Or the fact that I've stopped doing homework. Or anything else.

"I'm writing you a book." Proud smile—bigger smile than I've seen for a very long time.

"You are?"

"It's called Dad's Big Book of Advice. All the things I don't want to forget to tell you."

"Like what?"

"Don't forget to change the oil in your car. Remember birthdays. Never smoke. Always be careful with your money. Stuff like that. Maybe some funny stuff, too."

"You can just tell me those things, can't you?" This is weird.

"That way you can refer to them as you need them." His eyes tear up, but I pretend not to notice. "Dad in a book. Best thing ever."

"Yeah." My voice breaks, even though I don't want it to, and I look away. "Will it have bad dad jokes?" I feel my heart beating, and I will it with all my force back into Lake Superior. "Am I going to laugh?"

He nods. "You'll laugh your ass off." He wipes away the tears that have escaped. Crying happens two or three times a day now.

We stare at the lake some more, him lost in his head and me trying not to mind that he's lost.

"Do you want to do photographs for my book?"

I don't quite register what he says. "For what?"

"Dad's Big Book of Advice. It would be even better if you took photos to go with it."

It would rip my guts out to do that.

"I, um . . . I should focus on my portfolio for school. For the scholarship. You're going to need lots of doctors, and Ike must be expensive. I kind of have to get one."

"If you don't want to, that's okay."

I am such a shitty daughter sometimes. "I didn't mean it like that. I just . . ." I can't be a shitty daughter.

He pats my arm. "Just wanted to check. Help me up, would you?"

I grab his cane and hand it to him, trying not to be a shitty daughter, so he can stand up. Then I carry the chairs back to the house over one shoulder while he holds on to my other arm. We go really slow.

"Ike should be here soon, if he's not already." My dad isn't winded, but he's not breathing as easily as he was a week ago.

"On a Saturday?"

"We have to start doing some damn chart to check disease progress."

Ike's been around almost every day, and I'm getting used to seeing his bag of stuff next to the couch and his Bluetooth speaker on the side table.

Once we make it into the house, Ike takes Dad's phone from him and puts on Gordon Lightfoot. Wise move on his part. While Ike tests my dad's functions, he tells us the max score is 40, and the function test measures everything from speech to movement to salivation—ew—to handwriting. Dad gets a 33.

Ike is pleased, and he makes some notes in a big three-ring binder of paper. "Good stuff, Steve. Now I gotta do those bitches of dishes."

My dad laughs. "Rich always says that, too, in the break room—'Who's gonna wash these bitches of dishes?' But I don't think it's in your job description."

"It's allowed. Elena taught me well, even though, as the baby, I tended to get out of most chores." Ike points at me. "I know you were working on your portfolio today."

"Yeah. Thanks." It doesn't stop me from blushing again. Elena is his mom, and she's super sweet. She's a nurse at Gracie's school. She sent us the world's best enchiladas right after Dad told me about his diagnosis. If Ike can cook like she can, then he should do that instead of dishes.

Ike's long gone, and Dad's asleep on the couch. There's another notebook on the table. I risk it.

MEREDITH'S GRANDMA'S WILD RICE SOUP

1½ c. cream
3c. cooked wild rice

A cookbook? A very Minnesota cookbook, if it has wild rice.

I page through, and there are at least twenty recipes in there, all of them dated before I was born, all of them in his handwriting. No way am I letting this go. I spirit it up to my room and tuck it into a desk drawer, then come back down and rummage under the stairs until I find one with a long list in it—baby names? character names?—and nothing else. I leave it on the table. Maybe he won't open it before he puts it back in a box.

Now I have recipes to help me remember him, along with my great-grandma. And my mom.

Text message from Gracie, about 1 a.m.: *You up?*

Of course.

Things OK? Haven't chatted much lately. :(#GracieandSilentTobin

Life is stressful. But Ike did the dishes today. #downwithchores

Ike who? No male escapes Gracie's scrutiny.

Rich's son—Dad's ambulance partner Rich.

She sends a photo of Ike in his fatigues she must have found online: *This guy?*

Yes.

You're so lucky!!!!!!!! #hothothot #squadgoals

In the picture, he's tall and built, tawny-tan skin with dark hair and eyes, not smiling because soldiers don't smile, but handsome and hunky. Gracie would think he's the strong, silent type, even though in reality he talks a lot and is maybe the cheeriest, nicest guy I know.

You probably can't be that guy when you're deployed.

Gotta go.

I put my phone on my desk, wrap up in a blanket, and close my eyes.

Ike is here to help my father die more slowly.

How is that lucky?

Dad's Big Book of Advice #7
Do what you want to do,
not what others want you to do.

MAY 1

Yesterday at Trash Box I told Allison about Dad's birthday request. She picked up the phone and reserved the Beach House thirty seconds after I told her. She says she knows caterers and people who can make a cake in the shape of an ambulance, and we can talk more about the other details when school is out. Getting the place is the most important thing.

Party skills: she's got 'em. Thank god.

When she was up front and I was sorting dishes in the back room, I stared at Mama Duck. Then I googled her, and it turns out she's from Duluth—who knew? A homegrown six-story Zen duck. So I sent an email.

What could it hurt?

People have the end-of-the-year freakouts at school. Gracie is texting me every twenty minutes about which test she thinks she's going to flunk next. I've already been called in to see Mrs. Brooks, our assistant principal, since my grades are so horrible. That conversation went something like this.

Mrs. B: I hear your dad has ALS.

Me: How did you hear that?

Mrs. B: We're willing to be moderately easy on you this semester. ALS is a very difficult diagnosis.

Me: Um.

Mrs. B: [looking at the ceiling, trying not to act like I've really screwed myself] We don't want you to completely wreck your GPA, though we know you have to be very distracted. We want to make things easier. It's really for all of us.

Me: All of us?

Mrs. B: Nobody wants to flunk a girl whose dad is dying.

Me: . . .

In my head, I took a photo of Mrs. B, sitting sternly at her desk, hands folded in front of her, with the words DAMMITDAMMITDAMMIT framing her portrait.

I was so hoping nobody would notice.

Then I had to get my ass in gear and do homework for two weeks nonstop after teachers forgave a few assignments. Now I'll probably end up with Cs across the board. For a couple weeks, I was a straight-F student. Dad would lose his mind in an instant if he knew.

Which he's already doing, it turns out.

Ike gave me a pamphlet a few days ago, called "Pseudobulbar Affect," and it explains why my dad is always crying, aside from the fact that everything is tragic. Sometimes the neurons in your head that control emotions go to hell when you have ALS, so a person can have exaggerated crying, laughing, or smiling spells.

A laughing or smiling spell would be great about now.

Tonight, Ike is doing Dad's function test, and he's down to a 31. Walking is steady, so to speak, since he's not very steady, but eating is getting harder, as is writing by hand. Dad's lawyer, Mark, came by a week ago. I looked at the signature when he was done. I would swear someone else had written it. The changes aren't huge, but they're there.

Dad has to cry and hold my hand for a while when Ike tells him his score. He does that a lot, hold my hand, and usually it helps him stop crying. Ike's job is to pat his back.

Dad eventually grabs a tissue from the side table. Ike's taken to leaving boxes of Kleenex everywhere. "Well. Think this spell is over." Ike told Dad what's going on with the neurons, which helped Dad feel a little less self-conscious. "Resume normal conversation."

I try to look like I'm okay with what just happened. "You can hold my hand as long as you need to." Even though I want to run. "Is it time for a dad joke?"

His smile is watery. "What did the buffalo say when his kid went off to college?"

"No idea." He told me this joke two days ago.

"Bison! Isn't that a great pun?" He's laughing, and then he's laughing and laughing like it's a Robin Williams marathon on Comedy Central. He can't stop. His eyes are a little panicked, and he squeezes my hand again. Hard.

Ike touches Dad's hand. "Steve, maybe you could think about something serious for a minute. Though I know it's a good joke."

He takes a deep breath, trying to get himself under control while still chuckling. "I'm working on it."

He squeezes my hand one more time and lets it go. I try not to let him see, but I massage my fingers.

"Do you and Ike have a second?" Dad blows his nose. "I want to talk with you about something."

Ike shrugs. "I don't have anywhere else to be."

"My homework is done." Mostly.

"Stay here then. I'll be right back." He grabs his cane and hoists himself off the couch, then walks with careful, measured steps toward the back door and the junk room/mud room/humongous closet that holds that back door. We've never known what the house builder intended that room for, but there's space for a washer and dryer, and extra boots, hats, and outside stuff, along with all the other random junk. We call it the Everything Room.

"Do you know what he's doing?" Ike's eyebrows are raised.

"Not a clue."

Ike gets out his three-ring notebook and makes a couple notes on a different page than where he records Dad's scores. "Is your dad a secretive guy? Was he before the diagnosis?"

"Nope."

"Hmm." He jots another couple things.

Dad comes out of the Everything Room with a small box, held with care in his hand with the brace, the one that's not holding his cane. He motions Ike and me to the kitchen table, and he puts the box in the middle. His hands are visibly shaking, harder than normal.

"What's that?" I pick up the box. It's been opened and taped back up. There's a logo of mountains on it with a few birds flying over them. The box says CHOICE MEDICAL

SUPPLIES, and underneath it says SUMINISTROS MÉDICOS DE ELECCIÓN. And that's it.

Dad hands Ike a piece of paper that's been folded up. "You can read Spanish? I know you speak it with your folks."

"Yes." Ike takes the paper, reads it, looks at my dad, looks at me, and hands the paper back to Dad. "That's all that's in there?"

My dad nods, closes his eyes, and nods again.

"Did you order it online?"

He nods again.

"Judging from the packaging, I'm right, but I just want to check: you didn't get it from someone here in America, which would be illegal?"

Dad shakes his head *no*.

"Okay then, but I'm not helping you." Ike sits down at the table, clasps his hands together, and looks at my dad. "I'm not capable."

"Excuse me?" My voice is higher and more scared than I want it to be. "What's going on?"

"That box is from Mexico, Tobin, and it contains a drug called pentobarbital. It's his news to tell you what he's going to do with it." Ike's face and voice are calm, but there's something underneath it. "You probably want to sit down."

I sit. "What's pentobarbital?"

Dad clears his throat. "It's a drug people use to induce unconsciousness and stop their hearts."

"But your heart's going to stop too soon as it is."

Silence.

"Isn't it?"

My dad reaches across the table and grabs my hand again, the one that's still a bit sore from earlier, when he was in tears, which are flowing again. "The drugs are to help me."

"Help you what?"

"Decide when I want to be done with this illness, instead of letting the illness make the decision."

There are whistles in my ears. Traffic cop whistles and slide whistles and teakettle whistles.

"I've seen a lot of death, honey. Eventually there won't be anything left to save. CPR won't work on someone whose breathing muscles are shot to hell. You can't jumpstart my legs with defibrillator paddles. So . . ." He takes a deep breath. "This way I can choose when to be finished."

I can't hear anything. "Choose what? When?" He's miles away, behind the whistling and noise.

"Not soon." He points at the box. "Later in the year. I'll take some Zofran first, so I don't throw it up, then I'll drink the pentobarbital. Then I'll lose consciousness. Then my heart will stop."

Ike touches his hand. "I'm not sure Tobin needs the practical explanation right now."

The whistles screech on, but now there are rumbles, like landslides. Is the world splitting open?

"If this was a disability, I'd be fine. I could live the rest of my life doing wheelchair marathons, or whatever. That's totally workable." He looks at me and Ike. "But this bullshit disease is devastation. I'm so angry and sad I can barely see straight. So, when it's time, I'll stop the destruction."

Ike is still calm. "I will not help you. It's against everything I believe."

I stand and walk out the back door. I can't hear a thing, and I can't feel my body, but I push myself to move.

"Tobin?"

I keep going.

You'd think the temperature would get warmer out here, but it doesn't seem to.

I imagine my heart on the bottom of the lake, still black, still frozen, but smaller. Two months has eroded its size. Fish still nudge it from time to time.

My hands are blocks of unmoving ice.

He can't do this to me.

"Tobin?" It's Ike. "Your dad doesn't want to come out here in the dark, in case he trips. And he wants to talk to you a little bit more."

"Nothing else to say." I can barely get it out.

"He says there is. Could you be kind to him?"

I'm silent.

"I know this is impossible. Death always is. Please come back in."

I turn around. It's almost dark, but I can see Ike pretty well. He's got a fleece jacket for me.

I take it from him, putting it on as I follow him back into the house. The sand shifts under our feet. There's no way I'd want Dad walking out here in the dark.

He's still sitting at the table, and he's been crying, because his eyes are bright red and puffy.

"Tobin, I'm so very sorry." He reaches up to hug me as I stand there.

I bend down into the hug, even though every instinct in me is to head back out the door.

He pulls away and looks into my eyes. "I know I'm cheating you of more time. But I can't bear the thought of losing myself so completely."

I try to think of something to say to his hurt, agonized face, but my brain is stalled out.

"I love you so much, Tobin. I'm so sorry. It's all such a big mess." He pulls me into a hug again, and I return the gesture, but my insides aren't going to keep themselves together much longer.

Dad starts crying again, and then he's wailing. Ike comes around and carefully pulls him back from me. "Steve, Tobin will be able to talk about this soon. It's a big shock."

"She hates me, Ike! She just hates me!" And he's off, howling and wailing. Ike shoos me away over my dad's shoulder and mouths *go upstairs*, so I do.

Where I heave my guts up, then sit and stare out my bedroom window. Not that I can see anything, really, since there's no moon. The lake is a big absence of light, like the world just falls away into empty, deep space, as far as the eye can see.

I close my eyes and let that black absence of light flow into my body, deadening my limbs, my torso, and finally my brain. Stopping everything that was just vibrating itself toward light speed.

After Ike goes home, I go downstairs, and my dad's asleep on the couch, which seems to be the nightly routine. He's slumped to the side, mouth partially open and breathing slow. So, I take photos. His hands. His cane propped next to him. His face, which isn't really his face anymore. Too skinny. Too hollow. Like half of him is free-floating atoms. His eyes are still puffy from all his crying.

The box isn't on the table. I look in the Everything Room, and it's on the top shelf, next to the 20 Mule Team Borax detergent, like it's an ordinary box. Just a Box of Death, ho hum, no big deal.

When I go back to the living room, the tears almost rush out of my mouth in a howl, but I push them down into sub-mission with the black absence I absorbed from the lake.

My dead, black heart. That has to stay the same.

Then I sit on the couch next to him and take a selfie with my half-dead dad. Soon to be all dead. Sooner than I thought.

He's disoriented when I wake him, but I know he wants his own bed. He says sleeping on the couch isn't very comfort-able anymore.

Once I'm back in my room, I look at the photos and realize there are tears on my face in the selfie.

I didn't even feel them.

<u>May 3</u>

Sometimes I think about Mariette.

Finding love in the enormous, scary wilderness with some rough dude from far away, trying to figure out how the hell to live in the middle of so many trees. Stuck on the shore of a gigantic lake, trying  to force some order into her life. Making porridge, patching her man's trousers, watching her belly grow, hoping her Ojibwe neighbors are close- and will be generous enough to help her, the invader, the trespasser-when her labor begins. Hearing them laugh, watching them roll their eyes when she serves them inedible, undercooked wild rice-rice they gave her. Nodding in gratitude as they show her how to cook it properly. So many skills to learn. Carrying canoes and pelts and buckets and buckets of water. Weeping when her toddler dies.

Mariette had muscles and guts. She had good teachers. She had enormous balls and tenacious ovaries. And, thankfully, more kids.

Or I wouldn't be sitting here, Tobin Mariette Oliver, on the shore of the same lake, trying to figure out the twenty-first century equivalent of chopping wood and making beaver stew.

And living through death.

Dad's Big Book of Advice #8
Don't close off your heart, even when you're tempted.

MAY 5

The morning after Dad showed us the box, he was calmer than I'd seen him for a while. He was setting out cereal and milk for me when I made it into the kitchen before school. Now that I drive myself, since Dad's feet aren't coordinated, I get up earlier. Sometimes that means time for breakfast.

He's made all the arrangements, he said. He'll write a letter and give it to Rich, in case someone questions what happens. Nobody will get in trouble. It's all his choice. The house will be mine. The car will be mine. He's got it all worked out.

I kept my eyes on the Cinnamon Chex, silent as the grave. Ha ha, that's a pun.

Allison will be my guardian, he said, and there will be trust funds made from paid-out insurance money. He's taking care of me in the best way he can.

Can't I see that?

When I left for school, he was weeping at the table. Ike was on his way.

He begged me to talk.

I just left.

Now it's three days later. I'm still maintaining my freeze.

Text on the way to school. Gracie. *Doing ok, hun? #missyou*

I'm OK. #missyoutoo

We haven't hung out for forever. Like two weeks. Can we soon? #GracieandTobinGetTea

I hope so. #teasoundsgood

I don't say, *My dad's going to kill himself. He'll die sooner rather than later.*

I don't say, *My life is completely upside down.*

A cargo ship is arriving as I get to the bridge, so I call the school's office and tell them. After the ship blows its horn, the bridge blows its horn back, saying hello and letting folks know the bridge deck is lifting. The office hears the bridge horn, so they know I'm not lying.

I'm happy for the pause, though I'm probably the only one in this line of twenty cars who is. The chatter and hum of school jangles my nerves. The longer I stay away, the better off I am.

Another text. Sid. *Where are you?*

Stuck on our side of the lift bridge.

Lucky you! Can't wait till school is out.

Me either.

How's your dad?

Holding his own. Mostly.

It's more info than I gave Gracie. But he's calmer—quieter—than Gracie.

While I wait for the ship to get through, I google it. If you search "ship" and its name, it usually shows up. This one is named *Trudy*, and she's from Liberia, on the west coast of Africa. I can't get to school, but it can get here, in the middle of the country, all the way from Africa? I know there's a way, through the St. Lawrence Seaway and all that, but I just can't imagine it. How long does it take? It would feel like a million billion years.

In my mind's eye, I see my dad on a map, pushing a wheelchair through all the Great Lakes, on his way to Africa. Right before he gets to England, he and the chair sink.

I check my email, and there's a response from Chip, the guy who takes care of Mama Duck: *We don't generally honor Make-A-Wish requests. We are very busy and cannot be fair to all inquiries we receive.*

I reply. *The man has ALS and will be 50. Isn't that unique enough to consider this request? August 15 is also the weekend after the Tall Ships Festival, and you're normally in town for that, aren't you? The party's on Park Point, so Mama Duck has familiar territory to float in. Can't you do a kind thing for a dying man?* Send.

I may have been too blunt.

It's the first time I've written the words *dying man*.

There's another ship right after the first one, this one going out. I shut the car off, and my mind drifts.

Dad's at a twenty-seven now on the functionality scale.

Instead of discussing that fact endlessly, like Dad and Ike do, I work on my portfolio. Peapod Baby has been replaced by Little Rey. She's sat next to Professor X, learning his wisdom at his feet, and she's also hung out with Mystique. I built a school out of cardboard, too—it has a flagpole and a flag outside, plus a swing set, so you know it's a school—and they all took family photos there. There are also shots of Mystique leaving with a suitcase, and Little Rey looking after her. Then shots of Little Rey on the dunes, looking at the lake, reading a little tiny book I made for her, building a beach fire with Lando and Professor X. A tiny family doing family things.

At supper some nights, I watch my dad and Ike talk and laugh. Sometimes Rich comes over with food from Elena, which is always delicious, and the three of them tell stories of bad wrecks, people they helped, times they avoided disaster. I just listen.

Sometimes I think, *Our tiny family has expanded.*

Then the second ship is gone. People start honking. It's morning rush.

I check my own ice, to be sure it's solid, start the car again, and go to school.

After school, I park in the back of the shop, dreading the next two hours. The earliest summer tourists are showing up to paw through our stuff, so Allison tweaks even more about dusting and arranging. Thankfully, Paul also comes downstairs more, because he knows Allison tweaks.

I need to get addresses from her, for far away family. Aside from them, I have no idea who to invite to this shindig. Maybe I should look at the contacts in Dad's phone.

Maybe I should actually get some invites.

Ike texts: *Can you take your dad to the marathon meeting tonight? Gotta do some shopping for him.* My dad's on the board of directors of Grandma's Marathon, and it's six weeks to marathon time. All the planning gets him out of the house.

He won that marathon in 1992. This year, he won't be able to walk to the starting line without a cane. Maybe even a walker.

I text back before I go inside: *Sure thing. See you later.*

Allison hands me a duster the minute I walk in the door. "We've already had ten customers today. Business is picking back up!" She's practically singing. "The glassware needs to look at sharp as possible, all right, Tobin? And check out our new pop-up shop. It's right outside the window."

"Our what? And why right outside the door?" She's not making sense.

"You'll see." She smiles.

I look out the front window, and I see a table covered with records. Then I see a tall, broad man in a sweatshirt standing behind a chair, and I think there's a skinny guy in a red jacket in the chair, but I can't quite tell, because the broad guy covers him up. There's a sign on the sidewalk, on a sandwich board. It says MAMA DUCK'S RECORD STORE, with a drawing of Mama Duck on it, sitting next to a record player. Notes float all around the sign.

Seriously?

When I go outside, Ike hears the door, turns to look, and smiles. "Hey, Tobin! How was school?"

"Moderately okay. What is this? Didn't you just text me?"

He gestures. "Yes, and your dad was bored, so Allison said we could set up a pop-up shop."

Then I notice, on the other end of the table, there's a milk crate with a sign that says GORD'S GOLD, ALL ALBUMS $5 on it. There might be ten Gordon Lightfoot albums in the crate. Vintage record collections always have some Gordon Lightfoot.

My dad turns and sees me, and his face lights up. "Like my sign, Tobin? We've sold five albums to three people. Even one Gordon Lightfoot album!"

"Very nice." And I can't help it. I laugh.

My dad is interacting with the older couple standing in front of the table, telling them what he knows about the albums he's familiar with. They're listening, then all three of them start talking about big band conductors. My dad knows a lot about interacting with people but not much about music. They don't seem to notice. They hand him a five, and he hands them two albums. They wave, he waves, and they continue down the sidewalk with a smile at me.

Dad turns to me. "I could do this all day."

"Not in July, when it'll be hot without any shade." I frown.

"I bet Paul might have an old umbrella around somewhere. That back room is full of crap." He jerks his thumb back toward the building.

"Allison said we can sell albums whenever we want. She'll set the table up and everything." Ike smiles at me, trying to fix my frown. "Don't you want company when you work?"

"If it makes you two happy, who am I to say?" And I go back inside.

He could end up weeping if someone buys his favorite Gordon Lightfoot album. Or he could end up cursing them seven ways to Sunday for taking it away from him. Or it could all be just fine. This one's on Ike, not me.

Then I realize I just busted up my freeze. I look back out the window, over my shoulder, and Ike is grinning and giving me a thumbs-up.

Dammit.

Allison chirps at me from behind the counter. "What do you think? It's a good way to keep him busy, and we've got records for days. He can be out there all summer, if he wants to be."

I nod.

"Have you given up talking permanently, or just for a while?"

I shrug.

She rolls her eyes at me. "Dust, then."

She has no idea about my dad's Box of Death. I heard him tell Ike he's not going to tell her, and that the only three people who will know are me, Ike, and Dad. I guess I can thank him for that. I don't want Allison's opinion. Or her pity.

The duster and I become one with each other, and the glass sparkles when the light comes through the big window as the sun gets lower.

My trips through the glass aisles also result in some rearranging, and soon I have a rainbow down one aisle. Who knew we had red, orange, yellow, green, blue, and purple glass?

"Really nice." There's a chuckle behind me. "Wonder if Allison will leave it there for Pride month?" It's Paul.

I almost drop a green piece, because his voice startles me. "She might not even notice."

"It's hard not to notice a rainbow of glass filling up an entire shelf. Looks great, hon."

"It was kind of for you, and kind of because it was there, and kind of because I was bored."

Paul had a partner when I was born, a man named Edward. I don't really remember him, but I've seen pictures. When he died, I was two. Paul said he'd never have another love like Ed, so he quit relationships, which is too bad. He's a really nice guy, and cute besides, even though he's in his seventies.

He gives me a squeeze around my shoulders. "How's your dad? Hanging tough?"

"His numbers haven't gone down a whole lot. He was a twenty-seven last time."

"They didn't have that scale when Uncle Robert had ALS." He picks up another piece of green glass and puts it into place.

"Uncle Robert?"

"Your dad might not remember him. He was pretty little when Robert was sick. Robert was his great-uncle, and he got sick really fast." Paul's face is grim. "But Robert was the original couch potato, and your dad isn't. So that will help."

"I hope so." I wonder if Dad remembers. Paul's face tells me he remembers it all.

Maybe I should tell Paul about the Box of Fuck You I Hate You Worse Than ALS.

Allison comes back from wherever she is and looks over the glass rainbow with a frown. "Where's the glass that should be on this shelf?"

I gesture to all the other shelves. "Nothing got lost."

"So you can talk to Paul but not to me?" Her frown doesn't move.

I don't answer that but move my little dusting self on to the crocks and boxes and decorative plates.

Paul's voice is gentle. "Give her some space."

Allison doesn't have anything to say to that, so she goes back behind the counter to add up the day's receipts. It's about 5:15. Dad and Ike brought in their records and their sandwich board sign about 4:30 and headed home. They waved. I waved my duster at them.

Paul gives me one more side-arm hug. "You need an ear, I'm your guy."

"Thanks." I will the ice to clog my veins, but it's not working at the moment.

Allison looks up from the cash register. "You can head out whenever you want, Tobin. I like the glass rainbow. Let's keep it for a while." She smiles, and it's involuntary: I smile back. That makes her smile more, and Paul is smiling, and we're all smiling, and I remember my dad is going to kill himself, so I bolt out the back door before I can smile again.

When I finally get home, after getting stopped by a sailboat—a cargo ship is one thing, but a sailboat just pisses everyone off—Ike's already gone.

When I open the door, all I hear is Dad singing, at the top of his lungs: "First of May, first of May, outdoor fucking begins todaaaaaaaaaay." And he repeats it, with the same weird tune, in the time it takes me to get from the front door to where he is.

He doesn't see me, because he's in the kitchen. His cane is leaning against the sink, and he's getting a glass of water, singing the entire time. His voice sounds like someone I don't know.

"Dad?"

He drops the glass. Good thing the sink contains the shatter. "You scared me, Tobin!" His face is white.

"Ike asked me to take you to the meeting tonight. Ready? I'll clean that up later."

He grabs another glass, fills it full of water, chugs it, then sets it next to the sink before he picks up his cane. "Ready. My race notebook is on the coffee table. Will you grab it for me?" He starts heading toward the door, almost striding, if a person could stride and use a cane at the same time. No ricketing anywhere. In this moment, he looks close to being Steve Oliver again.

I drive him to the meeting, which is back over the bridge at Grandma's Restaurant. Yes, the marathon is named after the restaurant. We don't get stopped by any kind of ship. Then I head home and clean up the glass after I make us a salad for supper, complete with grilled chicken. Life is always better when you can grill.

My before-ALS dad would never sing a song like that. He likes to pretend I don't know what sex is. Periods are one thing.

There's another notebook sitting on the coffee table by his usual spot on the couch.

Dear Tobin:

I'm going to try and write a picture book for you, one you can take to kindergarten in three years and show all the other kids. Maybe your mom will take photos for it.

Once upon a time, there was a water witch who lived in Lake Superior. She lived way, way down at the bottom. Her hair was long and dark, and fish swam in and out of the strands that floated in the currents.

The story stops there.

As a kindergartener, I would have been scared shitless.

That water witch is probably sitting next to my black, lumpy heart.

It's Saturday. Dad's taking a nap. I went to breakfast with Gracie and didn't tell her about Dad's Stupid Box of Death I Hate It. Then I cleaned the house, took some really dumb pictures of the Star Wars X-Men Fam, and made lists of stuff I'll need for the party.

Then I sat down at the table with another notebook from under the stairs, one Dad left on the table. This one is notes from Paul's Tall Ships Festival presentations and copied passages from Mariette's journal. Notes about how Dad wants to write a history of Park Point, Duluth, and the fur trade. He's even got an editor's name jotted down—an editor who worked for the University of Minnesota Press in 1997, that is.

I don't hear Ike come in.

"You know your dad wants to keep his notebooks private."

I jump. "Dude! Yes, I know, but this one is history. No feelings at all."

He gives me skeptical side-eye. "It's still private stuff."

My face colors. "I haven't got a lot of months left to know him."

Ike sits down. "I see your point, but still." He gives me a long look. "Speaking of knowing someone, you seem awfully reserved these days."

"Emotions are useless at this point."

"But they still matter. And what he said is a shocking thing to think about."

"You were pretty against it."

He sighs. "I'm Catholic, for one thing, so suicide doesn't work for us. We can talk about my feelings some other day, okay? Time to talk about you and him."

I don't say anything.

"The disease is messing with his brain. Maybe you figured that out by now. Not just the pseudobulbar stuff." Ike glances into the living room at Dad, who's sawing logs, snoring louder than most freight trains.

"Is there a rating scale for that part?" I look at my dad, too. Today it's almost hard to recognize him. His hair's still his hair, still wavy and golden blond and thick, but that's about all. His face is even more drawn, and he's getting way too skinny.

"Not really. He'll still have good moments, for sure, but there might be times when he seems like a whole other person."

A chill runs up my spine, and I hear the tune for his outdoor sex song. "Great. Thanks for the heads up."

"I can't imagine how much this all sucks for you."

"Yeah."

"And this is where Stephen Hawking had an advantage." This thought amuses him.

"Huh?"

"Stephen Hawking was amazingly good at thinking, and thinking was the one thing he had left. It may have been all he needed. Stephen Oliver, on the other hand, lives in his body more than his brain—running, saving people. And it's all failing him. I can see why he'd want to end it before his body's completely stolen from him."

My brain pauses several beats while the anxiety stops whirling and Ike's words sink in. "I see your point." Not that I want to say it, but it's fair.

We don't say anything for a while. Dad continues to snore loud enough to be heard in Canada. Ike and I work on supper together—frozen lasagna and a salad—and then we wake Dad. He's groggy, but clues in once we get him walking. He perks up when he sits down and Ike pushes the Cholula over to him. "Smells so good!" He drizzles it on his lasagna. Gross.

Since Ike's been with Dad, we've had a bottle of Cholula Hot Sauce on the table next to the salt and pepper shakers. New family members have new condiments. It's way too hot for me, but Dad and Ike are liberal with it.

Supper discussion is basic. The marathon. The annoying tourists. The weather. Rich is working on getting a new partner, though he's sad about it. Dad sheds a few tears, but Ike keeps him calm and the storm is quick.

After supper, Dad heads back to the couch. "Come sit with me, Tobin. Just for a minute." He pats the cushion next to him once he gets settled.

So I do.

He picks up my hand and squeezes it, stronger than I'd expect him to be. "I love you, daughter. I'm going to die soon."

"Yes." I look at Ike. He nods, as if to say, *It's fine. Let him be how he is.*

"But I'm going to kill myself first. I'm sorry about that, but I'm too angry to live with this body forever."

His cheeks are red with fury—his eyes glow with hate for the whole world, it seems.

"Do you know how awful this is? How tired I am? How furious and jealous I am that you and Ike can still do the things you normally do? *Do you?*"

I can't even nod to reply as his energy assaults me.

Then his face literally shifts from furious to tired. "But right now, I want to go read in bed." Crisis over, just like that.

Then he gets his rickety self off the couch, with the help of his cane, and heads toward the stairs. "Ike, will you help me for a moment?"

Ike and I look at each other as Ike follows him up.

His emotions are like the storms on the lake—intense, then gone.

But you gotta take shelter when they happen.

<u>May 12</u>

When people die, do their stories end?
Or do the words switch to other tongues
only the dead can understand?
We start our lives with cells talking to nerves
talking to brains talking to muscles,
telling us to go and do, here we are,
laughing and fighting and crying and kissing,
until miscommunication
sends us sprawling up steps, down stairs,
breaking wrists, and then we're planning our death,
having good-bye parties, signing papers,
yelling at people who love us.

People try to decipher this new narrative,
the one your tongue stumbles through,
but once dying is an active verb in your life,
the story jumbles.

Maybe it's never over.
Maybe it just goes on in languages
those left behind can't read
but long to,
ones we desperately wish
a quiet voice would speak in our ear,

comforting us in the darkness.

Dad's Big Book of Advice #9
Don't take yourself so seriously.

MAY 17

No answer yet from the Mama Duck guy, so I send another email: a photo of Mama Duck and her haiku, in the back room of Trash Box.

During first hour, Mrs. Brooks calls me into her office. I brace for the worst, but she's smiling. "Are you looking forward to your trip?"

"My what?"

She's still smiling. "Your family trip to Hawaii? Your dad called yesterday. You'll be missing the last two weeks of school. Next Monday, you'll have your finals, and then you're off! Have you been there before?"

When the flip was someone going to tell me we're going to Hawaii?

"Um, no."

Her expectant face looks like this is all just wonderful, a dad and daughter going on a trip. She stands and holds out her hand. "Enjoy yourself. See you in the fall. Thanks for getting your classes back on track." When I extend mine, she pumps it like she'll never see me again. If I look closely, I'm sure I'll see tears in her eyes. I don't look.

"Yeah. Sure. Thanks."

She sits back down and busies herself with papers. "Talk with your teachers and get your exams arranged. You may go."

I scram out of there before it can get any weirder.

My dad will just trip over the sand. Or try and surf and drown himself. Or he'll cry the whole time.

Listen to me, crapping all over Paradise.

I text Ike: *Are we really going to Hawaii?*

Return text: *yes! :)*

WHY DIDN'T ANYONE TELL ME?

Shrug emoji in return. *We can talk when you get home.*

Grrrrrrrr. 100% not impressed about being left out.

No reply.

I talk to teachers, finish the day, go to Trash Box, dust more shit, wait on people, and think about all the ways a vacation could go wrong. Paul comes downstairs before I leave and gives me a snorkel and a waterproof disposable camera. I hug him tight and thank him, but it still pisses me off that nobody told me.

I make pork chops and rice—bake them with cream of mushroom soup, supper of Midwestern champions, thank you very much—and Ike comes in while we're eating and talking. Well, *I'm* eating, and Dad's getting some chewed up, but not much. *He's* talking, while I'm being a silent asshole again.

Ike grins as he sits. "Got a new joke! A combo: Stephen Hawking and bad dad. I know how you like bad dad jokes, Tobin."

"Pork chop, Ike?" My dad waves a shaky hand at the cupboard with the dishes. "Grab a plate and sit down." He seems very clued in tonight, which is nice. "What's the joke?"

Ike dishes up, then sits and puts Cholula on his pork chop, eyes twinkling. "Guess what, Tobin? You matter! Unless you multiply yourself times the speed of light squared. Then you energy!"

My dad laughs. Like outright belly-laughs, not even uncontrollably. "Stephen Hawking would love that joke. And hand that hot sauce over here. Good idea." Ike does, and Dad adds a generous dollop to his pork chop.

I chuckle, because the joke is funny. And because my dad is coherent and eating hot sauce on the most Midwestern dish ever. My crabby-ass bitch stance takes a momentary break.

"When was someone going to tell me we're going to Hawaii?" I try not to frown, because it's Hawaii, but I'm still annoyed.

Ike talks with his mouth full. "It was supposed to be a surprise. Bucket list for your dad, and a break for you."

"Except that I looked like an idiot in front of Mrs. Brooks today." My internal bitch's smoke break is over.

"Well, that wasn't supposed to happen." Ike looks at Dad. "Next time we take a trip, we make a list of things to do, and one of them is to clue Tobin in about everything."

My dad nods. "I'm sorry." I see his eyes start to well up.

I have to derail those tears, so my brain grabs for anything. "Have you been looking at pictures of Hawaiian fish? What's your favorite one?" I make it sound like he's six and into animals, which isn't quite right, but he does know a lot about Lake Superior fish, so maybe he's been studying Hawaiian ones.

"The humuhumunukunukuapua`a." My dad says it with no hesitation or stumbling.

"The what? That's a word? And a fish?"

Ike laughs. "Oh. That one. I'm sure we'll see a lot of them."

"If I'm remembering right, Kahalu'u Beach has a ton of them. At least they did twenty years ago, when we were there. Have you snorkeled, Ike?"

"It'll be my first time. I'll tie myself to you and let you show me around." He smiles.

My dad smiles in return. "Here's a bad dad joke about Hawaii, Tobin. Knock knock."

"Who's there?"

"Hawaii." He's trying not to laugh.

"Hawaii who?"

"I'm great, how are you?" And he loses it so hard he almost falls out of his chair. Ike has to prop him up.

"Good one, Dad." I roll my eyes at Ike.

Ike shrugs. "I liked it."

"We leave when?"

Ike goes to the living room and grabs a stack of papers from beside the couch. "We'll drive down to the Cities next Monday night. We leave Tuesday about 7 a.m., and the airline will have a wheelchair waiting for us at the Delta desk. We just have to get your dad to the desk."

"Wheelchair?" It's the only word that registers.

My dad slaps the table with his hand, which isn't loud and hard, but it's still a hit. "Stephen Hawking would get his ass in a wheelchair and take that ass to Hawaii. So that's what we're going to do, too."

A wheelchair.

Airports are some long walking. Long ricketing, that is. It makes sense.

But if I had a heart in my body, it would flip over.

Ike's reading the stack of papers. "Just like your Professor X, Tobin. Sometimes even super mutants need some help."

"My what?" My face is hot.

"I know you're doing weird stuff with action figures, but you're an artist, so I figure you know something I don't." He looks over the paper he's reading, and his eyes crinkle, like they do when he smiles. "I'm just a dumb medic."

"Right. A dumb medic. So leave the artist alone."

"Tobin!" Dad's not having it. "Don't call Ike names! We couldn't live without him." He glares.

"No offense meant, Ike."

"None taken." His eyes crinkle again over his papers. "Pack by Monday morning. We'll take off right after school."

"How much packing am I doing?"

"Ten days' worth."

"Who the frack is paying for this? We don't have that kind of money." My voice is louder than I mean it to be.

Ike sets down his papers. "My dad took up a collection and raised enough money for plane tickets, with the help of a doctor's frequent-flyer miles. Another doctor donated their condo."

The tears are running down my dad's face, but he's calm. "Rich is so kind. For us, it's about five hundred dollars. We have that."

"But we'll need it! You're only going to get sicker."

"I need to see some new fish. You need to have fun. Ike wants to visit Hawaii. Who are we to deny him the chance?" He sniffles. "So let's just take a damn trip before I can't walk across a room or open a door. When I lose my skills, they're gone. Forever. So let's just take a goddamn trip."

He rickets up off the chair, picks up his cane, and heads into the living room. Case closed.

Ike looks after him as he goes. "Guess you got told."
All I can do is nod.

After Ike and I clean up supper and do the dishes, I notice there's a box by the front door. From France.

I text Gracie. *Box came for you. I'll leave it on the front porch.*
Can I come in and see you? #longlostBFF
Probably not wise. Dad's resting.
Can you hang out soon? #GracieandLongLostTobin
I don't really have the strength to be a high school girl, but I can't tell her that.
Hopefully. Turns out I'm taking a trip to Hawaii. Before we go?
Let's do pedis! #prettytoesfortheocean
Good idea. #forgothowtobeagirl

The next day is Friday, and my teachers tell me my fate. Only two are making me do multiple choice, sit-in-the-testing-center tests, and the other three gave me short essay exams to write over the weekend. It was very clear they feel sorry for me, since I'm only getting to go because my dad is literally on his last leg. *Poor, sad girl* was right there in their eyes.

Pity sucks.

On Sunday, I pack my camera, lenses, swimsuits, shorts and tops, and six pairs of flip-flops. Then Gracie and I go for a pedi. She assaults me with a million questions, about Hawaii and my dad, which I try to answer, and I promise to bring her home something with a Hawaiian print on it.

So. Many. Words.

Gracie acts like nothing's wrong, like nothing's changed, like we haven't seen each other for a long time because of school, homework, work, whatever. Not because the world is upside down. I nod and smile, nod and smile. Nod. Smile.

Monday morning, before I go to school, I look in the Everything Room, and the box of drugs is still next to the 20 Mule Team Borax. One ordinary Box of Death, ready and waiting.

Fuck you. We're going to Hawaii.

I hand in my essays and take my tests, and we get everything into the car, including my dad, by four. Paul and Allison help us load up.

Allison gives my dad a kiss and a hug. "Be careful, Steve. Don't give Ike trouble. Same goes for you, Tobin." She kisses my cheek, though I shrug away from her hug. "Help your dad out."

"No. I'm gonna push him into the ocean and leave him there."

She steps away with a horrified look. "Why did you say such a thing?"

"Why did *you* say what *you* said when I help him every single day?"

She retreats and gives Ike a look, like *good luck*.

Paul moves to hug me, and I let him, though I see Allison's scowl over his shoulder. "Take care, Tobin. And have fun."

"We will." I give him a gentle squeeze.

My dad's in the back seat, looking like an eager puppy, and I turn to Ike. "Do we have it all?"

"If we don't, we can buy it there. Get your butt in the car." His grin is contagious.

When I look in the review mirror, Paul and Allison are actually waving at us, so I wave out the window at them. This could be awful or phenomenal. I'm not going to guess which one.

The trip to the Cities spools out in front of us. Three hours, including stops. What to do with three hours?

"Tobin, will you read a book?" My dad, from the back seat.

"What book?" I brought my Kindle, of course, but I don't think he'd like anything I have on there.

A book comes slowly over the seat.

"The first Harry Potter?"

"Gracie came over the other day while you were working, and she convinced me I should read it. She read me the first chapter and I was hooked."

Gracie can talk anyone into being a Harry Potter fan. I send her a quick text with six hearts: *Thanks for reading to my dad.*

Any time. #hestherealmvp Six hearts and three kissy faces.

"Will you read?" His voice is half of what it used to be. Maybe less than that.

Ike's looking excited, too. "I listened to Harry Potter when I was in Afghanistan. All seven books. Three times straight through."

"Seriously?" I try not to look surprised, but I fail.

"You're no Jim Dale, but you'll do in a pinch. Now read."

I start on chapter two. By the end of chapter three, Dad is asleep, and I put the book down on the seat between me and Ike.

"Nope. Not Jim Dale. But that's okay." He pats my hand.

"Gracie and her stealth HP domination moves. I'd swear Rowling pays her." My mouth is dry. "It takes a lot to read out loud. Who knew?"

Ike chuckles.

I take a swig of water. "You get to read next if we do it again."

"I'm on it."

Silence for a while. I drink more water and think about what Minnesota used to look like, before all the white people came. When Daniel and Mariette got here, I'm sure the trees were thick. And in clearings, there might have been Dakota tipis or Ojibwe birchbark houses. I'm also sure Daniel and Mariette never made it this far south of the lake. They probably went less than ten miles from their camp for the entire time they were alive.

And that makes me realize something.

"Ike, what's your origin story?" If he's a part of our family, I should probably know this.

"Origin story?" He gives me a confused look.

"That's what I'm doing with my action figures. So, if you're gonna be hanging out at our house, all parts of the Star Wars X-Men Fam have to have an origin story."

He raises his eyebrows. "That's a bit weird, but okay. As I understand it, my great-grandparents came to America in the early 1950s, as part of a thing called the Bracero Program. Mexican field workers who got to come here legally. They picked sugar beets, but never went back, so they got their green cards, then became citizens. My grandparents met each other in St. Paul, where they grew up after their families left sugar beet country, and then they moved up here because my grandpa liked the woods and the lake."

"A Mexican dude who likes the woods?" I chuckle.

He nods and smiles. "All the great-grandparents came from a warm, dry place, so everyone thought my grandparents were weird, but Grandpa Marcelo liked to fish. He moved to the biggest lake he could find. Rich was born in Duluth and went to college in the Cities. He married Elena after he met her on a blind date in Minneapolis and convinced her to come up here by telling her the sunrises over the lake were pretty. Then my two sisters were born, and then I was, and then there were five brown people in Duluth." He laughs.

"There's more than five brown people in Duluth!"

He gives me side-eye. "Not very many more. Have you looked? Then I graduated from high school, then I went to Afghanistan, and now I'm here, on my way to Hawaii with you."

"Do you have any superpowers?"

He ponders. "I'm pretty calm under pressure."

"That's way more useful than writing books or taking photos." Then it hits me that right now I can ask Ike what I can't when Dad's around.

"His brain is worse, isn't it?"

Ike nods. "Frontotemporal dementia. It can happen with ALS."

Fuck. It has a name. My mind blanks into terrified static, but I wrestle it back to reality as quickly as I can. "So what does this mean for him? For us?"

He considers again. "He might get stuck on a word, which you've seen him do, or be childish, or rude, or say the wrong thing. He'll lose words and act selfish and make shitty decisions, but there's no real way to predict when those things will happen."

I can't keep the anger out of my voice. "Wasn't it just supposed to be his muscles?"

Ike gives me a patient look, which I may or may not deserve. "The only blessing is he won't realize how his brain is deteriorating. Sometimes he might, like when he's in the middle of too much emotion, but not the other stuff—the rudeness, the bad decisions, whatever. Which sucks for us, of course."

For two seconds, I'm pissed, but then it hits me. "Imagine how pissed he'd be if he understood his brain was quitting, too." It almost takes my breath away, it's so awful. Especially on top of losing his body.

"Which is why I can understand his choice for suicide, even if I don't support it."

"What do you have against it, aside from the fact that you're Catholic?" I've been too chicken to ask.

"Want to know how many people I've seen die?"

"No."

"Two guys in my squad. Unexpected both times. Not going to tell you about it. Completely excruciating."

"I can't even imagine." I consider climbing in the back-seat, because I can feel the waves of sadness and anger and hurt coming off him, but it would be unsafe to unbuckle my seatbelt while we're going seventy-five down the interstate.

"Those guys didn't have a chance to save themselves. But suicide is a little different. There may be choice involved, and it can be stopped sometimes, if the illness isn't too intense."

"Illness?"

"Depression. Or whatever brain imbalance makes them think suicide is an option."

I hadn't thought about it that way.

"Science says living organisms are consistently oriented toward survival unless something's wrong. So, when a human is convinced that death is the right choice, you know something's off." Ike sighs. "Except in cases like your dad's."

"When people are going to die anyway?"

"Right. And people like me take oaths to fix brain imbalances. To save lives. Not to end them."

"Fair enough. But how can you think it's okay but not okay at the same time?"

"Cognitive dissonance and critical thinking are my friends. And my values don't have to be other people's values. We all get to choose."

Silence settles over the car again. We're getting closer to the Cities. There are more fields here, flat open spaces people fill with crops or buildings or billboards. An occasional pond, sometimes a horse. Sometimes a hawk. One billboard looks like it says SAVE BIG MONEY ON FRONTOTEMPORAL DEMENTIA. But when I blink, FRONTOTEMPORAL DEMENTIA has been replaced with MENARDS.

My mouth is dry again, and I take another gulp of water. "Do you . . . flip-flop? Ever think the opposite is the right answer?"

Ike doesn't hesitate. "No. But it's truly not my business. People get to make decisions. And your dad's being tortured. It's pretty horrifying."

Torture. Horrifying.

I can barely hear myself. "I don't support him."

"I don't blame you." Ike gives me a sad smile.

Silence again.

A new awareness creeps into my brain as I watch the road roll by.

What if he can't do it on his own?

He might shake so badly he can't pour the liquid into a glass. He might not be able to hold it to his mouth and drink it.

And Ike won't help him.

My dad's not the first dying person, or the last, to choose this option, I've discovered. It's amazing how many places—in America, in other countries, wherever—sell pentobarbital online. What he wants to do is legal in lots of other countries. But if he can't do it himself, then things change. If my research is correct, I'd be committing a criminal act in the state of Minnesota.

The road hum of the car is suddenly really loud. My dad's snoring is really loud.

Ike touches my arm. "You need to understand there's some bad shit coming down the pike. Feeding tubes. Ventilators. No ability to talk. No way to move. Maybe no ability to even think for himself anymore. Or constant laughing or crying, with no way to stop it."

Snoring. Snoring means he's breathing. That's good. I look at the billboards going by. Visit St. Paul! Visit Minneapolis! Buy a boat from this place! Build a log cabin! Happy things. Family things. Outdoor things. Smiling people doing things together. Nobody dying.

"He's not trying to ignore your needs. He's just . . . he's in pain. Mostly mentally and emotionally, but there will be physical pain, too. He's got to do what's good for him."

"That's how my parents roll, isn't it? Doing what's best for them?" I spit it out with way more anger than Ike deserves. He looks away.

"I'm sorry, Tobin." Ike is quiet. "I don't know how it feels to be your kind of alone."

People going and doing and being. Happy mothers and fathers and kids.

"Let's just go to Hawaii right now." I say it to the window.

"Yes. Let's do that." He reaches across and puts his hand on my shoulder. "It's not fair. To either of you."

Signs. Looking at them. My dad snoring in the back.

"So what? It's happening." I say it, but barely loud enough to hear it myself.

"Yes." Ike sighs. "It's happening."

My dad snores all night long.

Except when he's tossing and turning, which is every other minute.

I'm exhausted when morning comes around, and of course we have to be there at the ass crack of dawn. But we get everything into the airport, despite the impossibly long ricket from the parking garage to the Delta desk, and sure enough, there's a wheelchair. My dad audibly sighs when he gets in.

I take a picture of him in his wheelchair and send it to Gracie: *Like a boss.*

She texts back: *He looks happy. #GoSteve #Ilovehim #have-fun #loveyou*

I'll try. #loveyoutoo And I will.

Maybe I should chip the ice off my heart first.

It's eight hours to Hawaii, because it's in the middle of the freaking Pacific Ocean. Like the middle. Lake Superior is a drop in the bucket compared to the Pacific Ocean. I don't know who managed to get us direct flights, but I sure am glad.

Ike plays a game on his phone. My dad sleeps and reads. Nobody tries to talk to me about anything deep or weird, which is good. So I think. Which is bad.

I want to stand up and go to each passenger, asking if they know how I should behave. How should someone act when their father is dying—when he's going to kill himself so he can die faster? How does a person just go about their day while they carry that knowledge? How do I cook supper, go to school, go to work, all the time knowing my life is shattering, tiny crack by tiny crack?

I truly don't know. Maybe the strangers do.

But I imagine what would happen if I actually did it. People would frown, look horrified, turn away. Someone would call the flight attendant. Nobody wants to think horrible thoughts on the way to a tropical island. And the flight attendants might tie me to my seat or something if I actually tried.

So I don't do anything. I concentrate on thawing my heart—just temporarily, of course. I imagine a blowtorch and some blue flame, deep in the depths of the lake, working on a black lump.

Then I read a dumb mystery that my English teacher gave me. Eight hours is one thing when you're sleeping. It's another when you're on a plane. The book's not great, but it's enough to pass the time.

Every so often, Ike passes me a mazapan with a knowing grin. He's right. They're delicious. I scarf down each one of them.

About once an hour, I think: *I don't know if I can help him. If that time comes. When that time comes.*

But how can anyone know if they've never been there? How could it be possible that death is better than life? I could ask the other passengers that question, too.

The flight attendants would lock me in the bathroom.

So I read some more.

When we're landing on Oahu, the plane looks like it's going to skid right off the west side of the island, the airport is so close to the water. I text Gracie a photo of the airport, since half of it is outside, like gates and baggage claim are just . . . outside. Super weird. Then we wait for *another* plane to the Big Island, which is actually named Hawaii, but nobody calls it that, and that ride is short. They give us free juice.

Ninety minutes from the time we get on the second plane in Honolulu, we have a rental car and are driving into Kailua-Kona. The doctor's condo is nice, in a place called the Keauhou-Kona Surf and Racquet Club, not fancy, but nice. But the place is on the first floor, so my dad rolls his rented wheelchair into the apartment, and we've arrived.

It's the longest day and the longest trip of my life. But I'm in Hawaii. And my dad is still alive, looking out the sliding doors at the patio, where there are green geckos climbing the wall in the glare of the motion-sensing deck light.

I feel the warm air working on my heart. It's dripping in my chest. And on my face, but thankfully no one sees. There's no crying in Paradise.

Here are the top ten things I take photos of in Hawaii, in no particular order:

1. Sea turtles. Way more Zen than Mama Duck. I stood next to one for an hour—you can stand on the lava, at the edge of the ocean, in calf-deep water, where the turtles like to hang out—just watching it float and peace out. Incredible. I stuck my underwater camera in and took pictures of its face. I want to be a sea turtle in my next life. I want to live on this beach. I want to pet one, which is illegal.

2. Fish. Lots of fish. Including the humuhumu-nukunukuapua'a. We snorkel every day. Ike ties a clothesline to Dad, so they float along together. I buy three more disposable underwater cameras and use them all. I see transparent stick-like fish, fish wearing lipstick and eyeliner, lots of parrot-fish fish, a few Marlin/Nemo fish, a bunch of fish I don't know the names of, and an eel, which scares the shit out of me.

3. Hibiscus flowers. Gorgeous. They have hibiscus hedges in Hawaii. And plumeria trees. So many kinds of flowers.

4. Lava. So many textures and shadows in lava.

5. The ocean. So many textures and shadows in the ocean.

6. Sunsets. Totally cheesy but true. Amazing. They look like someone painted them on the sky.

7. Everything else outside.

8. Volcanoes National Park. Holy shit. The grass burns from the ground up. Stay on the path, or

get fried instantaneously? Yessir, Mr. Park Ranger.
Live lava in other places, though not in the park,
but the steam from the caldera is scary enough.
9. Food.
10. My dad.

I take so many photos of my dad. Laughing, swimming, smiling, eating at the luau, where there was tons of food, including poi, which isn't as horrible as people say it is. Dad watching the hula dancers. Dad looking at the ocean. Ike rents this bicycle for two with a chair in the front—someone with a disability can ride in the chair while someone else pedals—and I take pictures of him looking like a four-year-old in the front of the bike. Ike loves pedaling him around.

My dad never mentions that he and Meredith honeymooned here. Not once. Ike tells me.

We all buy Hawaiian clothes—I buy two dresses, and Ike and Dad each get a couple shirts. I find a dress for Gracie, after texting her a million different fabrics so she can pick one.

We eat whole fish—like, whole on the plate, with eyes and scales and everything—in a Thai restaurant on the top of an old shopping center that's part of an even older hotel. The whole thing is wood framed, like a house, very humble and weathered. Ike carries my dad up the stairs, and Dad doesn't mind. He does throw his napkin and a fork at the wait staff because he's mad he doesn't have any water, but they're nice about it after Ike takes them aside and explains. They bring me free sorbet, completely out of pity, but I don't mind. It was rose petal sorbet, and it was delicious.

We don't go back, even though the food is the best we have in all ten days.

The official Ironman triathlon is held in and around Kailua-Kona, so we check out the T-shirt shop with posters of every year of the triathlon since it's been held there—1981 on. It's the only time my dad cries, and it isn't even uncontrollable. He's just sad. I know a triathlon was a goal for him.

We're there during a full moon, so one night Ike and I put him in his wheelchair and push him out to the tiny rock beach by the condos. It's so bright we can see each other's faces perfectly. Ike and I sit in some crap-ass plastic chairs someone's left behind, on either side of my dad, and watch the water while the moon gazes down on us.

The air is thick with vibrations—from the ocean, from the moon, from whatever vibrates, which is all of life. I sit and watch the waves and feel the energy.

After a while, Dad turns to me. "Thank you for being the best part of my good life. You're my favorite person on Earth."

I don't say anything. I hug him, then sit back down and feel the vibes some more.

Torture. Horrifying. I hear Ike's voice in my head.

I shove the horrifying part into the waves, close to Japan, far away from us.

My dad is lucid, calm, and happy the whole time we're gone, except for tiny moments here and there, like when he threw the fork. Almost as if the warm air and salt waves and barren lava fields restored his brain.

It's the best ten days of my life.

Dad's Big Book of Advice #10
Keep your nudie pix to yourself, goddammit.
And do not trust a guy who sends a dick pic.
He'll end up without a job, sleeping on your couch
and eating your food.

MAY 28

It's Memorial Day weekend, and there are tourists *everywhere*. In the back room of Trash Box, looking for a bathroom ("Um, no, we don't have bathrooms for the public here . . . oh, it's an emergency? Just around the corner . . . oh, you have an emergency, too?"), knocking glass off the shelves, scattering magazines into every corner, leaving their garbage on the shelves for me to find. And they're all crabby, because it's not warm. "It's Memorial Day weekend! It's supposed to be warm! I saw a snowflake!"

Um, have you ever been to Duluth?

I'm standing in the back room, pulling out what looks salvageable from our maybe-this-stuff-will-sell corner, when I hear Paul's voice: "Hey, Tobin! You have a guest!"

Paul lets Allison partake of his services on Memorial Day and Labor Day weekends, but that's usually it, unless she's in a serious fix. His solution for rude tourists is a lecture on the historical details that relate to the piece they're purchasing. They tend to stop being rude and hurry out of the shop after that. Paul enjoys the hell out of it. Occasionally a tourist will engage him, and then he's stuck for a while, but he doesn't mind.

When I emerge from the back room with three picture frames, four antique books, and one lamp on our transport cart, I see it's Sid. With his violin.

"Hi, Tobin." He's got his violin out, on his shoulder, and he gives it a flourish.

"What are you doing?" It's not like Sid to just wander around with his instrument.

"I give concerts on street corners." He gestures with his bow out the window. "When I'm not slopping up puke at Vista Fleet, that is." Big grin. "I made thirty-five dollars already today. By the candy store."

"Better than Trash Box."

Paul shushes me before Allison hears. "Young lady, you know that name's not appreciated round these parts. And that's not illegal, young man?"

"Not as far as I know." Sid looks around, like someone might be following him. "But I guess I haven't seen a police officer yet."

Paul nods. "What do you play?"

"I know, I know!" I wave my hand like I'm in Professor Paul Oliver's history lecture.

Sid rolls his eyes at me, then turns to Paul. "John Williams tunes. Everybody loves it when they can identify *Star Wars* or *Jurassic Park* or some other famous movie. But I've only had one person guess right for *Empire of the Sun*."

Paul's smile is amused. "Do you do requests?"

"Sometimes, if I know it."

"Any Charlie Daniels?"

Sid puts bow to strings, and "The Devil Went Down to Georgia" erupts out of them. There are maybe ten people in the store, and they all stop what they're doing to watch. He doesn't play the whole thing, but when he stops, slightly sweaty from the exertion, there's loud, long applause. Sid blushes.

"Tobin, you've got some pretty talented friends." Paul is ringing up a grandma-looking lady, and she's giving Sid a big smile.

"It seems so."

The grandma lady hands Sid a five. "I'll look for you in a symphony somewhere." Sid blushes even harder.

"You're going to get recruited right off the streets of Duluth." I go back to the cart where I've left the merchandise. "Did you come in for anything in particular, or just to serenade us?"

Sid pulls his violin off his shoulder and walks over to me. "I came to make sure you were still alive. You weren't in school for the last two weeks. And you're a crappy texter. Can we ... talk?" He nods his head toward the sidewalk.

"Paul, can you cover for me for five minutes?"

Paul looks at his watch, then at the door to the back room. "Make it snappy." He smiles at Sid. "You've got some chops. Best of luck."

"Thank you, sir." He extends his hand, which Paul shakes, then heads out the door, me right behind him.

It's not that cold out here. People are just wimps.

Once we're away from the windows, Sid looks me straight in the eye. "So?"

"Yes?"

Then he drops his eyes. "I . . . um . . . just wanted to check on you. Like I said, I hadn't seen you." He looks like he's going to either jump out of his skin or drop his violin.

"Life's not great right now, but I'm okay."

"You were gone for so long." Still looking at the sidewalk. "And you didn't answer my texts."

"I was in Hawaii—I don't know why I didn't get them, but I didn't." I mentally make a note to check my phone. "I didn't mean to ignore you—not at all."

"How did you get to Hawaii?"

"The normal way—by airplane." I grin.

No answer.

"People donated a condo and money for plane tickets."

"Did you see all the amazing stuff they show on ads? Was it the most incredible place on Earth?"

"Yes and yes, and please look at me. You can come over and see my photos sometime."

"Okay." He raises his face, and it's a mix of emotion that I've not seen before on a boy: scared, happy, hopeful, nervous, and a little bit of sad.

"Hanging out is good, Sid. Any time."

"With you. And your dad." This time he doesn't drop his eyes.

"Right. I'm working and doing a photo essay for the college I want to go to, plus Dad takes a lot of time, so I'm busy. Might not happen a lot."

Sid's face dissolves into one emotion: disappointment.

"But I'd like it. I really would."

His eyebrows go up. "Really?"

I laugh. His eyebrows. "Yes. Hang out with us and be my friend, just like you've been forever."

His eyes don't leave mine. "I'll play for your dad. And you and Ike."

"We'd love it. You're a dork."

"A big fat music dork." He's utterly sincere.

"And that's great." I grin in response.

Then the shop door opens, and Ike comes out, carrying a table. He sees me and Sid. "Whoops. Didn't mean to interrupt." He grins big and wiggles his eyebrows at me. Thank god Sid's back is to him.

I stick my tongue out. "Nothing to see here, dork. We were just talking."

Sid blushes.

"Pop-up store time. Your dad's coming in a second." Ike points inside. "He's discussing which albums he wants to sell today."

"I saw his Gord's Gold crate in the back. Looks like someone's been loading it up." I look through the window. Dad's talking to Paul and Allison. He's got his walker, and aside from that, they all look sort of normal. Sort of like my family has always looked.

Sort of. Definitely not the same.

Ike pops the legs out on the table, then opens the door and grabs the MAMA DUCK'S RECORD STORE sign. He places it on the sidewalk at one end of the table. "Want to help me grab the albums, Tobin?"

"Sure."

Sid raises his violin to his shoulder. "Gotta go back to my spot. See ya." He smiles and nods, and just as suddenly as he was at the store, he's walking back toward the Rocky Mountain Chocolate Factory, violin under his chin, playing Darth Vader's theme from *Star Wars*. People are staring, and he just nods and walks. I wonder where his violin case is. Maybe the Rocky Mountain people agreed to keep it for him, if he agreed to buy a bunch of chocolate.

I go back inside.

"Here you are." Paul hands me an armful of albums, and I take them out to Ike, then come back in for more.

"Nice young man." Paul gives me one of his serene but knowing smiles.

"Yes. He is." And I mentally send Sid a big hug, for being a reliable, true friend.

Dad throws an elbow as I hold the door for him. "Out of the way, Tobin." He grins a very pre-rickety grin as he turtles by me. "This badass is coming at you. Duluth, you better watch out."

Ike comes back in for a chair and the Gord's Gold crate, and then my dad is ready. There are already tourists gathering around the table.

There are worse ways he could spend his time.

What we make at Trash Box on Memorial Day and Labor Day weekends balances out what we make in January, which might be all of $100. Winter tourists aren't big shoppers. Eight-hour shifts get long, especially on holiday weekends, but walking home is nice, once I get past the lift bridge and all the gawkers on both sides. Dad and Ike stayed until about two, then packed up their shop again. "Wouldn't want the customers to get too used to us," my dad said. Nope. Can't let the magic die.

When I get a couple blocks away, I can see there are pick-ups in front of my house. There's a bed in the back of one, and boxes in another.

What if he died in the last three hours? Would they wait to tell me?

I'm out of breath from running when I heave myself up the stairs. There's nobody in the yard. "Dad!" I scream it. "DAD!"

Ike comes out of the kitchen. "Tobin, what's wrong?"

"Where's Dad?" I'm panting.

He points out the back door. "Sitting on the back porch, staying out of the way. Talking to my parents and Mark, another EMT buddy of theirs. Why?"

He's not dead. That's good.

"What's up with the pickups?"

"He didn't tell you." Ike rolls his eyes. "I should never believe him when he says he has."

"What the hell is going on?"

"I'm moving in. I hope that's okay." It's clear he doesn't know how I'll take this. "He was good in Hawaii, but he's getting weaker every day. His numbers are down—he's at a 23 now." He pauses. "I won't boss you around and I'll stay out of the way."

I close my eyes. "How do we afford you in the first place?" I've never specifically asked.

"Your dad has a long-term care policy for some of it. I work cheap for the rest of it."

"How old are you?"

He furrows his forehead. "Twenty-six. Why?"

"Just checking. Gracie is going to ask."

"Your Harry Potter friend?"

"She thinks you're hot."

Ike laughs with a belly laugh that's deeper than almost any I've heard. "She's way too young for me. No thank you."

"I'll pass that on."

"Can you help us finish bringing in the rest of the stuff? Use those photography muscles?"

"Sure. But who's cooking now? Me? You?"

"We'll make a chart or something." He grins. "But you're gonna eat some Mexican food—huevos rancheros and tacos, not gringo ones, some pozole—on the regular. Got it?"

"I'm in. Dad will love it, too."

Dad's on the back porch, chatting with Rich, Elena, and Mark, looking tired from his pop-up store excursion. Elena hugs me and tells me there are three dozen homemade tortillas in the fridge. I hug her again. I'd skip bread for the rest of my life if I could have homemade tortillas instead. I have no idea when she has time to cook.

Finally, we get all the stuff hauled upstairs to the spare room, and I fix burgers on the grill with some potato salad from the store. Everybody's kind, but we have a new person in our house.

Someone who will cook now and use our bathroom all the time.

Someone who brought a small Jesus statue, photos of loved ones who've passed on, a rosary from his grandma—his *abuela*—and a tall candle with glass sides and the Virgin Mary on it, all set on a special table in the spare room. His room.

Someone who's helping my dad die.

No matter how much I like Ike, Hawaii didn't prepare me for this.

"Tobin, come here." Dad calls me into the living room while I'm finishing the dishes. Ike's upstairs unpacking boxes.

"Need something?" I wipe my hands on a towel as I go to him.

"Look. I've got a lot of pages now." He holds up a stack of paper, with writing on it that looks like an eight-year-old kid's. "Your Big Book of Advice." He's excited. "Ike's going to type it. It's going to be so good, Tobin." Then he bursts into tears.

I sit next to him on the couch and offer my hand. He clutches it like he's drowning, and he sobs. And sobs. And sobs. All the sobs he didn't cry while we were gone. All the sobs I threw in the lake the instant I got back to Duluth, right along with my heart.

When he's down to just sniffles, I pat his shoulder. "Can you tell me one of the bad dad jokes in there?"

"It's a surprise." He reaches for a Kleenex and blows his nose. But then he caves. "Why do chicken coops only have two doors?"

"I don't know. Why?"

"Because if they had four, they'd be chicken sedans!"

I smile in spite of myself. "That's not terrible."

He smiles back. He's so tired. "Can you help me up the stairs? Ike can take it from there."

"Absolutely." I get him off the couch, and we ricket toward the stairs, leaving the walker behind in the living room in favor of his cane. "Ike! Lipstick Fish coming your way." Hawaii's state fish, the one with the long and wild name, looks like it has lipstick on. And they were *everywhere*, tons of them, every time we snorkeled.

"Ready to receive The Fishly One." Ike's at the top, smiling down. "You're still miles ahead of Stephen Hawking if you can climb stairs. Eventually we'll have to move your bedroom to the living room."

My dad frowns. "Hell no. I still deserve some privacy."

"Fair enough, if you don't mind me carrying your ass up the stairs." Ike smiles, but I know he's extremely serious.

"Whatever, asshole. I care about not having to sleep in the middle of the goddamn living room." The frown is as deep on his forehead as it is on his mouth.

Ike keeps smiling. Dad's brain doesn't faze him.

"Lipstick Fish launching." I help Dad get up the first step, and he can usually go from there, using the rail and his cane.

Once he's at the top, Dad turns around and looks down at me, all signs of the anger gone from his face. "Love you, Tobin. Favorite person. On the planet. Never forget."

"Goodnight, Dad." Smiling back at him pulls against the edges of my frozen insides.

He and Ike shuffle into the bathroom.

I leave his book on the coffee table, where he can find it in the morning. Underneath it, there's another notebook, which I hadn't noticed.

It's photographs.

I flip through it. The shots are gorgeous. The lake, the bridge, the dunes. Me as a tiny baby. Me as a toddler—at the max, I'm three. Me in a pink Power Rangers Halloween costume. Me as a pumpkin. Me and Dad. So many photos of me and Dad.

In the very back of the notebook, there's a note.

I love you, Steve. Thanks for this sweet life, this beautiful baby girl.
Meredith took these. My mom.

I look through them one more time, then slip the notebook back under his manuscript.

What happened to these people?

I make sure the kitchen is settled down, and then I get the action figures from my room, waving at Dad in bed as I go by. Ike's door is closed already. In the living room, I manage to perch Professor X's chair on the edge of Dad's walker, with Rey pushing him. It takes twenty minutes and a lot of tape. Then Mystique spends some time in the middle of the coffee table, with her arm around Rey's throat, strangling her with her elbow. Rey is on her knees. Then I make two little tiny cardboard phones, strung together with dental floss, and pose Rey and Mystique talking to each other at opposite ends of the coffee table. I shoot from both ends and then in the middle. I also make a little cardboard camera and find Little Rey. Mystique takes some photos of her. I can insert them earlier in the story.

This will be the most messed-up entrance portfolio anybody's ever seen at that college, but I don't care. Realism works for me, if my mother were blue and my dad were bald, that is. And they were both mutants. Or if I were a badass Jedi warrior who didn't realize she was a Jedi.

That notebook. Those photos.

Between them and Hawaii, my insides are thawing.

I can still see my heart, on the bottom of the lake. It's getting smaller and smaller.

Just like my dad. Just like our life together.

<u>June 3</u>

I drop a glass, in the sink. Again.

Dad calls me a bitch, then a *FUCKING* bitch who shouldn't scare him like that, because it makes him jump. Then he hurts because he had to move. He says it all with white-hot heat, pounds his fist so the table rattles, then he asks me to pass the peanut butter, goddamn it.

Ike's eyes say *HIS MIND DOESN'T KNOW.* But those words flash-thaw every single nerve in my body.

I can't do this.

I can't. I CAN'T.

IT'S TOO HARD. I WON'T.

But there's no other choice. It's my life. My wreck of a life.

Dad's Big Book of Advice #11
Always put the TP *over* the roll (Not!! Under!!).

JUNE 10

Now that it's mostly nice outside, Dad and Ike take a constitutional—an old word for "walking around and looking
at stuff"—every day they're not running their pop-up shop,
which they do at least twice a week. Allison has cleared out
a lot of albums, and it's freed up space in the back room for
all sorts of new crap.

My dad loves having Ike push him everywhere, even
though he said, "I was just running marathons eight months
ago, and now I'm in a wheelchair," ten times an hour for
three solid days. But sometimes Ike straps him in and jogs
while he pushes, so Dad can finally go fast again. That's Dad's
ultimate. Ike wraps his abuela's rosary around the wheelchair
handle, right in front of his hand, "just for extra protection,"
he says. It must work, because they never wreck.

He still walks in the house, with his walker and his cane. The wheelchair is just for outside and being away from the house. Just those times.

That's what I tell myself.

Today, when I come out of the back room after fishing out more antique books for all the weirdos who think antique books are awesome, Dad and Ike have arrived with Subway for lunch. Mama Duck's Record Store was outside from nine till noon, and then they got hungry. They're going for their constitutional after lunch.

Ike holds up a bag. "Your favorite—BMT with salt and vinegar chips and a Sprite."

"I'm all about it."

Allison nods from behind the register. "Go eat outside. It's gorgeous out there."

Dad reaches out of his wheelchair for a porcelain statue of a bulldog wearing a top hat. "Where do you get stuff like this?"

Ike swipes it back from him. "We didn't come back here to shop, *viejo.*" He puts it back on the shelf, out of Dad's reach. I've seen Dad rearrange whole shelves of stuff, which pisses Allison off completely. Nothing like brotherly help.

"Don't call me an old man, you young fool." Dad smiles at Ike, and he smiles back.

Allison fixes Dad with a look. She's been reading our Yelp reviews. "You might want to talk with your daughter about arguing with customers. Not very helpful."

"What did you want me to do? He was going off about how Superior is a much better city than Duluth, and I couldn't let that stand." I do admit I'd gotten a little snippy with him, but it was after a long night of Dad's misbehaving brain.

Dad grins. "We may be twin ports, but there's only one *win* port."

"Send that to the chamber of commerce, Dad."

Ike laughs.

Allison frowns. "Go eat, would you?"

Ike pushes Dad back out the front door, and I follow. There are picnic tables by the restaurant next door, so we sit there. We can see Grandma's Restaurant from here. Dad's having marathon meetings every other day, it seems, which is good. He needs focus. Ike must be bored out of his mind while he waits for Dad to be done. They have the meetings upstairs in the bar, and it must give Dad strength to pass his photo—they have all the marathon winners' pictures in the stairwell—because other than that, I have no idea how he climbs them.

I hear notes from a violin wafting over the summer-ish air.

Ike turns toward the sound. "Wonder how much your friend Sid is pulling down each day."

"Fifty-ish bucks a day?" When we texted yesterday, he told me he'd earned forty-three dollars the day before.

"Puts gas in a car and buys some Subway for lunch. Not horrible."

"Better than Trash Box."

Dad points at me. "Allison is very kind to you, and always works around your school schedule when it's the school year. And if you're messing with her Yelp reviews, that's not good."

"But she's crabby and bossy all the time, not just because she got a bad review."

"And also your guardian, at some point, so get it together." Dad's look is stern over his Philly steak and cheese.

"Why can't Ike be my guardian?"

Ike chuckles. "Because I'm a big kid, and you're a middle-sized kid, and people would think you were my girlfriend, and if there's anything Rich taught me, aside from everything else in the world, it's to be proper around women, especially young ones. So no. We don't need gossip."

"It's good to be with family." Dad chews the little bits of sandwich that Ike pulls off the big sandwich. It's getting harder for him to swallow.

I banish that thought to the place I keep all his ALS changes: right next to my heart on the bottom of Lake Superior.

"Ike's not family?" Now I raise my eyebrow at Dad. "He's the son of a man you've known longer than you've had a daughter. He helps you wipe your ass."

Ike spits his Coke. My dad frowns. "Vulgarity isn't necessary, is it?"

"It's only vulgar if you say it is." I raise my eyebrow again.

Ike grins. "Yes, I'm family. But Allison is your aunt, and better equipped to be a parent than I am, since she already has grown-up kids, and I might be a wandering vagabond once I'm done caring for your dad. I don't know." Ike's finished with his sandwich and is eating the other half of Dad's Philly steak and cheese.

Once I'm done caring for your dad. Shove. Onto the bottom of the lake, right next to not being able to chew or swallow well.

"What's your plan, Rambling Man?" My dad's arm shakes as he holds his Coke up to his lips to find the straw. Ike steadies him.

"I need to get my ass into college before I go gray, but I haven't decided when or where."

"Speaking of college, Tobin, is there anything we need to do for your entrance portfolio?" For just a second, he sounds like my dad, strong and capable.

"Gotta take more photos. Caption them so they make a story. Fill out a form."

"As long as you're working on it."

I nod.

"How's my birthday party coming? Only a couple of months." He smiles. "Got my duck yet?"

"Allison's helping with invites, and I think she has the cake lined up. I talked to her friend who's a caterer, so we have the food ordered. I've got a set of photos that are being blown up for decorations. I have to buy streamers and plates and do a couple other things. No luck with the rubber duck."

"You've already done all that?" Ike's amazed.

"I don't want to forget anything."

"You're incredible." He stands and bows.

"Whatever."

Dad gathers the trash, and Ike deposits it into the garbage can. Now there are fiddle-like notes wafting our way. Sid is studying up on country music, obviously.

"Is Sid aiming for a music scholarship somewhere?" My dad adjusts his shades as Ike pushes him back toward Trash Box.

"I think so." I should ask him. I've been a little self-centered lately.

"He's damn good." Ike points, and we can see Sid, a block away, outside the candy store with a huge crowd around him. "Gonna make some bank today."

We're at the door. "See you Lipstick Fishes when I get home."

Dad's shaky hand blows me a kiss. "Don't give Allison too much hell."

"I may call Paul down to run some interference."

"He doesn't mind that. Now do a wheelie, Ike, and let's go to the lighthouse and write some graffiti."

"Your wish is my command, sir, but I don't have a marker."
Ike rolls his eyes at me.

"Probably better not to engage in defacing public
property." Dad starts singing Gordon Lightfoot's "Carefree
Highway," like they're going on a big road trip.

They head down the street, toward the jetty and the
lighthouse, along with a billion tourists. I see Ike bend down
to listen to something Dad says, then tilt his head back and
laugh at the sky. I see Dad's shoulders shake. Then I hear Ike
holler, "Cholula Maaaaaaaaaaaan," and he starts jogging. My
dad's hands are clamped on the sides of the chair.

They're having fun. And if I watch them for too long, I'll
start to melt.

I open the door and Allison is right there. "Looks like
your dad's enjoying himself." She clears her throat. "How are
his numbers?"

"He's not giving you regular updates? I don't remember
the last number, exactly."

She busies herself with something at the register, clicking
keys and opening and closing the cash drawer. "Not really."

"He's having trouble swallowing, but his breathing is still
okay. He climbs the stairs to his bedroom each night, with his
cane, even though it's really hard. His voice is relatively weak
but still there. Sometimes it's really hard for him to pick up
his phone because that requires fine motor skills. Sometimes
his emotions are really intense, and sometimes he gets stuck
on a word and repeats it for five minutes." I'm a robot repeat-
ing facts.

Allison nods. "Okay. Thanks. Yeah. Tough. Yeah, just . . .
I'm sorry. So tough." Her head is down, and I don't realize
she's crying until she looks at me. "I'm so sorry, honey."

Here's what I want to say: *There's nothing we can do about this stupid situation, and we're handling it, so stop with the pity. I end up feeling bad because I'm not crying and sad like you. If I feel those feelings, I'll self-destruct. So quit stressing me out. Take your tears somewhere else.*

But I don't, because she'd lose her shit. And I can't handle another person in my life losing their shit.

"Yeah. Me too." And I escape into the back room so I don't have to see her face anymore.

I text Gracie: *Would you like an extra aunt?*

Nope. Got four already. #fournosyaunts #foursassyaunts #enoughforme

Can you introduce them to mine?

That I can do. Is she being crabby? #fourcrabbyaunts

She's got too many feels. Don't need anyone else's.

Your own are enough. #feelingssuck Sad face emoji. Three hearts.

She has no idea, but the hashtag works for me.

When Allison goes to the post office, I make two signs on printer paper, with a bunch of colored markers. The first one says WHAT IS YOUR FREAKING PROBLEM? HE'S DYING. CAN'T YOU HELP US? The second one says HE JUST WANTS TO SEE YOUR DUCK UP CLOSE. WTF. BE KIND.

Then I tape them onto Mama Duck's portrait in the back room—carefully, so I don't smear the chalk—take a photo, and email it to Mama Duck's handler. Way too smart-ass, but whatev. I won't get an answer anyway.

It's 10:30, and my dad's snoring up in his room. Pop-up shop days make him sleep hard, which is good. I'm sitting at the kitchen table, shoving my action figures into various contortions. Nothing's happening.

Ike sits down across from me. "Need some ideas? Cholula Man is here."

"Who came up with that nickname?"

He grins. "When we jog, your dad says it's the hot sauce that gives me my extra strength."

"Guess that's your superhero name now."

He picks up the bottle and shows it to me like he's showing it off on a game show merchandise showcase. "Mexican superpowers in a concentrated, easy-to-use food additive."

I laugh.

"Back to the question." He puts the bottle next to the salt and pepper, where it belongs. "Want some help?"

"I'm failing big time, so, sure." I tumble the Star Wars X-Men Fam across the table to him. He moves them around a little bit, his mouth twisted up like it's the biggest puzzle in the world. Then he gets up, goes to the fridge, and takes out an apple and a can of the liquid protein stuff Dad sometimes drinks instead of forcing himself to eat. He puts them down on the table and goes for a knife and a cutting board.

"What the hell?"

"Watch."

Ike cuts up the apple into pieces the size of big dice, then gets a fine-point Sharpie from the can of pens in the Everything Room. He puts a heart on one, then a frowny face on another. A smiley face, a lightning bolt, and a money sign go on some others. He puts the symbols on every side of the pieces. Then he puts Professor X on top of the can of Promote.

"Got your camera?"

"Not on me."

He gives me a look. "How you gonna take photos, doofus?"

His laughter follows me up the stairs.

When I come back down, he's made a background for Professor X and his can of Promote with a dish towel draped over a cookie sheet, propped up by the toaster. "Our new photo studio." He's proud.

You think you sculpted a bear, but it's really a moose. You think you drew a caterpillar, but it's really a turtle. You think your photos are just action figures, but then you add in apple chunks. Art is like that. You gotta go with it.

I click off a few shots, up close and far away. Then I take Professor X out of his wheelchair, leave it on top, and splay him in front of the can. That seems a little bit more realistic.

"Nice." Ike's behind me. "Your dad hates that stuff."

"It tastes like shit."

"Yup."

I take a few more shots, then Ike clears away the Promote. He changes out the kitchen towel, so we have a different background, then sets up Mystique and Rey. He sets Mystique's and Rey's arms so they look like they're throwing things between them. "Get your action setting ready."

"You're gonna have to angle it just right to make it look realistic."

"How does the word *realistic* even enter your mind if you're representing your mother as a blue mutant?"

I change the settings. "Go."

First, he throws the heart cube. Then the frowny face, then the dollar sign. Then the smiley face. Each time he throws, I capture about ten shots.

"Let me draw one more." I grab an apple piece and the Sharpie and draw two stick figures, tiny ones, but female ones with dresses, a mother and daughter. Then I draw an X through them. Then I repeat it for all sides and hand it to Ike. "Throw this one next."

He looks at it, then at me.

"Not kidding."

"Okay then." He throws, picks it up, throws from the other side, on and on. I take a crap-ton of shots.

I move Lando in front of Rey, even though he's the same size as Little Rey. They didn't make action figures very big in the eighties. "Lando is Paul. He protects me."

Ike picks him up and studies him. He makes Lando's arms look like he's throwing/catching, and we get started again, using all the cubes. I shoot a ton.

When I look at the clock above the sink, it's 1:30.

"Do you realize we've been doing this for three hours?" I stand up from where I've been kneeling behind my camera on the table. "Why didn't you tell me it was so late? You know he's going to wake you up early."

Ike yawns. "I got good at sleep deprivation in the army." He stretches his arms above his head and bends and twists. He's been kneeling on the floor, too, to get the throws just right between the action figures. It was a really small arc.

I yawn, too. "Was it horrible? The war?" As soon as I say it, I blush. He already said no talking about it. "Sorry. Foot in mouth. And duh, of course it was."

"Depends on which part, but yeah, it was bad. I wasn't there at the worst part. Plus, Afghani temps get above a hundred and ten on a regular basis. Compare that to Duluth."

I shudder. "It's so much easier to get warm than to get cool."

"Exactly." His look is solemn. "The army itself gave me discipline and focus, which helped me become a man I like. Someone who can function in the real world. But deployment was awful." He pauses. "Though ALS is on a pretty close par."

"Do you really have to say that right now?"

He comes to me, where I'm rubbing my knees and the small of my back and puts his arm around my shoulders. "Running from the truth only compounds the problem. Yes, ALS is as bad as the army. In fact, ALS is way worse than the army."

"Can we not say any more truth for the rest of the night?"

He grabs the apple cubes from the table—the ones with the symbols on them—and eats them. "Truth all gone."

"You're a weirdo. Is Sharpie ink poisonous?"

"You've just noticed? And I have no idea. It probably won't hurt me too much."

We go into the living room so we can sit on the couch, and we check out our work. In the series with Mystique and Rey throwing the mother-daughter X-ed-out cube, there's a perfect shot. The cube is upside down, frozen right between them, and the entire shot is clear. I couldn't have done it better in Photoshop.

"That one's going in."

"Most definitely." Ike nods.

There are some good Lando ones. There's one where he catches the heart cube almost perfectly between his hands, or at least it looks like that. Photos are illusions, after all.

"Does Paul know you're representing him with a Star Wars smuggler?"

"Remind me to tell him."

"He'll be honored." Ike yawns again. "For all my talk of sleep deprivation, I need to get some. See you in the morning, Voyageur."

Hearing that name sets off a warm glow somewhere close to where my heart used to be, and the glow travels up my spine to my brain. It's the first time anybody not biologically tied to me has called me Voyageur. And it's nice.

Our tiny family is complete.

"Thanks again. Some of these are really brilliant."

"My pleasure." He heads up the stairs.

I scoop the rest of the apple into the trash, after I eat a little more of it. It's 2:30 now. I'm sure my dad will be up by six.

I make sure everything's put away, then head for my room. My teeth will survive one night. I have to get up at nine to be at Trash Box by ten. I'll brush them in six hours anyway.

Having a big brother is a good thing.

Even if I got him in a really crappy way.

Dad's Big Book of Advice #12
Peer pressure is both useful and bullshit.
Make sure you know which it is.

JUNE 14

The marathon is in four days, and Dad and Ike are moving as fast as they can to keep up with the details. I was right to wonder about the stairs in Grandma's Restaurant—turns out he gave up on them the day we ate Subway outside. After he and Ike came back from their constitutional, he tried them again and couldn't do it. The marathon committee has been kind enough to come to our house every day. They've known him for years, so they were cool with moving. Dad was embarrassed, and he cried, but they insisted.

It's the worst. When stuff just . . . slips away.

It's my job to serve drinks, so I get the beers that three of them want, and the glasses of water that three of them want, and the coffee another wants. Lucky for me Ike can go to the liquor store.

The windows are open, and the lake is humming its evening song. Not too many tourists come this far out on Park Point, so the traffic is light. It's very pleasant in our living room. And Dad's excited and happy, too, which is a welcome change. Lots of tears and anger these days. Even Ike can't always take it. I caught him on the back porch yesterday, breathing very deliberately and slowly. When I asked him what was up, he said he was taking a break. Too much emotional energy.

They feel like arrows, Dad's angry words. And his tears can burn.

"So, folks, have we got all the things we need? We're down to hours now." Kerri looks around our living room at Rachael, David, Kevin, Chris, Ken, and Layla. They nod. "Then we have a request, Steve."

"What's that?" His voice is weaker than it was even last week.

"Will you please say a few words at the beginning of the race? Kick us off?"

He's surprised. "Nobody wants to hear from me."

"You've run this race for how many years, and been involved with this committee for how many years?" Kerri spreads her arms wide.

"Too many to count, and thirteen."

I see Ike move the Kleenex box toward Dad, because a statement like that could bring on a gale of tears, but nothing happens. Ike is leaning on the doorway to the kitchen, outside their circle of chairs. I see him relax a little.

"So I think it's your time." She reaches for his hand, avoiding any other statement.

Dad looks around the room. "A cripple with a weak voice, a walker, and a sidekick like Ike should start the race?"

Solemn nods. Ken speaks up. "Nobody else I'd rather see do it. No offense, dear spouse." He's married to Kerri.

Ike adds in. "It's an honor to be your sidekick. Please do it."

"Yes." Layla and Chris say it at the same time.

"Nobody better." From Rachael.

My dad hangs his head. "This is . . . well, this is a real honor. Thank you all." And the tears start coursing down his face. Nobody bats an eye. Ike hands him Kleenex, and I come over, so he can hold my hand. David and a couple other folks grab a Kleenex, too.

"All right then." Kerri stands after everybody's blown their noses and gotten themselves settled down. "I officially declare the planning over. Everyone ready for another zany weekend of racing?" She puts her hand out, and everyone stands up to join her with a hand in the center of the circle. Ike helps Dad up from the couch, and they put their hands in, too.

"Teeeeaaaaaaam RUN!" Everyone shouts it at once, then flings their hand out of the circle. My dad's hand goes the slowest of all, but he's probably smiling bigger than any of them.

Once they're gone, Dad turns to me and Ike. "What am I going to say?"

"Whatever you think would be inspiring." Ike pats him on the shoulder. He can see that Dad is already slumping. "Just welcome the out-of-towners to the North Shore, tell them how much they're going to love the course, and tell them how much you love the race. Keep it simple."

"Yes. Simple." His voice is already fading.

"Maybe you should write it down, too. So you won't forget. You might get nervous." I give him a kiss on the cheek. "Be sure to brush your teeth, Dad."

"Hey, that's my line." He's almost asleep, but he smiles.

Ike takes his arm and helps him up the stairs. "Gotta keep that killer smile." Dad is so thin; 180 is now 140. Ike's almost dragging him. Dad's strength is gone for the day.

"Like I'll be alive long enough for it to go anywhere." Dad gives a weak chuckle.

Not funny.

The Box of Death is still there, in the Everything Room.

I want to throw it away.

He'd know if it was gone. He'd make me dig it out of the trash. He'd order more.

I check my email to see if a camera part's been shipped, and there's an email from Mama Duck's team: *We're talking it over, to see if we can fulfill your dad's wish. His circumstances are rather extraordinary.*

The drawing and the haiku are very clever. We appreciate fan art.

Well.

I write back: *The man was a paramedic until March. He's done so much for this town. His uncle is Paul Oliver, the history guy who gives talks at the Tall Ships Festival. Could you please make an exception for him? He's DYING. Do you not get that? He is RUNNING OUT OF TIME. Mama Duck is the one thing he wants at his birthday party. Can't you help us?*

Maybe there are uses for pity after all.

I sit down on the couch to watch some Netflix, something I never do, and Gracie texts: *Want to go to Fizzy Waters?*

Total tourist trap. It's a store with vintage candy and any kind of soda you could want, ranging between candy from when my dad was a kid to a soda with Osama Bin Laden on the label. Who knew?

I text back: *Sure*. It's only 8:15.

"Ike! Going out with Gracie for a little bit." I holler it up the stairs, but not too loudly, just so he knows.

As I walk through the yard to wait for Gracie on the sidewalk, I notice how much it needs to be mowed. Our yard is sloped and hard to deal with, because there's beach grass and regular grass. It ends up patchy and odd every summer. Now that Ike lives here, he mows. And I'm glad.

Gracie pulls up and I get in. She starts talking right away, like it's not awkward that we haven't seen each other in a month. "We're seniors now. Seniors! Can you believe that? I thought this day would never come!" She's bubbly and happy as ever. "You should text me more. We need to hang out—and act like seniors!"

"I take care of my dad and work and take photos. That's all I have time for right now." I watch the houses going by, so I don't have to look at Gracie.

She notices. "Look at me, would you?"

I turn. She's got a kind smile on her face.

"I know shit is tough right now. Can I come over and read to your dad again? Help him pass the time?"

"That would be great." I don't know what else to say, so I look back out the window. "Are you working?"

"Yeah. At Fizzy Waters, actually. I'm going to grab my paycheck and this grape soda that I really love. It's from England."

"Eeew."

"I know it's not your thing." She laughs. "But there's some really good peach stuff I thought you might like. And you need to get out."

"True."

There are a ton of people we know at Fizzy Waters, which is weird, since town kids don't usually go where tourists go. We're there until it closes at ten. It's good to be a high school senior for ninety minutes.

Gracie drives us home while we sip on a 1919 Root Beer. I've got a bag of ten different sodas on the floor between my feet—Gracie insisted on using her discount to buy me whatever I wanted: strawberry, peach, five different kinds of root beer, two different ginger ales, and one I don't remember.

"You'd better not let Ike drink all that stuff." She gives me the eye. "Or maybe you should, since he's so cute."

"He's basically a big brother, and I'm sure I'll share."

She stops at a stoplight. "If I had a cute guy living in my house that I wasn't related to, I'd be making moves all the time."

"Because I have lots of time for romance." I sigh. "Brother, remember?"

"Your dad goes to sleep at some point, doesn't he? You could be quiet."

That comment is at least three steps over the line. "You just don't get it, do you, Gracie?"

"Get what?" She's genuinely surprised.

"Ike is there to help my dad eat, poop, and get up and down the stairs."

"Tobin, you can't think . . ."

"I'm out." We've started moving again, and we're almost to the lift bridge, almost out on Park Point. "Stop the car, please."

"Tobin! I didn't mean anything! He's just so sexy." She's got that grin on her face that says *I'm so cute, you can't be mad*, but yeah, I can be mad.

"Stop the car or I'll jump out."

She pulls over to the curb and I lurch out.

"I'm sorry!" She yells from behind me. "And you forgot your soda!"

"Keep it." I shout it at her, but I don't look back. I just walk.

She passes me thirty seconds later, going toward my house, since she can't turn around yet, and I see her flash me the peace sign out the window.

"Not interested in your crap right now!" I yell it as she goes by. I have no idea if she heard me.

I have no goddamn time for cluelessness right now.

I don't look at her when she's driving back toward Canal Park. Back toward her house, and being a teenager.

When I come in, looking like a thunderstorm, Ike raises his eyebrows at me.

"Thought you went out to have a good time, not a bad one."

"Yeah. Me too." And I stalk through the house, out the back door, and onto the dunes.

If you drive up the west side of it, the lake is loud all day and night, crashing on the rocks. But here on the south, if there's no wind, the lake almost purrs.

I let its hum wash over me. I concentrate on freezing out the anger. But I can't do it tonight. Everything hurts.

Please.

Somebody.
Take this away.
There are no feelings that will help me right now.
None.

Dad's Big Book of Advice #13
Bad things will happen to you. That's life.
The amount of optimism you have
determines how bad you feel when they do.

JUNE 18

Anybody who's normal should be asleep right now. It's 7:02 on a Saturday morning. But normal people don't run marathons.

The lake's already showing off her beauty with shimmers and a clear blue sky to reflect in her ripples. Mornings are so fresh and clean, especially sunny ones. They make me never want to leave.

I'm sitting between Allison and Paul in the back seat. Dad's being anxious in the front seat.

"I'm going to forget. I know it." He's breathing kind of hard and shuffling his speech from hand to hand.

"No, you won't." I see Ike reach over to him to pat his shoulder. "I trust."

Dad looks out the window. "All the times I ran this damn thing. No better marathon in the country. Just gorgeous."

We're on the fast highway, not the highway where they'll run, so we can't see the lake right now, but I know she's moving into her sparkly mode as the sun gets higher, like someone's scattered a million diamonds on her surface. The runners will have a beautiful morning. Even though I hate running, I would do a couple miles just to take it all in. When Lady Superior shows off, she does a good job.

When we pull up to Sonju Motors in Two Harbors, where the race starts, runners are already gathered, like a million of them, and it's only 7:15. Dad and Ike were here at 5:30 this morning, making sure all the signage was clear, and making sure no assholes had stolen them. They only came back to get Allison, Paul, and me. Driving on race day is a pain in the ass, but they have a GRANDMA'S MARATHON STAFF sign on their dashboard that gets cops to let them through the traffic jams.

"Tobin, will you help your dad get settled while I park the car?" Ike turns around to look at me. "Maybe you and Allison want to wrangle. Paul and I will join you in a second. It's a good time to breathe deeply." He shoots me a grimace, and I get it. Dad's been intense this morning.

"I'm on it." I hop out the door, then get my dad out of the front seat as carefully as I can. We have his cane, because he wants to walk up the stairs and stand on top of the announcement stand thingy, which is tiny. Ike wanted to bring his wheelchair, but Dad was adamant the cane would be fine. His direct quotation was, "I'll be damned if I'm going to sit down in front of people I've run with."

Dad's testy when I help him get out. "I don't need to be wrangled."

I try and smile. "You just need a handler, then?"

He jabs his cane at me with a crabby look. I dodge it, since he's pretty slow, and since he needs it to balance, while I breathe in, as deep as I can. Then I exhale with a *whoosh*. The sound is lost in the crowd noise.

Allison clears the way in front of us as I escort Dad to the base of the announcer's stand. He's talking to people close by and waving at other people he knows. Some of the marathon committee is here, too,

I just stand there, watching my social butterfly dad, when someone touches my elbow. When I turn, it's Rich.

"How's Medic 3464 today? We're on duty." He cocks his thumb back at the rig he and my dad used to drive.

Dad turns and smiles when he hears Rich's voice. "Glad you're here."

"You'll be brilliant, I know." Rich hugs him.

Rich's new partner, Lexi, raises a hand to us. She's maybe Ike's age, maybe a little younger, blond and pretty but strong-looking, like she could lift Paul Bunyan if he needed help. She came over with Rich one afternoon, and I think she passed Dad's inspection, even though he told her she was too young for the job. She punched him in the arm when he said it. Rich told her to.

Allison takes Dad from me, and after Dad says goodbye to Rich, they ricket over to a group of Duluth runners.

Rich watches them go. "Wow. He's . . . diminished. I didn't know it would be so soon." Then he kind of shakes himself. "I mean, he looks good. He's holding his own." Rich slaps me on the shoulder, like he was just kidding about what he said before. "Where's Ike? You all doing well in the same house?"

"He's the big brother I never had."

Rich grins. "He always wanted a baby sister to spoil, since his big ones pick on him."

Just then Ike and Paul arrive, and Ike gives his dad a hug before we go toward the announcer's stand.

Paul takes my dad's hand. "Ready? The race starts in five minutes."

Dad pauses and closes his eyes. "Let me review my speech one more time." He keeps his eyes closed for about a minute, then opens them. "Ready. Ike?"

Ike comes around to my dad's left, and then steers Dad by his elbow over to the three steps that will take him to the top of the announcers' podium. He follows behind Dad as he starts up.

It's agony watching him climb. Last year, I'm sure he was bouncing at the starting line. He was always a bunny at the beginning of a race—hopping and moving and trying to get the nerves out, remembering to pace himself. Pure energetic joy.

The crowd hushes, because folks in the front have watched him climb, and they know something's going on. The stillness ripples back into the runners a block away and more, and soon the whole pack is still. As still as a pack of 9,500 runners gets.

Ike takes hold of the mic, makes sure it's on, and hands it to my dad, who's leaning on his cane, trying to catch his breath. My dad closes his eyes, steeling himself, and opens his mouth.

"Welcome to the North Shore." His tone is suddenly angry, and his face matches his voice. "My name is Steve

Oliver, and I have ALS, or I'd be running right alongside you. Do you realize how lucky you are to have legs that work? So fucking lucky you'll never know."

This isn't his speech. He's almost shouting now, as much as his voice will let him.

"I'm on the race organizing committee, and we've done all we can to make sure you have a great experience before, during, and after your marathon." He's so mad he's spitting. "Grandma's Marathon is the most beautiful race in the country, and we've got a gorgeous morning to show that beauty off. This race will kick you in the ass, but I want you to enjoy every single fucking step of it, because I can't. And you fucking suck because you can. See you in Duluth!"

I'm going to throw up.

A beat of the most complete silence I've ever heard.

"Oh my god." Allison's voice is barely audible. "Does he do that a lot?"

One yell, maybe a hundred yards back: "Hey! The only person who gets to tell me I suck is my boss!"

Another beat.

And the air horn sounds.

The mass of humanity that is Grandma's Marathon bolts down the road, and my dad waves his cane at them, barking commands and scowling with the mic in his hand: "Run, fuckers! Like your life depended on it!"

He gets a lot of glares.

I look at Rich. His hands cover his face. Lexi watches Rich, Dad, and me, wondering what's next.

Ike takes the mic from my dad and shuts it off. "Let's get you down. It's going to be a lot harder than up." He and Dad move toward the stairs from the front of the platform, but before they get very far, a woman is at the bottom, shaking her fist up at Dad. I've never seen anyone do that in real life.

"How dare you say those kinds of things? How dare you say the word—" She covers her mouth and whispers. "—*F-U-C-K* to a group of strangers in our city? Free speech only goes so far, you know. You've ruined their morning!"

My dad is surly. "Ma'am, you have no idea what it's like to be in this body. It fucking sucks. But I wanted to welcome them."

I hear her draw in her breath. "If that's your idea of welcoming friends, I'd hate to hear you talk to your enemies!" And she stomps away.

Dad stares at her as she goes. "Whatever, bitch." His face is a picture of frustration.

Ike tightens his grip on Dad's arm. "Let's focus on getting you down."

Dad lurches down the first stair and makes it maybe an inch before he's tumbling in a tangled heap of legs, arms, cane, and metal edges.

Rich is right there, picking him up and soothing him, crooning to him like he's a hurt child, because once he hits the bottom, Dad starts yelling and crying.

Ike is on Dad's heels, clattering down the stairs. "Steve!"

Rich carries him over to Dad's old rig and checks him out for injuries while he and Lexi patch up his scrapes. Ike and Rich talk over Dad's head in Spanish, almost identical worried looks on their faces. Dad's sobbing like he's five and someone's run over his dog. "Get your stupid fucking hands off me! I hate this body!" Over and over and over.

Allison and Paul are on either side of the stretcher. Allison's holding Dad's hand, and Paul's patting his shoulder.

I'm standing down by his feet, holding them and watching the very last runners move off the starting line.

Kerri approaches Dad, and he bursts into more wails. She's as understanding as she can be, given that a man just dropped the f-bomb more than once in front of almost ten thousand people who were not expecting to be cursed at. She gives him a hug and reassures him.

Then she comes to me and hugs me. "Does this happen often?"

"It's unpredictable, but it's never been like this. I'm so sorry."

She sighs. "We'll get nasty letters, I'm sure. I'll just send a mailing to the runners about what can happen to your brain if you have ALS. It's not like your dad meant to do it."

We both look at him. He is the picture of misery on his stretcher. I've never seen anyone so sad. The things he used to be able to count on—his legs, his brain—are abandoning him.

"Tell him we love him. Don't ever let him say we don't." She gives me one more hug, hurries over to give him one, too, and then she's gone. She's got a race to keep on track, no pun intended.

Paul brings the car to where we are, and we load Dad into the front seat. Rich gives my dad one more hug through the window. Dad is still weeping and raging, though it tapers to silence as we leave Two Harbors.

Nobody says a word on our way home.

We drop Allison and Paul off at Trash Box—they're going to watch at the finish line in a while—and Ike and I take Dad home. When the car stops, Dad gets out, under his own power, bandages on his face and arms, and walks into the house by himself, stabbing his cane onto the ground each time he picks it up. It takes him about a year. He rickets through the house to the stairs—I'm sure he'd give a million dollars to be able to stomp up them—and goes up to his room. The door slams with as much force as Dad can muster, which isn't a lot, but enough to make his point.

The next day is Father's Day. He won't come out of his room. Ike goes in to check on him, and to make him use the bathroom, but that's it. He won't eat. He won't talk to me.

I sit in front of his closed door and tell him bad dad jokes.

After Ike and I have a silent supper, one Dad refuses to eat, I clean up the dishes and go into the Everything Room. The Box of Death is still there, next to the 20 Mule Team Borax.

I take it down.

I put it back up and stare at it.

Then I take it down again and put it on a low shelf by the back door. At my dad's elbow level.

Not like he doesn't know where it is.

I guess I need to let him know I know where it is, too.

Either way, it might be his last Father's Day.

I knock when I go by his door, on my way to bed. "Love you, Dad. You're my favorite person on the planet."

Very faintly. he replies. "Love you, Tobin."

"See you in the morning."

No answer.

Gracie texts: *Can we talk? Please?*

I don't answer. I have no words. For anything.

Sid texts: *How are you? Doing OK?*

No. Dad skipped Father's Day. Blew up Grandma's Marathon. Long story.

Oh shit. Big eyes emoji. *That sucks. I'm sorry.*

Yeah. Me too.

I guess I have words for Sid.

Three sad face emojis. One with a tear. *Talk to you soon. Take care.*

You too. And I put my phone, face down, under my bed.

I don't sleep for a long, long time.

Dad's Big Book of Advice #14
God is much too big to fit inside anyone's box called "religion."

JUNE 25

My dad didn't come out until late Monday afternoon. He ate supper with us, let Ike check all his owies, and went back up to his room. He didn't say a word the entire time.

Tuesday morning, it was back to business as usual. He was cracking bad dad jokes, some of the ones I repeated to him on Father's Day. Ike took him to the doctor, I went to Trash Box, and life started again.

When he came home from the doctor, he told me his functionality number is a 19. I see it everywhere: painted on the kitchen wall, on his bulletin board of race mementos, draped on the stairs, a neon red 19, framed by the word FAILINGFAILINGFAILINGFAILING, written in stark red letters.

Today I notice the box is gone from the Everything Room.

I don't mention it to anyone.

Nobody mentions it to me.

I check on my heart, at the bottom of Superior.

Still there. It's tiny, though.

Black, cold, and still.

Now it's Saturday, and Trash Box is swimming with people. Why the hell would you want to be inside, fighting over knickknacks and doodads, when you could be outside? It's gorgeous out there. Go eat chocolate and caramel apples, people. Walk out to the lighthouse. Fight with the seagulls. Do something, anything, everything. Be alive. And get out of this freaking shop.

Dad and Ike are on the sidewalk, with Mama Duck's Record Store, and they're both busier than a one-legged man in an ass-kicking contest, as Paul says sometimes. But Dad is just exhausted. He moves slower and slower as the morning goes along. I watch through the window even though I shouldn't, because I want to cry when I look at his tired face. Ike picks up the slack every time, smiling at Dad like he's Ike's own father.

Allison stays sweet to customers no matter what. She greets everyone with an angelic smile as she talks about Duluth history and what she knows about various pieces. I sit behind the register trying not to frown. She's gotten another bad review on Yelp about me. It said, "The counter girl was quite surly, and I didn't appreciate her attitude." Yeah, well, I don't appreciate the attitude of people who don't understand teenagers who are occasionally surly, especially when their father is fading away in front of their eyes.

Paul's come downstairs to help, most likely at Allison's request to try and prevent more bad Yelp ratings, and has ferried out new glassware, antique newspapers, which smell musty and gross, a couple cool Red Wing crocks Allison found in Canada last year, and a rocking chair to fill in a hole where there used to be another rocking chair. A guy bought the first one this morning. He walked in and said, "My wife wants that chair. How much?" Then he plunked down three Benjamins, put the rocker over his head, and carried it out the door. He must like his wife a lot.

A couple of older women have been mooning over a set of bowls for the last hour. They can't make up their mind whether to buy these rare pieces for their other sister, who lives down in Blue Earth and couldn't make it this year because of bursitis in her ankle, isn't that a shame, she never misses our Duluth trip. A true shame, I say, *and can I tell you about how my dad's planning to kill himself before the ALS eats him alive? Now that's a shame.*

The ladies finally buy the set. They live in Chanhassen, so it's only a couple hours to Blue Earth, and they say the bowls match her kitchen perfectly. I wrap them extra carefully, just like they ask me to, and they leave with big smiles.

"You were very patient with them, Tobin. Thanks for that. Maybe we should ask them to leave a Yelp review." Allison smiles, too.

"Maybe so." I slump on the stool behind the counter.

Paul comes out of the back room with a New York Seltzer, lemon lime, my favorite kind, and hands it to me. I drink it in about three swigs.

Allison goes in search of more merchandise to plug the holes on the shelves. "If you need me, just holler."

"We will." Paul answers for me.

He studies me, looking at my face like he's trying to decipher it. "So, Tobin. What's up?"

"Nothing. I'm fine."

His voice is kind. "How long did it take your dad to recover from what happened at Grandma's?"

"He didn't come out of his room except to pee until late Monday afternoon."

"Skipped Father's Day, did he?"

"Yes." There are hands around my throat, choking me.

"Sad for both of you."

"Yes." The hands get tighter.

He reaches out and pats my hand. "Maybe every day can be a celebration from here on out."

"Good idea." I'm going to pass out from lack of oxygen.

"He brought me a small box with mountains on the side."
WHOOOSH. The hands are gone.

"He told me what it's for, and he asked me to keep it until he wants it." Paul's studying me, to see if I know.

"I'm glad it's out of our house. I hate it." I spit the words like venom.

"What do you think about its contents?"

"What do you think I think?" The hands are back. And squeezing.

"I can be there instead of you. I know what it means to be looking at the end. I've thought about the same thing, actually."

"Paul!"

"What's wrong?" Allison's voice from the back room. I didn't realize I was that loud.

"Nothing. I just told a dirty joke, and Tobin objected."
He chuckles.

"When the hell did she get bionic ears?" I glare toward the back door while I pitch my voice slightly above a whisper. "And don't you *even* talk like that. Who'd defend me against Allison?"

"I'm not ready to go." He gives me a one-armed hug, his specialty. "But your dad's hurting. He also knows he's hurting you enormously by considering it."

"Yeah." I feel the hands creeping around my neck again.

"Maybe you get it a little better now, after what happened at Grandma's?"

"Maybe." The hands ease momentarily. "But I am fucking pissed."

"Understandable." He gives me another sidearm hug. "He'll let you know when it's time. Until then, make every day Father's Day, and get ahold of that six-story duck, all right?" Paul knows Dad wants Mama Duck at his party.

"I'm working on it."

"Grief is just love turned inside out. It's how we know we've loved someone. And grief is a long process, different at every stage of the situation." His face has gotten sadder with every word.

"I'm guessing you know what you're talking about."

"Firsthand." His eyes are glittery, but no tears slip out. "You're a good kid. You don't deserve this."

The hands are back and squeezing so hard I can barely get the word out. "Thanks."

One final sidearm hug, and Paul disappears into the back room. Faintly I hear him clump up the stairs, back to his place.

I take deep breaths to unblock the lump in my throat.

"Has your dad recovered a little bit, Tobin? When I talked to him on Thursday, he seemed all right." Allison comes out of the back room with a couple of kitchen canisters in her hand and she arranges them on a shelf in a bare spot. "I hope the race people aren't angry with him."

"Kerri's really kind. She understands."

She shakes her head. "He doesn't deserve this illness."

"Who does?"

"I can think of a few people who I'd like to suffer for a while." And she's gone again before she looks at me, so she misses all the daggers I send her with my eyes.

I wouldn't wish this illness on my worst enemy. Hitler and a couple other dictators, maybe. Nobody with a real heart or a real life.

She doesn't come out again. When five o'clock comes, I do all the closing stuff, and I'm out of there by 5:15.

Summer arrives slowly in Duluth, so instead of being warm and muggy at the end of June, it's really great outside—not too hot, everything still smells good—and the farther I walk away from the lift bridge, the quieter it gets. Getting away from tourists feels like taking off a sticky wet suit—once you peel it down, your skin can breathe again.

I'm about a block from my house when I realize I'm walking in time to the music I hear, which is the cantina song from *Star Wars*. Sure enough, when I climb over the dune to the backyard, Sid and my dad are sitting on the porch, and Sid's got his violin. As quiet as I can, I creep up the stairs and slither into a plastic chair next to my dad, who's in his wheelchair.

Sid's got his eyes closed, and you can tell he's really into what he's doing. The music courses out of his violin and pours into the grass on the dune, flowing toward the lake. If the sun was lower, I'd be able to see it. Liquid gold.

When Sid's done, he opens his eyes, and then opens them wider. "Tobin! I didn't hear you come up the stairs."

My dad's clapping, which is awkward, and he looks a lot like a Muppet when he does it. "You're going to be at Carnegie Hall someday. I know it."

Sid blushes. "I'm trying, sir."

The tears start pouring down my dad's face, which surprises Sid but not me. "Can you play the Olympics theme for me? It's John Williams, and I won't get to see another Olympics." He swipes at them with jagged motions. "Is it its own song, or is it just a couple phrases?"

"It's a song." And Sid puts his violin back under his chin and plays.

Of course, it sounds different when it's one instrument, but my dad loves it. The tears keep pouring. I get a box of Kleenex, and my dad takes one to push against his face, trying to mop up the wetness. Then he bonks himself in the nose without meaning to, so I wipe his cheeks. He closes his eyes and lets me.

Then Sid's done, and my dad Muppet-claps again. I clap in the human way.

Sid is gracious. "You're too kind." He stands up and bows, then reaches around the chair he's sitting in for his violin case. "I've got to head home. I'll be back, Steve, okay?"

"Please. Come back anytime. I would stand up to see you off, but my legs don't work so well these days." He's still got a Band-Aid or two on his forehead from where he fell down the stairs at the marathon. "Thanks again for the music."

"It's my pleasure." Sid's got his violin in the case again, and he reaches to shake my dad's hand. I can almost see my dad get taller in his wheelchair.

"Tobin, you want to walk me?" Sid's smile is shy.

"I can go see if Ike needs help with supper." Dad's smile is much bigger than Sid's. "Go." He wheels himself over the threshold. "Ike, what can I do to help?"

"You can keep me company while I chop the cilantro. That's enough." Ike's voice is right inside, through the kitchen window. "Fifteen minutes, Tobin."

"No cilantro for me, gross gross gross." I hate that stuff.

A chuckle floats out the kitchen window. "I wouldn't even think of it."

I point at Sid. "I can walk to your house and back in fifteen minutes, can't I?"

"You can do it in ten." I don't notice he doesn't have on any shoes until we get to the water's edge. I leave mine there.

We don't say anything, just splash through the edge of the lake. The water's maybe fifty-five degrees now. It's still cold enough to kill you fast if you fall off your boat. His mom sees us coming—she's sitting on their back deck—and she waves with a smile. I wave back.

"I'm, um, not going to come up and talk to your mom, if that's okay. It was a crap-ass day at the store, and I'm just ... you know. Brain-dead." I say it fast, so it doesn't seem too rude.

Sid nods. "She knows you have a lot going on."

"Thanks for coming over to play for my dad. It helps the anger stay away."

"Yeah." Sid digs his toe into the sand. "Ike told me what happened at Grandma's."

"Yeah."

More toe digging. "I'm sorry."

The hands are back, closing up my throat. "Yeah."

"Yeah." Sid reaches around me, violin case and all, and hugs me.

An enormous wall of sadness falls on me, and it's all I can do to stay upright. Being touched with kindness is too much.

"What if we . . . hung out? Did something fun?" Sid says it in my ear.

I pull back. "Fun like what? Like a date kind of fun?" I am not emotionally equipped to go on a date right now.

Sid chuckles. "Not a date. Just something that doesn't include Duluth and tourists, or worrying about your dad."

My brain immediately replies *There is no activity on this Earth that doesn't include worrying about my dad*, but I don't say it out loud. "Well . . ."

"We'll have a nature day. Or a nature hour, even. How about four hours—an afternoon? Can we do that? I'll plan something cool, or at least sort of cool." His face is open and kind, just like it's been his whole life, just like it was when we were ten and he showed me a DVD of his favorite movie at the time, which was *The Good, the Bad and the Ugly*, and he wanted me to love the music as much as he did. It was one time he fell in love with a soundtrack that wasn't John Williams. Though ten-year-olds shouldn't have been watching that movie. Waaaaay too much death and blood, way too many guns.

He can see he's surprised me. "Tobin?"

"I'm in." I say it before I can chicken out, because that's my first impulse—to say no.

A huge smile breaks across his face. "Text me your work schedule, and I'll match it up with mine, and . . . and then we'll do something."

"Okay." I smile back, because he's just too cute at this moment to do anything else.

He hugs me tight, and quick, and heads toward his house and his mom. His regular mom. Who lives in his house, not in Paris. Who doesn't send gift boxes. Who is someone Sid likes, as much as any teenager likes their parent.

I turn around and walk back toward my house, ankle-deep in the lake, thinking about hailstones. Icicles. Icy roads. Ice cubes. Igloos. Icebergs. Anything to solidify myself again, because I am leaking feelings against my will.

By the time I get back, supper's on the table. Nothing fancy. Non-gringo tacos, as Ike calls them. But they're delicious. We tend to trade off cooking, depending on when I work at Trash Box, and my choices are much less inspiring. Yesterday I cut up bratwurst after I grilled them and threw them into some baked beans. Add an apple and a glass of milk, and you've got a summer supper in Minnesota. Ike's tacos are so much better. Elena taught him well.

Dad starts talking about the Tall Ship Festival in August, and his birthday party, and how he'd really love it if Mama Duck would come to visit, and how Paul's voyageur history lesson won't be the same without his assistance—Dad always dressed up like a voyageur during Paul's public lecture—and wasn't Sid good tonight? Ike and I just let him talk. It's more than he's said for a couple days. His voice is weak and there's a wheeze. I watch Ike evaluate him.

"The taco meat was delicious. Easy to chew, too." Dad tries to wipe his mouth with a napkin. "That helps."

"Glad you liked it." Ike stands to clear the table, and I stand, too. "The more we can keep you away from a feeding tube, the better we are. I want to watch your wheeze, too."

"Not going on a . . . ventilator." Dad has to catch his breath in the middle of the sentence.

"Since you just had that lovely demonstration of how out of breath you are, why don't you go rest in the living room while Tobin and I get things cleaned up." Ike shoves the walker close to the table from where it was resting by the counter. "Tobin, help your dad up."

I guide the walker to him. "Sure you don't want your wheelchair?"

"Nope." And he turtles his way into the living room, to creak down onto the couch and watch some TV on his laptop. Somewhere he's found this old EMS show called *Adam-12,* so he's watching people from the seventies save lives with dinosaur equipment. Sometimes he laughs and talks to the computer: "Good god, man, put that thing down!" and "Really? You're going to use *that?*" It's hilarious. He told me he used to watch it when he was a little kid, but he didn't get it then. Now he says he knows more than the actors and the writers combined.

My phone buzzes, and I check it before I start putting away leftovers.

Please can we talk? #sosorry Gracie.

Not right now. #hurt #lifeisdifferent #sickdad

I use the hashtag summary trick. My brain can't hold another thing right now, including her.

By the time I get the table cleared and Ike gets the dishwater going, Dad's asleep and the snores are drifting into the kitchen.

Ike and I fall into rhythm pretty quickly—I wash, he dries.

"You know the box is gone, right?" Ike looks me in the eye. "You know he gave it to Paul?"

"Paul told me." I almost drop a glass but save it at the last second. "He doesn't deserve to have that happen again. What happened at Grandma's." My hands are shaking. I almost drop a second glass. "He wasn't Dad."

"No." Ike puts the towel down. "He told me today he wants to wait until September. Until he can see the leaves change a little bit. Then he can go. Maybe after your birthday."

My birthday is September 22.

I mentally settle a huge ice cube on top of my stomach, holding everything in. "September, huh?"

He puts the dishes away that he's dried. "Two months to goof off. Two months to write down his advice."

"He's still working on that?"

He smiles. "Advice for you until you're eighty-five."

"Hopefully we'll be able to check Mama Duck off his bucket list before September. And we'll celebrate another birthday." I force myself to smile back. Then my hand slips and I really do drop a glass as I hand it to Ike. It bounces on the floor and rolls away.

"Don't wake the dude up, klutzy fingers. He's had a long day." Ike retrieves it from where it's rolled under the table and puts it back in the dishwater. "Your hands, Tobin."

Shaking like I've never seen them shake before.

"I know." Ike puts his hand on my shoulder. "I know."

"No, you really don't." I shrug his hand off.

"You're right." He goes back to drying dishes. "I don't."

Everything's washed and dried in less than ten minutes. I hang up the dish towel before I go check on Dad. He's slumped to his side, walker in front of him, laptop on the coffee table, like a broken rag doll. His face is even thinner, which I didn't think was possible.

I get my camera from the kitchen counter and snap a few shots: from the floor, lying down and shooting up, so he looks like the three-story World's Sickest Dad.

Ike brings me my action figures, almost like he read my mind, and I rest Mystique on one of Dad's knees and Rey on the other. They have a stare-off while Dad snores, softly for once. Then I line up all four on his thigh, which is tiny, since he has no quad muscles now, and they all stare up at his face while he sleeps. Then it just feels creepy and wrong, so I put my camera away.

"What do you think happens after we die?" Ike's voice is quiet.

I'm getting a Coke out of the fridge and turn to look at him. "You're the Catholic, Ike. You tell me." I take a swallow and the Coke courses over the ice cube on the top of my stomach.

He sighs. "Hell just seems made up. And dumb besides."

"I thought it was mandatory for your crowd."

Ike shakes his head. "Not when you've actually been there, or you've seen people who live there permanently. Hell is here on Earth. I do think there's a heaven, though probably not one with a big-bearded God who looks like Zeus. I think our animals are there." He looks around, like someone's spying on him, but he's gonna tell me a secret anyway, which makes me smile. "Just don't let on that I don't believe in hell. It's a biggie for us. Gotta keep people under control, you know." He sighs and shrugs. "I just think about heaven."

I take another drink. "All the people we loved, and all our animals. Any food we want to eat. It's always the perfect temperature and sunny, but with good shade, if you want it. And you never have to pay for anything."

"You can kayak every day, or surf, and the waves are always perfect. And the water's just the right temperature. And you never get sick or sore or fat." Ike gets himself a Coke and drinks half of it, then pats his stomach, which is a bit less round now than when he started.

"You need to keep that devil mazapan out of this house." I point at him and then the cupboard where I know it is.

"If you jog and push your dad on the days I don't, you too can eat mazapan with no consequences." He grins.

"My definition of heaven is Dad being able to run again, and not being so whacked out. I want him to be himself."

Ike drains his can and puts it in the sink. "I will tell you this—it's very clear when a soul leaves a body. Very clear."

I sit down at the kitchen table, because my legs are starting to shake. "Good to know, I guess."

Ike sits down across from me. "It's just like people say it is—the body's a husk. A shell. Not the person. A meat sack."

"Meat sack." The words make me want to vomit.

"Maybe souls just go into the Universe, and not to heaven, I don't know. All I know is that they're not in the body anymore." Ike burps.

"Very reverent."

"Death is a process, just like birth. If it's not an accident or a trauma, that is." He burps again, which kind of makes me want to punch him. "Totally natural. Sad and gut-wrenching, but natural. Like burping." And he does it one more time.

"You're gross, first of all, and this is one million percent serious to me."

"Me too. And your dad. He's been there for a few deaths."

"Can we just stop now? If I have to talk about this for two more seconds, I will lose it. No hell, delicious food, hopefully running and dogs. Good talk."

I go out on the deck and breathe. And breathe. Then Dad wakes up, and Ike comes to get me, and we all watch *Adam-12*, and Ike takes him upstairs to get ready for bed.

I have no idea if there's a God, or a Higher Power, or Anything anywhere to help us out. But if there is, I hope She oversees a heaven.

Running on clouds. Running with our dog Ranger, the dog we had when I was in kindergarten. Crossing the finish line of Grandma's in Canal Park. Running among the stars of the Big Dipper, over the lake. In his favorite shorts and shoes, waving at people he knows.

Running.

Laughing.

Free and happy.

Being himself.

<u>June 30</u>

Here's the one thing I ask of
heaven-aside from the fact that it looks
like the time Sid's dad took us way out
into the middle of the lake at sunset,
and everything was magical and still and
gorgeous, with fish jumping in the warm
air from the cold water, or maybe that
time Paul took us over to Fargo for a
history conference, and we got to see
a sunset on the Great Plains, and the sky and the land
were enormous and the sunset was literal stripes of
color-aside from that, let it be like this:

Let the boundaries be permeable.

Let his voice filter through to me somehow. Let
me find him in random places, and let me know he
was there. Random running shoes, left by some dumb
tourist on the beach. Random men with hair just like
his. Random messages or songs or billboards, his voice
quietly whispering from the Other Side. Whispering
with purpose, to reach me. Whispering because he
loves and misses me.

Will he hold on to some
of his Earthly self? Will he
remember me, like I remember
him? Or will his... mind? soul?
self?... be a blank slate, free of
Earthly attachments?

Let him be happy. Let him be
joyous. Let him be free of pain
and sadness, and free from his
tumultuous mind.

But please let me see him.
Even from that far away. Let
me see his outline, hear his
voice, smell his smell.
Let me know he's here with me.

And let him remember me. Please, if You're there.
Please let that one thing be real.

Dad's Big Book of Advice #15
Sometimes you gotta chuck it in the "fuck it" bucket and move on.

JULY 4

On Park Point, we watch the Duluth fireworks at the Beach House. Usually there's at least a hundred of us. Some folks are spread across the dunes, and some are on the lake in boats— canoes or kayaks or sometimes speedboats. Everyone eats and talks and laughs until 10:30, when the fireworks start. Duluth puts on a good show, with big fireworks, not little puny ones. It's one night we share with each other. There are community tables set up with hot dog fixings and plates. Another table has a bunch of salads and snacks. All sorts of people show up, and nobody fights. Everyone is happy to live in the United States, at least for one day.

My dad and I have been going since before my mom left. Tonight is Ike's first time, since he's never lived on Park Point before. He's always watched them from Duluth. We get there about 8:30, with our wheeled cooler. I stay with Dad in his chair up by the Beach House while Ike grills us some dogs and Dad chats with folks walking by.

Sid's mom and dad are there, but Sid's visiting his older brother in Minneapolis, finding a new violin for his senior year. Who knew violins had to be test driven before you bought them? Gracie's here with her family—they've come every year since they moved away from Park Point. She keeps her little brothers busy at the edge of the lake and doesn't look at me, which is fine. I'm not ready to make up.

We push Dad to the edge of the concrete patio, but he isn't happy, because we didn't bring his cane. We try to compensate by feeding him chips and s'mores, which take forever to get to his mouth. Ike makes him laugh by telling him paramedic jokes: What happened when Waldo had a heart attack? He died, of course—nobody could find him! People come by and tell him how glad they are to see him, and he's completely polite. Charming, even. But he's got an edge to him. Maybe only Ike and I can tell, but it's there. In his words. In his eyes.

Last year, he'd organized Frisbee tag between about twenty kids at the shoreline. He was laughing and catching Frisbees, and they were pulling him in all sorts of directions.

I go inside to use the bathroom, and Gracie's mom starts talking to me, which is awkward, but I escape, only to be trapped by Sid's mom, who's a little easier to talk to than Gracie's mom, but she's still a mom.

Then I hear Ike: "TOBIN!"

I bolt out of the Beach House at a run.

"TOBIN, WHERE ARE YOU?" Ike is almost screaming.

"Right here! Where are you?" I'm trying to keep my cool.

The crowd is parting to let me through, and then I see Ike, crouched at the shore. I look behind me at the Beach House patio, and my dad's wheelchair is there. Empty. I went right by it.

The form is hollering. "Goddamn it, Ike, you don't have to shout! Just fucking help me up!"

"Get his chair!" Ike points. I grab it and run.

By the time I get it down to the edge of the lake, which is almost impossible in the sand and the dark, Ike has my dad on his feet. He's trying to shake off the water, like a dog.

"What the hell were you thinking, Steve? You could have drowned. You almost did." Ike is working hard not to blow his cool. I can see it. He carefully guides my dad out of the water, onto the damp sand. A woman brings over a blanket, and Ike wraps it around my dad, turning him into a shivering, angry burrito.

"You have no idea what the hell you're talking about." Dad's breathing fire.

"You were facedown in the water. Thank god you could pick your head up enough to keep breathing." Ike is rubbing my dad's shoulders, trying to help him stop shaking and trying to breathe deep at the same time. He rubs, breathes. Rubs. Breathes. Then starts talking again. "Thank god I saw you fall, even if I didn't see you get out of your chair."

"Some fucking help you are, huh?" The poison Dad spits at Ike is unreal.

Ike gets him into his chair and takes over pushing it as the crowd re-forms into little clusters, waiting for fireworks and pretending not to notice the family drama.

"Learned my lesson about leaving you alone, huh?" Ike's trying for lighthearted.

"You should have let me drown, you asshole."

"Dad, knock it off." I try so hard not to react, but this is too much. "Why did you even try it?"

"Don't tell me what I can and can't do, young lady."

Ike tries a soothing tone. "Let's save walking for the house, when you have your cane, and where the ground is level."

"*I can walk to the goddamn lake! I am not an invalid!*" Even though he can't holler like a regular person anymore, he's still loud enough that people turn around and stare at him.

"We'll talk about this later, okay?" Ike's trying to smooth things over, but Dad's not having it. He tries to stand up while Ike's pushing.

"Dad! No! Sit!" I grab his arm and pull him backward into the chair. The motion shakes the chair, which shakes Ike, which doesn't help.

"*Goddamn it.*" Dad is furious, a different kind of furious than I've ever seen.

And then the fireworks start.

"Down in front!" Dad hollers it, in his semi-loud way, and a woman with dark hair turns around and glares. We've finally made it back to the concrete patio behind the Beach House, so of course folks are standing in front of him.

"Steve, maybe you could lower your voice." Ike pats his arm.

"I can't see the fireworks around her, or that chick with the rag on her head!" Dad points at a woman in a hijab. Luckily, the fireworks are booming a bit, and folks are oohing and aahing, so the Muslim woman doesn't hear him.

"Steve, I know you're upset, but please don't take it out on other people." Ike's got a stern tone under his words, but it's too late.

"If people thought men should fuck other men, the Roman Empire would still be a thing!" Dad's on a roll now.

The dads with two kids are just to my right, and both guys look at him, mouths open in shock. Thank heavens their kids are paying attention to the pretty lights and colors. One dad flips him the bird, which I totally agree with.

Dad yells at anyone and everyone, moving his chair back and forth. He doesn't have enough strength to roll over people's feet, but he's annoying. People start to whisper. Every time Ike asks him to settle down, he shouts, "Don't shush me, you asshole!"

Ike points to the sky. "Check out the cool lights, why don't you?" His teeth are almost gritted, he's so frustrated.

"The booms are kind of great, aren't they? They rattle your ears." It's all I can think to contribute.

"Stop being such a cunt, Tobin!"

That's it. We grab our cooler. It was a gorgeous night to walk down, so we did. Not such a great choice right now. There are intermittent street lights out here, so we move in and out of shadows as we walk home.

My dad keeps hollering. "This is kidnapping! You're kidnapping me!" Cars slow down to see what's going on. Ike says, "Dementia," because the truth is too complicated, and each driver nods and moves on.

Under his breath, I hear Ike mutter, "Mother Mary and Baby Jesus, if ever there was a time I needed you, it's right now. Please help us make it home. Thank you. Amen."

"Shut up, you fucking greaser! We don't need your stupid fucking prayers!" Dad's relentless, but Ike just pushes him along, and all I can do is follow. "I hate this body, and I hate you!"

We walk through some pretty dark spots. Not exactly what we need right now.

"I'm scared! Where are we?" Dad's voice carries, even though it's not that strong.

"You're okay, Steve." Ike tries again.

"Shut up, you wetback!"

"*Shut the fuck up!*" I don't even recognize the voice that said it.

"Tobin." Ike is quiet. "That doesn't help."

"*Just shut the fuck up for one minute!*" Then my shame stops me in my tracks.

Dad keeps yelling, Ike keeps pushing, but then a baritone singing voice slides out into the darkness. I don't know the words, but the notes are soothing and calm.

Duérmete mi niño
Duérmete me amor
Duérmete pedazo de mi corazon.

The only words I know for sure are *child*, *love*, and *heart*, the words at the end of each line. The song is quiet, sure and steady. One more shout from Dad: "Where the fuck are we? I'm scared!" but then it's over. He's quiet. Maybe Ike's prayer helped.

Ike keeps singing as he pushes Dad up the ramp and into the house. Dad is wild-eyed, but we get him settled on the couch with a blanket. Ike keeps singing.

"Could I . . ." His voice is hoarse. "Could I have a drink?"

I pull the blanket over his feet. "Be right back."

Ike keeps singing.

Thirty seconds after he drinks the water, Dad is sound asleep.

Ike goes up to bed. I sit on the back deck and look at Duluth and think about all the life going on over there. How I should drown myself for being a shitty daughter who yells at her dad who has no control over his brain. Then I cuddle into the chair in the living room and cover up with another blanket. I don't want him to be alone down here. It's probably 12:30.

I say my own prayer: *Dear Universe, please help me tape my mouth shut if it gives me patience with him. Please give him peace. Thank you.* No idea if Anyone hears. At this point, I don't care. I just need help.

Three a.m.

"I hate this body!" Dad's voice is hoarse and quiet, since he's already used up a lot of his energy, but his brain's on round two. "I can't stand it!" Then there's a *thump*, and I realize he's fallen, trying to get out of the chair we put him in. The room is dark enough that it takes my eyes a minute to adjust.

"*Ike!*" I scream it. I can't get him off the floor by myself without breaking him, he's so fragile.

A sleepy voice answers me. "On my way."

"Are you all right? Are you hurt? Ike will be here in just a second, Dad, to help you up." I kneel to check him as Ike makes his way to us in the living room.

"I'm fine! Get your fucking hands off me!"

We get him off the floor and up the stairs to bed. Ike sings the whole time. Once we get him laid down, he's asleep in less than thirty seconds.

Ike and I retreat to our separate rooms. Nobody shuts their door. Just in case.

When I come downstairs around 11, Dad's at the kitchen table, eating a piece of toast torn into tiny pieces and looking through the photos on my camera.

"Did I say you could do that?" I don't want him seeing my thoughts.

"Tobin!" He's startled. Then he smiles. "Just looking. That's not permissible?"

"They're not for public consumption. Everything's raw." In more ways than one.

"These are interesting." He points to the back camera screen where there's an image of him sleeping, with a couple of action figures. "Unusual series."

"A little bit, yes." I take the camera and put it on the stairs.

"If I'm in a photo, it's my business, you know." He's not the screaming banshee he was last night, but he's plenty edgy.

"I get that, but these are for my entrance portfolio. I'm not going to do anything with them besides that."

His face changes. "I'm not sure you want to do that." His voice is angry, but quiet.

"Excuse me?"

"I'll be fucked if you use them. They're ugly, and they won't get you into college anyway, so no. Permission denied." He stands, with his walker, and starts to make his way toward the stairs.

I swoop for my camera and head out the back door.

"*Come back here, bitch! We're not done!*"

"Hey, Steve. What's going on?" Ike's voice comes through the open window. "How was the toast?"

From the way Ike's voice is fading out, I'm guessing he's steering Dad toward the living room, maybe toward his computer and some more *Adam-12* episodes.

I'm guessing Ike talks to Mother Mary and the Baby Jesus way more than just last night, judging from his level of patience.

Ike comes to find me on the back porch. I'm flipping through the photos on my camera, kicking myself for not downloading and then password protecting them.

He touches my shoulder. "You hanging in there?"

"Do I have another choice?" My voice cracks, but I get it together.

Ice. I'm made of ice.

"That yelling, name-calling guy is not your dad, and of course you know that, but it's still all right to be hurt. It's been a pretty gross eighteen hours."

"It's not one bit helpful to be hurt."

"But it's all part of the grief process. And ALS grief might be crueler than most. That and Alzheimer's." He looks as hurt as I feel. "Watching it happen is awful."

"Fuck this process." I stand. "Fuck it twenty ways to Sunday."

Ike nods with a sad smile. "Anger is part of the process, too."

I slam into the house with my camera and vow to download the photos tonight.

When I go back downstairs after I've stowed away my camera—those hot dogs were a long time ago and I'm famished—my dad calls to me from the living room. "Tobin? Will you bring me an apple?"

I consciously remove the bitterness from my voice. "Sure."

"Can you cut it up for me?" He sounds like regular Dad right now. Just a weakened, ill version of himself.

"Really small chunks, right?" I try and think of what I've seen Ike do.

"Yes please. And maybe bring some peanut butter?"

"You got it."

I cut the apple into chunks—just like the ones in my photos—and grab some chunky peanut butter and slop it on the edge of the bowl. Then I deliver it, along with a fork.

"Will you sit with me?" He pats the cushion next to him on the couch with a very clumsy hand. "Just in case I need you to retrieve apple pieces? And because you're wonderful?" He can see on my face that something's not right. "What? Did I yell?"

"A little."

He sees the tears in my eyes before I slam them away. "Oh, honey, I'm so sorry. So sorry. I don't know when it happens, and . . ."

The tears I want to cry fall down his face, and I grab his hand, hoping to avoid a full-on catastrophe. But it never arrives. The water just keeps flowing.

"Let's watch *Adam-12*." I grab the laptop from the coffee table with my free hand.

"Hand me a Kleenex, please." He pulls his hand out of mine, with the speed of a snail, and I hand him a tissue. "I finished that yesterday. I'm watching *ER* now. Just the right amount of guts and blood. Makes me feel like I'm working again." A small smile. A honk on the Kleenex.

"There are some cute guys on that show." I point at a super-young George Clooney frozen on the screen.

"I know!" Now Dad's smile is more his normal smile. "They're just babies. But I was, too, back then."

We laugh, and we watch. I help him get little nibbles of peanut butter on his apple before he stabs it. I ask Mother Mary and Baby Jesus if they'll please keep the peanut butter from sticking in his throat. Ike doesn't usually let him eat it, but I forgot that when he asked.

Ike comes and looks at us from the doorway. Then I hear him make a sandwich.

A small peace is a good peace.

Dad's Big Book of Advice #16
You've got to decide what you don't want
so you can focus on what you do want.

JULY 10

It's 1 p.m. on a Thursday, and miracle of all miracles, I'm not working. Neither is Sid. It took a long time to find this afternoon. And I mostly want to stay home under my bed—I am just not capable of being a regular human right now—but I can't break my word. Plus, Dad and Ike know Sid's taking me somewhere, and their shit is endless already. If I skipped out, they'd never let me hear the end of it.

Sid picks me up in his mom's RAV4 instead of his beat-up Saturn, and we head north on Highway 61. Sid's got his aux cord, and the theme song to *E.T.* is blasting from the speakers.

"Gonna tell me where we're going?" The small talk has been awkward thus far. Might as well get to the point.

Sid looks startled. "Um, well . . . I kind of wanted it to be a surprise." He keeps glancing at me as the trees whiz by. "It's not all right to have a surprise?"

"It's fine." It comes out surlier than I mean it to.

"I know you're tense, which is totally understandable, but I was hoping we could forget . . ." He glances again at my face. "Maybe that's not possible."

I slam my eyes shut before anything leaks out of them. He's being kind again. "I'm sorry. I know I'm terrible company."

Sid reaches over and grabs my hand. "You're not terrible." And that's all we say for a while.

He doesn't let go of my hand. I don't object.

We pass through Two Harbors, which takes a while because of tourists and stoplights. After Two Harbors, the highway is two lanes. We breeze by Castle Danger and Split Rock lighthouse.

"Not the lighthouse?" I'm surprised. That was my guess.

"Too many people." He smiles. "We're heading for nature."

We pass by Beaver Bay, then Silver Bay, then pull off at a tiny little parking lot, next to a cliff. The sign says PALISADE HEAD, with an arrow pointing up.

I look around, and memories start firing in my brain. "I've been here. With my mom, even. And maybe once since she left, with Dad."

Sid knows my mom was a photographer. "I'm sure she came here for sunrise photos more than once."

We climb the path, Sid carrying a basket—an honest-to-god picnic basket, which I don't know if I've ever seen in real life before—and then we're on top of a huge rock face. Just us and the basket.

It's gorgeous. Look north, and it's beautiful pines and shore-line views. Look east, and it's all lake. Look south, and it's more beautiful pines and shoreline views. Look west, and there are hills with more trees. We're up so high, we can probably see thirty miles in each direction.

"I remember her yelling at me not to get too close to the edge. And then Dad would go close, and she'd yell at him, and they'd laugh." I had no idea these memories were in there. "And it was just getting light. I was so tired. I laid down on the rock and fell asleep while they watched the sun come up."

Sid smiles. "Pretty early for a little kid to get up."

"Or a grown-up."

Sid kneels, opens his picnic basket, and spreads out a small blanket. Then he pulls out grapes, cheese sticks, a bag of mini Reese's Peanut Butter Cups, and two bottles of sparkling water. He looks apologetic. "I guessed."

"This is perfect." And it really is.

"Would you like to sit?" He gestures to one side of the blanket.

I sit. "You're really nice to do this for me. I . . ." I look away. "I'm not exactly a regular teenager right now." Suddenly I want to throw myself into his arms and cry until my head explodes.

He touches my hand again. "Just be who you are. Sad and scared and whatever. But look at me, okay?"

I do. And he looks as sad as I feel.

"I'm here for you. All right?"

"All right." I can barely get the words out.

"Have a Reese's." He hands me one, so nobody has to feel anymore.

We're quiet for a bit, just staring out at the lake. An eagle buzzes by, close enough that I see he has a fish in each talon.

"Do you know how weird it is to grow up with a Great Lake in your backyard? Literally in your backyard? Or front yard, or any part of your yard, for that matter?" Sid breaks the silence.

"It's weird." I eat another Reese's.

"There might be a million people who can say that." He spreads his arms wide, taking in the lake. "How many houses can you actually fit on the shoreline of five Great Lakes?"

"No idea." I unwrap another Reese's.

Sid frowns. "Maybe half a million?"

"That's tiny. There are three hundred million people in America, I think." I eat one more Reese's.

"Do you remember that storm we had last October? The one with the hurricane winds and the twenty-foot waves? The early one?" It's not normally that bad until November. "The guy who lives next to me got his lost canoe back. It washed up in the storm, after it had been gone for more than a year."

I scan Sid's face to see if he's kidding. "No way."

He nods. "He figured someone had stolen it. The day of the storm, he went out to check his beach, and it was back. Like she coughed it up again." He chuckles. "He told me he's hoping for a fishing boat next."

"Is he sure it's his canoe?" This is way too strange.

"His name is in it." Sid shakes his head. "She takes, but she gives."

"Weirdest story ever, but it also kinda doesn't surprise me."

"Agreed." Sid gazes out, toward the horizon. "She's like another person in my life. A presence. Is that dumb?" The blush rises in Sid's cheeks, very faintly.

"Nope. She's just . . . always there." I don't know how else to say it.

"And I can't quit her. Even though she scares the shit out of me." Sid unwraps a Reese's.

"Same."

We sit there, looking at the lake and its trees, boats, birds, bugs, fish, and waves. Mostly we're silent.

"How's your portfolio?" Sid hands me another Reese's. I haven't had one for at least twenty minutes.

"Mmm . . . coming along? Sorta? It's okay. Not done yet. But it will be."

More silence.

"How's Gracie?"

"Dunno. We had a fight." I reach out for one more Reese's and unwrap it.

"She told me."

"She did?"

Sid nods. "She's really, really sorry, and she misses you a ton. Maybe you miss her, too?"

"Maybe. It's just . . . hard to be a friend right now. Or a girl, for that matter. Everything is . . . overwhelming."

Sid squeezes my hand. I squeeze back. But he doesn't say a word.

Smart man.

More silence. More nature.

At one point, I fall asleep with my head on his shoulder.

Then the sun angle tells us it's time to go back to real life, so we pack up. Supper is calling. The ghost of my dad is already tugging on my leg, pulling me under the waves of sadness that threaten to plow me over as I walk down the path to the car.

When we're on the highway again, I pick up his hand.

"Thanks for this."

"You're welcome." He stares straight ahead. "My pleasure."

"Thank you for not trying to kiss me."

"I'm not that stupid." A smile flickers on and off his lips, and I laugh.

We hold hands until we get back to Duluth. Then real life takes over again.

But even when I go to bed, I feel his warmth.

July 14

For every moment of connection with another human, there are ten other moments custom-made to destroy you.

Negative words. Crabby interactions. The wrong look at the wrong time.

And then you decide—what else could you possibly conclude?—this person who chose to love you, or is supposed to love you because they're your blood, really doesn't care. They're only in it for themselves. They just want to hurt you.

Once you know that, you consider burning down the world.

But then you stand back, if you can. When you can. When the mad/sad/bad has faded a bit.

And you realize their pissy look, or their harsh words, might not be about you.

Maybe. Possibly.

So you have to decide.

You have to THINK in the middle of all the emotions.

(how to do this? I don't know)

And then what?

Maybe you freeze them out.

Maybe you don't text them back.

Or you find them, and hold their hand. Or give them a hug.

People aren't perfect. So you choose.

Is a relationship good if it's 50% positive?
Should it be more?
Can you even ask for 50%?
What are you willing to put up with?
In the meantime, you talk. Work. Laugh. Eat candy.
Watch the world go by. Try and forget the bad stuff.

People are human. Even if you wish they weren't.

Dad's Big Book of Advice #17
NEVER EVER NEVER EVER NEVER EVER SMOKE. Ever.

JULY 16

I get an email from Mama Duck's boss:

Tobin:

We're still discussing whether or not we can fit you into our schedule. You said your dad was going to turn 50? Don't Make-a-Wish wishes only go up to 18? :)

Chip

Not funny.

I write back: *Call it a bucket-list item. Shouldn't everyone's wishes come true when they're dying? Please allow me to rely on your kindness and generosity to bring joy to his heart. Mama Duck is all he wants for his birthday.* Maybe if I try to sound more like an adult he'll pay more attention.

An almost-dead man would like to see your ginormous-ass duck before he kills himself. I almost add it at the end of the email.

WHY IS THIS SO HARD?

It's Wednesday, and Sid and I meet up for lunch at Little Angie's, a Mexican restaurant in Canal Park. Allison doesn't usually give me this much time off for lunch, but I told her I was meeting Sid to talk about Dad's party. She thinks he's going to play his violin for Dad, but he's just going to help serve food—no planning required.

It's a nice day. We deserve to have lunch outside.

Sid is fidgeting with his fork and spoon, looking around like he's waiting for something while I eat salsa and chips. "Gonna tell me what's up? Someone after you? Did you steal a violin?"

"Osmo Vänskä." His eyes dart around, and he tilts his whole body to the side to see behind me

"A Swedish mobster?" I eat another chip.

"You dork. He's the music director of the Minnesota Orchestra, and he's Finnish."

Now I start looking around. "He's here?"

"He was standing in the crowd this morning, listening to me play Beethoven. I took a John Williams detour." He makes eye contact but starts looking around as quickly as he stopped. "He put a ten in the bucket, so I want to thank him."

Then our food arrives, so we're chowing down on enchiladas, but Sid's eyes never stop roving. "Is your dad's party all done? I guess we should have talked about that at Palisade

Head." He stops scanning for three seconds to look at me again. "Not much time now."

"Mostly done. I just need his birthday present to come through." I'm facing north, and I watch tourists scurry everywhere, like tall ants.

Then water gushes into my lap.

"Dammit! I'm sorry!" Sid's grabbing at napkins, trying to mop up what he just knocked over.

I sponge off my chair and my crotch with my napkin. "It dries." A server brings over more napkins.

While Sid's bent over the table, stabbing at the water underneath the salt and pepper shakers, a man walks up behind him. He's older, with a serious face, receding hairline, and glasses. The stranger smiles as he watches Sid work on the table.

"Sid?"

He looks up and I cut my eyes to the guy, so Sid will turn around. Sid drops the wet napkins as he jumps to his feet.

"Hello, young man." The guy's voice is gruff but not unfriendly. His accent is definitely not Minnesotan.

"He-hello. Um. Hello, sir." Sid can barely talk.

"What are you planning for college? Or do you know yet?"

"I ... um ... don't know." He's barely audible.

"I hope you'll consider school in the Twin Cities. I'd like to keep an eye on you." He smiles at Sid and then at me. "Though you might be busy here in Duluth."

"No! She's going to college in Colorado, anyway."

I blush.

"That will allow you some time to focus on your violin, then." Another smile.

"Yes. Yessir." Sid's a little louder now but not much.

The man digs into his wallet and hands Sid his card. "Let me know when you'll be down to visit, and I'll show you around Orchestra Hall." Sid drops it, because his hands are working as well as Dad's at this moment.

"Thankyousir." All one word. He can't take his eyes off the man.

"Enjoy your lunch." He gives us a small salute and walks off. I hand the card to Sid.

He flumps in his chair and stares at me. "Osmo Vänskä."

"I caught that."

"Holy shit." He rolls his eyes. "He's going to show me around Orchestra Hall."

"Guess you'd better get your butt to college in the Cities."

"Guess I'd better." He takes in a deep breath then exhales. "All right. That made my summer, right there." Then his eyes get wide. "And I forgot to thank him for the money!"

"It *should* make your summer, and I'm sure he can spare a ten."

"Probably." Then his face transforms to a combination of horror and embarrassment. "I'm sorry!"

"For what?"

"Because . . ." He looks anywhere but at me. "It's rude of me to be happy when things are so . . ."

Please not this.

I sigh. "Sad? Depressing? A complete mess?"

"Yeah." He looks at the sky, at the people seated next to us, anywhere but at me.

"Knock it off. You have every right to be happy." A small furry jealousy monster leaps around in my gut.

He finally looks at me. "I don't want to insult you."

"By demonstrating that life goes on? That's the truth." I look back. "I'm happy for you." I punch the jealousy monster in the head and smile, really big and with teeth, so Sid knows I'm for real. "Being happy for you saves me from being sad."

"Sad sucks."

"Yeah, it does. But mostly it just is." I look at my phone. "I've got five minutes to get back to Trash Box." A server is walking by, and I wave. "Can I have my check?" She nods. The last bite of my enchilada is cold, and the cheese is solid again, greasy and slimy.

Sadness tastes about like that when you swallow it.

But I'm still happy for him.

Sid shovels an enormous amount of lunch into his face. The server brings our checks. Sid grabs mine and puts money into both check folders. "You can at least let me do this."

"Fine. Whatever." But I blow him a kiss, which makes him laugh. And blush, just a tiny bit.

Then we head off to our afternoons.

When I sit at the counter, I can see out the window, and I watch the corner by Rocky Mountain Chocolate Factory. The crowd is big. At lunch, Sid told me he was planning to spend the afternoon playing stuff from the very first *Superman* movie, which was made in 1978. He figures nobody will know what it is, so if he makes mistakes, it won't be horrible.

Even though my life sucks, it's good that his doesn't.

Gracie texts. *Please can we talk? Please? #reallyreallysorry*
   My head is too full to be a friend right now.
   I am so sorry. I want to help. #reallysorry
   I know. Both things. It's OK. #forgiven #toohardtoexplain

Love you, Tobin. Thank you. #againsosorry
We'll chat soon.

Nobody can get it unless you've been here. But thank god Gracie *doesn't* know how it feels.

She's trying. We all are. Nobody knows how to do this.

The afternoon is full of magazines. At least thirty touristy ladies come into Trash Box and look at old ladies' house and garden mags from the fifties and sixties. No idea why. I sell at least one magazine to each woman.

Is the past fascinating because it was a simpler time? Because it's already happened? Because it's not the present?

Allison tells me she'll lock up. Fine with me. The tourists in Canal Park are three deep, looking for a spot to eat or checking out the shops. In July, people get here early and leave late.

My walk home is sweaty for the first time, which feels wrong. We spend so much of our year shivering around here, we don't really know how to be warm.

Ike's making Hamburger Helper for supper, which is about all my dad wants to eat these days. I'm not sure nutrition matters now. He points his spatula at me. "Good day at Trash Box?"

"What's up with the apron?"

Ike gives me a look. "Just getting my chef on. Like the ruffles?" He keeps the spatula aimed at me. "I've got something to show you after supper."

Dad's sleeping in the living room, and I hear a snore and a snuffle. "Should I wake him up?"

Ike nods. "Everything else is ready."

Supper is nice. We laugh about the women at Trash Box today, buying magazines from a life that doesn't exist anymore.

"Okay, Tobin, help me up." Dad looks around for his walker, which is in the living room. "I'm going to go watch some more *ER* and dream about when I could drive my own rig. Back when I did something important in the world instead of sitting in my goddamn living room watching a shit-ass computer." He grins a little bit, but his eyes are tearing up. "It sucks to be useless."

I help him to his feet, being as gentle as I can be. "You're still good for a laugh or two."

"Speaking of that, Tobin and Ike, have you ever noticed it's hard to tell a joke to a kleptomaniac? They take things literally." The old Steve is still in there.

Ike pats his shoulder. "That's one's actually good. Where'd you get it?"

"Your dad. Right before he ran off with my wallet." He sticks his tongue out at Ike.

"You should see him take money out of my mom's purse."

I steer Dad to the couch. "Rich isn't going to like this character assassination." And they both laugh at me.

"Go get your computer, Tobin. You need to see this." Ike puts the last plate in the cupboard after the dishes are finished.

I retrieve it and sit down. Dad's chuckling in the living room, and I hear him say, "Man, if you use that syringe, you'll get blood all over yourself."

"Head over to GoFundMe and type in your dad's name." Ike sits down across the table from me.

I am shocked.

Someone named "Love Warrior" has set up a GoFundMe page for him, and it's raised $13,000 and change. In two weeks.

I look at Ike. "Does he know about this?"

He nods. "He does. The money's going to be put into a trust fund for you to have after you're eighteen."

"Or we could use it to pay for the party." So far, we've racked up a good $1,200 in bills for it.

"A hat at the door, and it's covered. People love to give money to folks worse off than they are, so take advantage now. People forget soon enough."

I stare at him. "That's rude. And it's not like I want their charity, you know."

He sighs. "I know. And *you* won't forget, of course. But they'll want to give you money so they'll feel better when life goes on."

"People aren't assholes."

Ike sits back in his chair. "How long did it take you to forget when someone you knew died?"

"I don't know anybody who died besides Mrs. Nealy, and she was just a neighbor when I was a little kid, so that doesn't count."

"It counted for her family, though. Just not for you."

"Shut up!" My voice is higher and sharper than I want.

"I don't mean to be a jerk." Ike softens at my tone. "All I'm saying is let them give to you. Take it while you can get it, so to speak." He pats my hand. "People also give because they have good hearts."

"You make it sound like they don't."

"You know I'm full of crap."

"Yeah, and you suck."

I take my computer upstairs and consider not coming down for a while.

But then I get hungry again, so I do, and my dad wants to sit out back and watch the moon come up over the lake, so we get him out on the porch to wait for it.

And the lake is quiet.

And Ike is quiet.

And my dad is quiet.

And when it gets there, the moon is quiet.

And for just a moment,

my brain is quiet, too.

Dad's Big Book of Advice #18
Don't squat with spurs on.

JULY 25

Back when I was six and Marcy Castile lived next to us, I was convinced her seventeen-year-old life was glamorous. She was so beautiful, with her long blond hair, her purple high-tops, and her guitar. She had friends, boys, a car, cute clothes, all the things I figured a teenager would have. My seventeen-year-old life has narrowed itself to sick dad, work, home, supper, laptop, and bed. Repeat. A talk with Sid here and there. An occasional text with Gracie, now that I'm not mad anymore. Not summer fun. Not the future, except for Dad's slowly dwindling lack of one.

Not what I imagined.

About 1:00, Ike and Dad try Mama Duck's Record Store one more time. Dad's bored, and Ike's running out of things to keep him amused. *Why not give it one more shot,* Ike says when he texted me. Maybe his brain will appreciate the activity, too.

Yeah. No.

Dad lasts twenty minutes. Then he gets overheated, even with the umbrella Paul rigged up for their table, and he yells at a lady when she asks about taking a Gordon Lightfoot album out of the crate. Then he tells a woman she's ugly, and he tells another woman her baby looks like a monkey. After that, Ike shuts it down.

Ike brings the stuff in the shop and leaves Dad on the sidewalk. He probably should have reversed that order, because Dad's giving dirty looks to the people going by and muttering under his breath. I take records out of Ike's arms to ferry them to the back room. Then Allison notices Dad is outside by himself, so she goes out to keep him company, but Dad yells in her face, so she skitters inside and goes to the bathroom in tears.

I see Ike sigh as he pushes Dad down the street. I see Allison sigh when she comes out of the bathroom. I, on the other hand, want to knock every single piece of glass to the floor and smash the shelves with a baseball bat.

So yeah. Sigh, Ike and Allison. Sigh your heads off. It's way less destructive.

It's 5:30, and I'm maybe ten steps away from Trash Box when I hear a really loud "Hey!" behind me. I turn, and it's Sid, with his violin on his shoulder, playing away.

"What is that music?" I walk toward him, already feeling sweaty. It's a tad steamy out here. "It's like your heart's on your strings."

"Fifth movement of Bach's *Partita No. 2* in D minor. Just listen."

So I do. We stand on the sidewalk, and Sid gives me a concert, tourists flowing around us. Occasionally someone stops to give me a dollar or two, but Sid doesn't see, because his eyes are closed. Five minutes later, he's done, and there's sweat dripping off his hair.

"That's some passionate stuff." I don't know what else to say. "Intense." I hand him the cash.

He's puzzled, but he puts it in his pocket. "It's for college auditions. Been practicing for a year already." His smile is tired, like he's used up his whole day's worth of energy on the song. "You're not the only one trying to get your shit together."

"I haven't heard you today."

He points with his bow. "I was down by the Dairy Queen." It's way farther than his normal corner. "I was just walking back to Rocky Mountain to pick up my violin case when I saw you walking home."

"Get your case. I'll wait." I sit down on a bench.

"Deal." He practically jogs back to the store. If he falls and hurts himself, or his violin, I will never forgive myself.

Then he's back, and we walk home. Easy. Quiet. Peaceful. When we get to my house, he gives me a hug and walks on.

When I turn toward my house, I see my dad in the window. He waves in his Muppet-like way, and from his face, it looks like his brain hurricane has passed.

By the time I open the door, he's on the couch, and he grins at me. "He's a good boyfriend, to walk you home."

"He's absolutely one hundred percent not my boyfriend."

"It's not for lack of trying on his part." There's a Dad grin.

"He knows my mind is on you right now."

He frowns. "And that really, really sucks."

"No, it doesn't." And 92.8 percent of me means it. The other 7.2 percent of me is just tired.

Ike yells from the kitchen. "Time to eat."

"Time for a dad joke." He's getting up and I'm getting him situated with his walker.

"Okay."

Dad points himself in mostly the right direction. "Why can't you trust stairs?"

"No idea." I'm behind him, just in case something happens.

"Because they're always up to something!"

"Good one, Steve." Ike's hands reach for Dad as he crosses the threshold.

Supper is tomato soup and grilled cheese sandwiches, cut into the tiniest squares ever for my dad. More and more we feed him, which Ike does with some pretty serious precision, and Ike's so casual and cool about it, it seems almost normal. Dad will only let him do it close to the end of the meal, when he's barely gotten anything into his mouth and he's still hungry.

I can't make myself watch.

After supper, I clean up while Ike takes Dad up to bed. The pop-up shop fiasco tired him out.

There's a notebook on the table. It's poems again, but it's imitations. One page is a poem from a famous person, xeroxed and taped in the notebook, and the next page is a poem my dad wrote, in the same style. All the poems are about my mom. Before she was my mom.

There's one poem about a dude's cat, Jeoffrey—from the eighteenth century. Sort of like an ancient version of a cat video. Long lists of what the cat does, "firstly" and "secondly" and whatever. Mr. Smart's poem is pretty okay, but my dad's lines surprise me.

> *For fifthly, she never stops,*
> *eyes roving the world,*
> *in search of the perfection it supplies.*
> *For sixthly and on, to admire Meredith*
> *is to worship those eyes, the angel-spun hair,*
> *the June flower smell at the hollow of her throat.*
> *For she thinks in pictures*
> *she places on empty pages.*
> *For she is more beautiful*
> *than the sun rising over the lake,*
> *scattering jewels everywhere*
> *for her to find.*
> *For she walks with purpose.*
> *For she sweeps me along.*

I don't want to know that he loved her. I don't want to think his heart was broken, too.

And I don't want to know what happened, because I don't want to think I could have had a different life, one where she stayed.

He and I did just fine by ourselves.

Someone else—even her—would have messed it up.

<u>August 1</u>

Even though I can't see her, I stare into the blackness, where I know my lake is. I love her, even though she doesn't acknowledge me. Her soft voice sighs.

She is more present than the woman who gave birth to me. She is frigid. Bottomless. Gargantuan.

Glaciers carved the earth to make her—melting, filling, leaving behind scarred land—and to expand across horizons and lands I've not seen. Coves and secret places, landmarks everyone knows. This water is so much to so many.

Each time they arrive, I sacrifice a small piece of faraway Meredith's offerings, tucked under tiny rocks and icy waves just past the water line. I bury them in the pebbles my lake deposits on Mother Earth, this water more constant and elemental than any human. My lake keeps secrets as completely as any confidante. In return, she brings me sea glass, polished smooth and translucent.

Neither she nor my mother are kind. But her presence is unchanging, whispering out my back door.

I trust her to calm me. I trust she will hold what I give her. I trust she will not leave me.

Dad's Big Book of Advice #19
Water in all forms is your body's best friend, so always drink enough, don't forget to wash behind your ears, and cry when you need to.

AUGUST 7

There's an email from Chip.

Hi, Tobin:

Mama Duck will be in Lake Superior in front of the Beach House on Park Point at 8:30 p.m. on August 15. Will you feed our crew? There may be six or seven of us. That's all we ask.

I write back instantly: *OF COURSE. Thank you so much!!!*

What I want to say is *WHAT TOOK YOU SO GODDAMN LONG?*, but that would be incredibly rude.

Now we're gonna have a party.

Dad's in the living room, grasping a big marker with a pile of printer paper in front of him.

"What's he doing?" I pour a glass of water while Ike grabs Dad a Coke. It's already looking like a rough day, even at 9 a.m.

"Writing your book." He frowns. "It's not going well at the moment."

"I had no idea he was still working on it."

Ike holds up a piece of paper with Dad's latest piece of advice. "Forty-five. Never name your band Blasphemous Sex Toy Inferno."

The letters are big and look like they were written by a four-year-old who happens to know how to spell *blasphemous*. "That one I can do."

I walk toward the living room, but Ike stops me with his hand. "He doesn't want you around right now."

"Dad?" I knock on the doorframe.

"Listen to what Ike said." He's on the couch, hunched over the coffee table, paper and markers spread out in front of him.

"Can I help?"

"Go away, Tobin." I can hear the sob in his voice.

"Getting some ice for your Coke, Steve." Ike keeps his voice light and cheerful, but then he turns to me with a sad smile. "Maybe he'll have his next one figured out when you get home."

"I trust." And I walk out the back door, away from my father, crying over the fact that his hands aren't working well enough to write another sentence of The Saddest Book in the World.

I check on my heart. It's about the size of a stony, black marshmallow.

I walk to work along the shore, in the water, and my feet freeze into foot-shaped ice cubes. When I get on the sidewalk to go over the bridge—sorry, people whose yard I walked through to get there—I put my shoes back on, and it feels like my feet are cinder blocks.

Nine hours later, supper is a quiet affair. When Ike gets up to get another glass of milk, my dad finally turns and looks at me instead of staring into his soup. I will never get used to eating soup in the summer, but he can swallow it.

"Tobin, what does a thesaurus eat for breakfast?"

I can hear the breath in his words. I can hear how hard it is to talk.

"No idea, Dad."

"A synonym roll."

Ike and I laugh. Dad smiles, a tired and frustrated smile, but a Steve smile.

I smile back, trying to be encouraging. "That's really good. Where'd you get it?"

"Where does anybody get jokes? Online, of course."

"I'll help you write down some more tomorrow." Ike pats his shoulder as he stands to put the supper dishes in the sink.

"Sure."

There's a solid wheeze in that word that wasn't here a week ago. Maybe it wasn't even here this morning. Maybe it's just because he's tired.

"Tobin, will you get me back to the couch? I've only got one more season of *ER* to go." He stands, and I get his walker, and we get him settled with his laptop.

I give him a kiss on the top of his head. He reaches up and holds my hand. We stay like that for a minute, me hugging his shoulders with my head on top of his. Him just hanging on.

I am so wobbly from sadness I can barely walk into the kitchen, but I get myself straightened out before either Dad or Ike notice what's happened. Ike's got his back to me, doing dishes, and Dad's absorbed in another episode.

"Did he get any more writing done today?" My voice is low.

"Three more besides the one about blasphemous sex toys." Ike's splashing in the suds, covering the sound of our conversation. "It's hard to think when you're not able to expel all the carbon monoxide in your body." *Splash splash.* "He's going to need a ventilator soon. By the end of the month at the latest. So glad the party's coming up." *Splash splash.*

"Mama Duck is a go, by the way. Just found out this morning: 8:30 on the night of the party."

"Holy shit, you did it!" He hugs me with his sudsy arms, and I hug him back.

"What did you do, Tobin?" Dad has no way to project his voice, so we almost miss it.

"I got you the perfect cake for the party." Which is true, though Allison did it, not me.

"Thank you." Faintly from the living room.

"Of course."

Ike punches me on the arm and goes back to washing dishes. "Your dad will flip."

"Everybody will flip."

"You rock, Tobin."

"I get shit done." And I go upstairs to get more shit done, namely sort some photos. September 15 is soon. I make one more by posing Professor X and Rey just like my dad and I were in the living room. Her head on his, him holding her hand. You can see their faces, which are both surprised and sad. Like they're not quite sure how they got here.

In an hour, Ike has Dad in his room, because Dad's so tired. I hear his wheeze in the hall.

"Maybe your breathing will be better tomorrow." I kiss his cheek while it registers just how dumb a thing that was to say.

His hand grabs my arm, with what little strength he has left. "You know that won't happen."

"You have a party to go to first, so I command your diaphragm to last that long." I try and give him a good grin.

I see the panic in his eyes. "I hope it listens to you."

"I hope so, too. Good night, Dad."

"Tobin?" His hand grips me with all the strength he has left. "Yes?"

"When it comes time. If I can't, for some reason. Will you?"

I see the heat of his need. His eyes are so fierce, and so scared.

"Ike won't." He tries to take a deep breath, but it doesn't work. "Will you free me?"

If eyes could light fires, I'd be in flames. His cheeks are bright red.

I stare at him staring me down, as his question echoes in my ears.

Free is the word that gets me.

"Yes." I kiss him again on the hot flesh of his face.

His shoulders slump forward, and his forehead unfurrows, all at the same time.

"Thank you." The relief in his voice makes it stronger. "Just . . . thank you. I love you, Tobin."

"I love you, too." I kiss him one more time. "Get some sleep."

"More writing to do tomorrow." In less than sixty seconds, he's snoring.

I stare at him in the faded light coming in the window. He's so small now. Like a beat-up, sick teenager, not anybody's dad.

My dad was strong, with broad shoulders and a big smile. Lots of muscles. Blond and handsome and smart, with a resting heart rate of thirty-five, and the lung capacity of ten men. He could run fifty miles in a day and not even think about it. He saved people's lives and taught people things. He loved his family and his rig partner and this town and the lake and his ancestors and movement and joy and being alive. He was fierce.

The person in that bed is not the same.

He's not fierce.

He deserves to be free.

There was no other answer.

August 11

You don't really notice until you look,
but the sunlight is too slanted
and too far south.
We're losing daylight and warmth,
and it's always too soon.
Always.
Underneath the August heat,
chilly Canadian wind delivers the cold with a laugh,
here to stay for another ten months.

The top layer of air says
hey! it's summer! let's play!
let's walk to the lighthouse, add some graffiti,
get ice cream, give a tip
to that nice young man who plays the violin by the
candy store,
but the icy teeth of what's to come
growl over the lake, chomp at your neck
when you turn your back for just a second
to notice the sun has slipped even farther south

than the north that you already are.
The north that is too far away from the rest of
the world.
The north of the winter that will close you in.

You shout at the sun: *IT'S TOO SOON! YOU'RE PRECIOUS!
COME BACK.*

You know it won't.
It never does.
It's never overhead, on our faces,
in our lives for enough time.
Winter is just
      so
      long.

Dad's Big Book of Advice #20
Something wonderful is always about to happen—
no matter how shitty life seems.

AUGUST 15

The party is supposed to last from five until ten, but I get to the Beach House at one to decorate. My mind will not shut up about details. Do I have enough food? Plates and napkins? Will people come? Will the cake get smashed during delivery? It's like someone parked a tornado on my head.

Will Dad lose it?

It echoes in my ears. It's drawn around every single thing I put in my car to take. HEMIGHTLOSEIT framing the plastic silverware, on all sides. HEMIGHTLOSEIT written on the front of each roll of streamers—when I roll them out, the words will be feet long, over and over again. I say a quick prayer to Mother Mary and Baby Jesus. Ike is rubbing off on me.

When Sid arrives, I'm surprised to see his mom and dad. "What are you doing here?"

"Helping is the least we can do." His mom, Maggie, grabs the bag of plastic plates out of my hand and hands them to Sid, who's already grabbed two sleeves of cups and the bright-red streamers, Dad's favorite color. If it's his last birthday on Earth, he's going out in a blaze of fire. "What else is in your car? They can take this up."

We send Sid and his dad, Larry, up to the Beach House with everything from my arms, and we grab the coolers of fruit and veggies Ike and I have been chopping all morning. Lucky Duck Catering—no relation to Mama Duck, I don't think—will bring the chips, meat, beans, buns, and lemonade. Ike's getting a keg and some other alcohol.

"How many people are coming, do you know?" Maggie's huffing her way up the hill.

"I don't know. We ordered food for a hundred."

"Veggies are heavy." She puts the cooler down, not very gently, once we get to the top, and shoves it the rest of the way into the Beach House. I carry my cooler toward the fridge and ice machine near the built-in bar. We fill the fridge with fruit and veggie goodness.

Sid and Larry have made it back and forth to the car two more times. The two-liters of pop, which I was hoping I could put in the fridge, go in the coolers, and luckily there's some ice in the ice machine to put on top of them.

I feel like I've forgotten something. I slow the tornado in my brain to run through my lists, but it won't come to me until Sid and Larry decide to work on streamers. Turns out that something is tape.

Sid leaves to get some, and Maggie and I lay out table-ware while he's gone. We also find a table for gifts, and from somewhere Maggie produces a basket with a ribbon on it. She places it at the end of the gift table, and she puts a little sign in front of it. The sign says DONATIONS.

I'm trying to hide the redness in my cheeks. "There's the GoFundMe that someone started, and . . . I don't feel right asking for money." I don't look at her.

She takes me, very gently, by the shoulders and smiles into my face. "People *want* to help, because they want to make things better—any way at all. And you'll need it . . . someday." She looks like she doesn't want to say exactly when. "So let them give you something." She gives my shoulders a squeeze. "People don't like feeling helpless."

I think Dad wins the helpless prize, but I stay quiet.

When she realizes what she's said, it's her turn to blush.

I put up pictures of Dad on the walls with pins—which I did remember—while Maggie talks to the off-duty lifeguard. Sid comes back into the Beach House with tape right as his mom's getting out some folding chairs to put around the tables. "Where's the ladder, Tobin? We're in the streamer business!"

"I'll find one." Maggie scurries off.

She pulls one from a broom closet, and we get to work. The ladder is high enough to reach the top of the vaulted ceiling, if you stand on the top rung and hoist the streamers up on top of a broomstick. Sid manages it while I hang on to the ladder and keep feeding him streamer starts. Maggie stands at the edge of the room and twists, then tapes them to the top of the wall. We make an awkward but cheerful umbrella of red.

Larry walks in from the beach, where he's been setting up a few more tables and chairs. "It's gonna be dark. Nobody will notice they're weird."

"Thanks, Dad." Sid hops off the ladder and throws the roll of tape at him.

Larry catches it and throws it at me. "It looks great, guys. Seriously."

I check my phone. It's already 3:39. "I've gotta jet, so Ike can go and get the booze. Thank you three for helping me."

A pit opens in my stomach. It's huge, Lake-Superior–sized, and threatens to gush out all the weird feelings I've had about this party.

Maggie saves me with a quick hug. "We'll see you after five." Sid hugs me, too, quick and gentle like he's hugging someone else's grandma, and Larry pats me on the head, like I'm six.

One lifeguard comes inside as another one goes out back to the beach. "Looks good." He grins, a California-blond surfer dude somehow transported to a Great Lake.

When I burst into the house, Ike and Dad look at me like I'm from another planet.

"What's the rush?" Ike is brushing my dad's hair, getting it into its traditional Steve swoop. My dad still has some pretty amazing hair, though there are silver threads among the gold now, which is new since March.

"You told me to be home by 3:30, and it's 3:50 now. I didn't want you to be pissed." I'm sweaty from setting up and already exhausted.

"All is well." Ike smiles. "Doesn't your dad look great?" He points at Dad with the brush. "New duds and everything."

He's got on a new red polo shirt and a nice pair of khaki shorts, with a pair of flip-flops that look like they're from 1978, but hey, he's not going to be walking on them. He looks like a wasted-away runner, which is what he is. But he's smiling.

"I'm gonna be fifty tomorrow, and tonight's gonna be a great party. That's all I . . . care about." His eyes are full of tears, but they don't fall. His voice is wheezy and weak, so I have to come close to hear him. I have no idea how he's going to muster enough energy to talk to a hundred people.

Ike puts down the brush and walks around my dad in his chair. "All right, dude, you're as handsome as I can get you for now. Gotta go get some booze so we can have a real fiesta." He holds out his fist, and my dad bumps it, big grin still intact. Ike heads out the front door.

"You okay to stay down here by yourself, Dad? I need to take a shower."

He gives me a thumbs-up. "Can I have my laptop? I want to put a few more things down . . . in your book, before I forget."

I hand him his laptop, and I race upstairs to take a shower and get ready.

He can't type anymore. I know he can't.

When I come back down fifteen minutes later, my dad is sobbing, and his hair's a mess, like he's been punching himself in the head. My guess is he was trying to run his hands through it, which he used to do when he was thinking. Emotion storms get really bad if he's alone.

I move the laptop, grab the brush, and start on his hair again. Sometimes repetition will soothe him. "What's up, Dad?"

He can't talk, he's crying so hard. I stop brushing and put the Kleenex box in his lap. He takes a couple, which takes a minute, with his hands.

Brush, brush. "Can you tell me what's wrong?"

Honk. Blow. "This is my last birthday."

"What do you think Stephen Hawking would do about that?"

Honk. "No idea."

"He'd make it the best damn birthday party anyone ever had on Park Point." I keep brushing, even though my hands are shaking almost as badly as his are.

Honk. Blow. "Good point."

"I'm smart like that sometimes." Brush, brush.

His breath is hitching, like he's three and is just finishing a tantrum, which I suppose he kind of is. His poor brain.

"Shall we go outside and wait for Ike?"

A hitching sigh. "Yeah. Let's look at the lake."

I take him out the back door and park him on the porch. The day is really bright and clear, but the sunlight's already got more than a whisper of autumn in it. Lake sparkles glitter along the shore. She's clear, calm, and thoughtful.

He brings the Kleenex box, and goes through a couple more as he pokes at his face and blows his nose. He studies the lake hard, like it might disappear if he takes his eyes off it.

Ike finds us out there about ten minutes later. It's 4:30.

"Time to party!" If Ike sees it, he doesn't mention the pile of Kleenex in Dad's lap, which I scoop up and pitch in the garbage. "Let's get you into the car, Steve. Tobin, you probably want to grab some containers to put the leftover food in."

"Good point. You're the best housewife ever, Ike."

He grins. "Someday I'll get to stay home with the kids and my sugar mama'll bring home the cash."

Ike pushes Dad down the ramp and settles him into the front seat while I bring out a bag of containers. My camera case was waiting by the door, so it's over my shoulder now. I tucked my action figures into the side pockets, just in case.

Dad's breathy, quiet voice drifts over the seat to me. "Hey, Tobin."

"What?"

"A woman was standing in front of a judge for beating her husband with his guitar collection."

"Okay . . .?" I hope this is a joke.

"The judge said, 'First offender?' And she said . . . 'No, first a Gibson. Then a Fender.'"

Ike laughs so hard he swerves, and a car honks at him. There's not much room to move out of the way on our narrow street.

"Nice one, Dad."

He chuckles a wheezy chuckle. "I've still got it."

When we get there, the parking lot is nine-tenths full, and it's not even five. People are walking up the hill in twos and threes, chatting to themselves. There's a big truck with a cartoonish-looking mallard duck on its side, and the words LUCKY DUCK CATERING are painted over his head. He's got a four-leaf clover in his bill.

Because he's a strongman, Ike doesn't need my help pushing Dad up the hill, so I go ahead of them to make sure things are in place.

It's packed. The place has a pleasant, low hum from all the chatter. Gifts rest on the table, even though the invites clearly said no gifts, and a huge stack of envelopes and cash lean in the DONATIONS basket.

Ike wheels Dad into the door, and a cheer goes up. People are careful not to swarm him, but they're definitely waiting to talk to him, shake his hand, wish him well.

Sid's been pouring pop along with beer from the keg that Ike delivered, even though he's technically too young to serve. Dad has plenty of cop friends, so I hope they're not here. If they are, I hope they're looking the other way. Sid's having fun. People are complimenting him on his lack of foam.

He's already got Ike's booze delivery arranged, too, which he shows off to us. "The wine's on ice there, the glasses are here, the ice is there, the extra bottles are over here, and it's all ready for you, Ike." He smiles. "I'm tempted to put myself through college as a bartender."

"There are worse ways to roll." Ike walks behind the table and Sid steps out. "Thanks for minding the store while I was fetching the guest of honor."

Sid turns to me. "Anything else in the car?"

I put the camera case behind the bar. "I forgot the food containers, for leftovers."

"I'm on it, provided you share the leftovers with me." And he's out the door.

I look around the room, and there are tons of people I know, and tons I don't. Gracie is watching me, standing with her brothers and her parents, across the room. I wave at her. Her face breaks open, and she waves back. I blow her a kiss. She does the same. I start to move toward her, but there's a hand on my elbow, so I have to talk to someone else. I blow her one last kiss before I turn away. She nods. It's enough for now.

Lucky Duck's owner, Anne, is the person gripping my elbow. She's a friend of Allison's. "Everything look good?"

"Yes, for sure! Thank you!" She gave me a really good deal on the food, so even if it sucks, I have to say yes, but it won't.

"Your dad's partner, Rich, provided the absolute best cuts of meat to serve tonight. It was so nice of him. The pulled pork is awesome, as is the roast beef." Anne glances over to where Dad is, a circle around him of well-meaning friends, shaking his hand and talking to him. "Your dad holding his own?"

"He'll probably sleep for a week after this party, but that's not all bad." I had no idea Rich helped with the catering.

Her face is very serious. "Allison told me he's failing fast."

I keep the smile on mine, even though my insides are curling up. "Thanks again for catering." And I walk away.

Anne's workers have set up their food along the south wall, opposite the bar, and they're ready to go. There are five of them, with duck aprons on, and the tables look ready to feed thousands. A huge cake in the shape of an ambulance sits at the end of the food. I have no idea how they're going to cut it.

Everything seems to be handled, from eats to decorations to drinks. The tornado is still sitting on top of my head, but I shove it away. What's not done doesn't matter.

A hand lands on my shoulder, and I whirl around. It's Paul.

"How's it going, Voyageur? Hanging in there?" He sweeps his hand around the room. "Looks great. You should be proud."

"I . . ." And then I can't talk. I can't breathe. I can't see.

Paul notices the panic come over my face, and he propels me out the back door, to the beach. I let him.

When we get outside, Paul guides me down the path toward the lake's edge. Once we're off the dunes, he lets go of my elbow and turns me to face him, with gentle hands.

221

"Doing okay, honey?"

I lose it.

My whole body sags into Paul's arms, and I shake. And shake. Silent, convulsive sobs rip out of my center and fly into the air. But then there's noises, like an animal being attacked. And then there's silence again. My body never stops heaving.

There's a splash behind me. I know it's the world's ugliest, smallest, blackest heart leaping out of the water, from the deepest bottom of the lake. It slams into my back and claws its way into my body, which makes me stumble to my knees.

Paul kneels, too, and he holds me while the storm attacks. He doesn't say a word.

It's about 6:30, and there are at least a hundred and fifty people here. They ran out of food about ten minutes ago, with the exception of cake, which they just cut. But nobody's crabby. Dad's parked himself by the end of the table with the cake on it, and he's greeting people while Ike is trying to feed him in between conversations. They're getting crumbs all over everything. Ike's doing it fast, swooping in during quiet seconds, so people don't gawk any more than they have to, but Dad doesn't seem embarrassed. For once. He's radiating happiness.

My eyes are still red and puffy, and I cried off all my makeup. But nobody's asked me what's wrong. If they have to ask, they probably shouldn't be here.

My whole body hurts, like I've been tossed up and thrown back to Earth by the tornado inside me. But I also feel less freaky. Stronger.

That's new.

I put my hand on my chest, and my heart is beating there, after the storm.

When I grab my camera from behind the bar, I start with casual shots, but everyone wants to pose, like they would at a wedding instead of a man's last birthday party. Then Ike helps me set up the action figures so they're having a drink at the bar.

Then I hear a trumpet.

Maybe it's an angel, coming to take Dad.

Then a flurry of color and noise comes in the door, followed by Rich and Dad's ambulance buddies.

It's a fucking mariachi band.

Dad grins from ear to ear, Rich hugs him, and this fiesta amps up to a thousand.

The mariachis start playing songs that are impossible not to dance to, and women take Dad out on the dance floor in pairs, twisting and rolling his chair, one dancing in front of him, and one behind him, steering the chair. At least eight different pairs of women try it out, and then Ike and Rich do the same thing, and my dad can barely breathe, he's laughing so hard. People are dancing around Ike and Rich and Dad, everyone cackling and giggling, and it's the happiest thing I've seen in my life. I take so many photos.

The mariachis stop for some cake and beer, which sounds gross to me, but it's all we have. The catering women are gone, and the food containers I brought never got used.

Rich comes over to me, sweaty and smiling, arms out wide. I fold myself into his big hug.

"What do you think, *pequeña*? *Una buena sorpresa, sí*?" He's fading in and out of Spanish, which is fine. I know enough to understand him.

"*Muy bien*, Rich. *Muchas gracias* a million times. And why meat? I didn't know you were helping with the catering."

"A Mexican fiesta always has supreme cuts of meat. It was my honor."

"You're the ultimate, Rich. The absolute best." I hug him again. "*Muchas gracias*. I can never repay you."

"*Te quiero, mija.* You're my little girl, too."

I give him one last squeeze, so he can't see the tears in my eyes, then I give him a shove toward my dad. "Go hang out with your rig partner."

"*Sí.*" He goes, but not before I see the tears in *his* eyes, which makes me want to weep again, but I pick up my camera instead.

Sid comes over while I'm taking long shots of the crowd. "Mama Duck's gonna have to be on point to beat this mariachi band."

I check my phone. "Holy shit. She'll be here any time." I didn't realize it was almost eight fifteen. And then it hits me: we have no food to feed the Mama Duck crew.

I turn to Sid. "You have to run to Grandma's Restaurant and get some food for the duck people. I promised Chip, the owner, that I'd feed them. I'll pay you back."

Sid points to the door. "No need."

The Lucky Duck women are coming back through, with full food containers. Anne waves at me when she sees me staring. "We had more back at the kitchen. Might as well eat it, huh? You've got a big party going on." She smiles the kindest smile ever.

You'd think I'd get used to those.

Allison follows in the Lucky Duck crew, carrying a covered platter of something. Her face is red and blotchy, just like mine was a couple hours ago. But she puts a smile on her face as she puts the platter down, and she feeds the mariachis.

"Food problem solved." Sid punches me but with no force. "Good party, Tobin."

"Can you help me get folks out onto the back patio?"

"Sure thing. I've got lungs." And Sid opens his mouth and lets out an enormous yell. *"Hey, everybody, we've got another surprise for you, so when you get a beverage and a snack, why not head on out to the back patio so we can show you? It should be here any minute. Thank you for coming to Steve's birthday party!"* All in one breath, it seems.

It has the right effect on people, because they start meandering toward the back doors, gabbing and munching.

Dad and Rich are talking, and they both look very serious.

"Come out really soon, okay?" They nod at me.

People are scattered all along the dunes and the beach, pointing to their right, to the east, so I look, and there she is, just coming around the bend of the point, about a mile and a half away. It's not like you can mistake Mama Duck for anyone else. People start clapping and laughing, like they've just seen Santa Claus.

Ike finds me on the patio and gives me a big hug. I've been hugged more tonight than I've been in the last month. "She's so great."

I grin at him. "How rad is it to see a giant rubber duck coming toward your party?"

The sun has gone behind the hill Duluth is spread over, to the west of us. Layers of pink, blue, and white deepen and glow along the circle of the horizon, especially out on the lake, as the sky begins to dim. The world is rosy and peaceful, pearly and soft. And Dad's birthday gift, six stories of Zen with a Mona Lisa smile, is in place.

When Mama Duck's tugboat ties off at the dock in front of the Beach House, a huge cheer goes up. Everyone crowds onto the beach and the dock to examine her up close.

She's pretty impressive, glowing a mellow yellow against the pink and blue sky, the perfect benediction to this party. She smiles down on us as people laugh and talk about her skirting and her pontoon. A guy on the dock is talking loudly and gesturing, and people are nodding along. I'm guessing that must be Chip, her owner.

A woman, followed by five guys, walks up the beach and sticks out her hand to me. "I hope you're Tobin. We're Mama Duck's minions. Chip said you'd have food?"

"Right inside. Help yourselves."

Mama Duck's minions stop just inside the door. Then I hear the woman say, "You might want to see who's come to visit you."

My dad wheels through the door as soon as Mama Duck's crew is out of it, pushed by Rich. Then his mouth falls open. It's even better than the mariachi band.

Then he starts to sob.

Rich picks him up and cradles him like he would a toddler, then carries my dad toward the beach and Mama Duck. I follow behind with my dad's chair—neither of them see me standing there. They're about fifty feet ahead of me, and my dad is wailing like a fire siren. As they get closer to Mama Duck, though, he quiets down. He just stares. I get his chair on the dock, next to where Rich is standing with him. Rich looks surprised to see it appear, but he deposits Dad into it with slow, careful hands.

The talkative man comes over and extends his hand to Dad. "Happy Birthday, Steve. I hear you're going to be the big five-oh."

Dad shakes his hand in amazement. "Tomorrow. Is she here for my ... birthday, or were you just ... cruising ... along the shore?" His breath is so short.

Chip smiles. "She's here for you."

"How did you know?"

He glances over Dad's head to me and raises his eyebrows. I nod. He smiles again at Dad. "I'm sure you'll find out at some point."

Dad looks Mama Duck up and down, passing right by what Chip said. Rich elbows Dad. "Does she remind you of the Stay Puft Marshmallow Man in *Ghostbusters*? The first movie from the eighties? Every time I see her lit up like that, I think she's going to start smashing the city."

Chip throws back his head and laughs the heartiest laugh ever. "I promise you she's not into destroying things. She just likes to cruise around and be happy."

"You have the greatest job ever, don't you?" Rich looks at the duck and then at Chip.

Chip nods. "All the sadness and crap in the world, and I get to bring the joy. Luckiest guy ever." He walks toward me. "You must be Tobin?" He sticks out his hand again, and I shake it.

"Please have some food and some cake. You crew's in there already." I gesture back toward the Beach House. "Thank you so, so, so much for coming."

"Thanks for your hospitality. And congratulations on your tenacity. It will serve you well." He raises his eyebrows at me, grins, and walks past me.

Yeah, well. Don't patronize me, dude. I did what I had to do.

I turn around to check on Dad, who's gazing at Mama Duck like she's going to disappear if he takes his eyes off her. The crowd drifts around, talking to the crew, who's come back down with their plates of food. Mama Duck just glows her happiness over everyone. Dad stays on the dock with Rich. I get my camera and my action figures, then position them on a piece of driftwood so you can see their silhouettes against Mama Duck. She looks like she's been engraved with four shapes that might vaguely be people. She doesn't mind, though, because she's the biggest duck in the neighborhood. She can take it.

After a few more shots, I walk back to the dock and around my dad's chair to see his face. "What do you think, Dad? Happy birthday!"

He cranes his neck around me, so he can keep looking at Mama Duck. "She's amazing. Did you know she has a . . . pontoon underneath her?"

"I did know that."

Chip comes back, and he and Rich and Dad start talking mechanical stuff, what it takes to make her, or power her, or steer her, or light her up. I get a few pictures of the three of them, deep in the technical details and backlit by Mama Duck. They talk until it's completely dark. Peaceful, kind Mama Duck is the only light on the beach, watching over the partygoers with a calm smile.

Some things are still the same. This goodness that floats around my dad and me: it's always here, even when I don't remember it. Even when I'm an awful bitch. This feeling that surrounds us is the same as it was when he was healthy and strong.

We are safe, and cared for, and loved.

We get home around 12:30. Dad's still wired, talking about all the people he saw, how awesome it was to have Mama Duck there, how cool the mariachi band was, how delicious the cake was, when he could get it into his mouth, and every other little thing. Even though he can barely breathe, he never shuts up.

Ike and I are completely exhausted.

While Ike's getting Dad ready for bed, I click through my photos. It's a mixed bag of art, dumbness, and hilarity, as usual. One of them is my dad, with everything else blurred out, and he's laughing and looking like a man I used to know six months ago. It captures the fact that he's still in there, even if his body is barely present.

I didn't take that shot.

The next one is a pattern—bright daisies. Only one person wore that fabric.

I text Gracie: *The photo you took of Dad is brilliant. Thank you. #sosorry #loveyou #letsgetteasoon*

You're on.

This feels so much better.

Ike comes downstairs and flops on the couch, opposite from where I'm sitting.

"He in bed?"

"Yes. Still babbling about the party."

"Fantastic." I lean back and close my eyes. "It was a good night."

"The bucket of donations had eight thousand dollars in it."

I sit straight up. "How do you know that?"

"Paul told me. He's going to put it in your trust account."

I close my eyes and sink back again. "We're going to need that money for other stuff. We don't know how long he's going to live."

"Yes, we do."

My eyes fly open. "We do?" The words cut my mouth like they're broken glass.

Ike nods, slow and solemn. "He's hit his pinnacle, he says. The party was the ultimate. He's had a good life, so it's time for a good death."

"Did . . ." My chest is so tight it's going to implode.

Ike nods again. "August 22."

"That's a *week*." The blood in my body turns to ice.

"Yep." The tears are rolling down Ike's face. "Six days."

I stand up, without a word, and go to bed.

Where I don't sleep. I stare at my ceiling.

I hear Ike go to his room and shut the door. The gentle hum of his voice slides out from under his door. He's praying.

I hear my dad snoring. I lock that sound in my brain.

The only breaths I can take are shallow and tiny. My chest hurts too much.

What was I thinking?

My heart barged back into me, telling me how to feel, and I can't do it.

Not now. Not ever.

<u>August 16, 2:49 a.m.</u>

In the dream, I rip my heart out of my body one more time, then stumble out the back door with the dripping mass.

I paddle my dream kayak back to the middle of the lake and fling the betraying organ hard as I can toward the bottom. All the color it gained in the six hours we were reunited bleeds away in tendrils before it thumps into the silt. I watch the ice form. I watch the fish nudge it again, and nibble what had grown back.

When it's a lump of useless gristle, black and destroyed, I paddle back. The sun's just coming up, and the horizon around me is pink and blue again, shimmering and glowing. A new day. My dad's birthday.

And I am safely dead inside, one last time.

Dad's Big Book of Advice #21
You get everything you want in life if you lower your expectations.

AUGUST 18

I go to Trash Box at 10 a.m., and I last for three hours. Then I take Allison into the back room and tell her I'm sick, which is the closest word that makes sense.

She studies me, but then her face breaks, and she hugs me, sobbing.

I hug her back, which is the polite thing to do.

She finally raises her face from my shoulder, sniffling. "I'm so sorry, Tobin."

"Okay."

"Paul told me." She pats in her pockets for a Kleenex. "About what's going to happen on the twenty-second."

"Was he supposed to do that?" Paul is the one person who's never done anything to hurt me, and now I'm pissed.

Her face is shocked. "Your father is my *brother*. Of course he's going to tell me when Steve's going to die!"

I just glare.

"First of all, I am completely against you being there with him. You can't make a rational decision to help him. You're too young."

She is so full of shit.

"And I don't believe in it." She sniffs, like she's disapproving and also trying to get rid of some snot from her crying fit. "I'm not going to be a part of it when it happens."

How can she make this about her?

"Tobin?" She's waiting for me to say something, given the expectation I see on her face.

I take a moment to decide. Honesty or tact?

I opt for walking away without a word.

When I get home, there's a man in the living room I don't know. He and Dad are working on something. They both look up at me when I come in, but neither says hello. Dad doesn't seem to be doing much talking, just signing. His signature looks like a chicken wrote it.

I go into the kitchen, and Ike's doing up the lunch dishes. The box with mountains on it is back in the middle of the table.

"Where did that come from?"

Ike turns around to see where I'm looking. "Paul brought it over."

I walk straight out the back door.

Paul brought it for Kleenex Day.

I can't call it what it is.

A speedboat goes by, on its way to Duluth. Another goes by, on its way to Wisconsin. A seagull swoops around and lands on the beach. It caws and makes noise and drops a feather from its wing. Then it looks right at me and takes off.

Whatever, bird. I'm losing my mind here.

I almost can't find my heart in the silt on the bottom of the lake. And it's blacker, if that's possible. It's the size of a button.

"Can I sit with you?" It's Ike.

"It's a free back porch."

He sits on the other chair and hands me a glass of water. "Drink this. It will help."

"How?" But I drink it. Suddenly I'm incredibly thirsty and need to drink seventeen more.

"How many meals have you eaten since the party?"

I count in my head, and the number isn't good, so I add a couple. There have been eight meals since the party. "Four."

"That's why you need a glass of water. And a burger, maybe."

"Gross."

"I'm going to do some cooking in these next couple days and freeze it all. For fall, when you won't have time. Senior year will be busy."

"Senior year?" Then I clap my hand over my mouth.

I forgot.

Ike looks out at the lake. "When I came home from Afghanistan, I threw my heart out there. Metaphorically, of course." He chuckles. "It's the most reliable freezer I know."

He is not saying this. "Bullshit."

He nods. "Why not? Cold and quiet down there. Exactly where my heart wanted to be." He looks at me. "Why is your mouth hanging open?"

"How is it that two people who didn't know each other could come up with the same idea?"

He raises his eyebrows.

"I threw mine in the night Dad told me his diagnosis. Then it came back into my body at the party. When you told me what he said, about how soon Kleenex Day is, I threw it back."

He chuckles again. "Kleenex Day. Good name."

"How could it be that we both had the same weird idea?"

"Call it kismet. A mind meld. What you do when you live by an enormous, cold body of water. Whatever it is, you can't do it anymore."

"Fuck that." I look him dead in the eye.

"So you'll end up in the hospital." He gives me the same dead-eye stare. "Talking to a million professionals, doing a million things you could have avoided if you'd just decided to feel in the first place." Ike is stern.

"How do you know?"

"About six months after I came back, I wanted to kill myself."

"I thought you didn't believe . . ."

"Shut up, Tobin. I'm talking here." His mouth twists into a wry smile. "The feelings were there. Survivor guilt is powerful. I was in the hospital for a week, then I saw a therapist for about two years, and then I got my shit together and went back to school, but it wasn't the right program, and now I'm here, doing this for you and your dad. In the spring, I'll go back to school to be a paramedic like my dad. So don't doubt me. I know what the fuck I'm talking about."

He doesn't drop the f-bomb around me.

"Why do you think that would happen to me?"

"It might not. But I *do* know burying your emotions inside is a recipe for disaster, and it always causes self-destruction if we don't let it out the right way."

"Which is?"

"Through your eyes and your mouth. In big sobs and wails, the same way your dad does. With people who care."

"Speaking of him, is that lawyer dude still here?"

"No. Your dad's asleep on the couch. And you're not getting out of this conversation. Grieving people have to express that sadness. Or you'll get cancer, or crash your car, or drink yourself to death. Something."

I don't say anything.

"My grandpa died of cirrhosis. Rich's dad. Dude was a straight-up mess. Vietnam veteran who was abused by his mom. Rich made me go to therapy for two years because he didn't want me to end up like Grandpa Marcelo. So take a lesson from three generations of Navarros. You gotta let it out."

In my mind, I see myself shatter. Nothing left but Tobin atoms, floating into the sky and over the lake. "What if I . . . can't put myself together again? Once it comes out?"

"Some days you'll fall apart, but we'll help put you back together. Some days the pain will be manageable. And those days teach you how to deal with the rest." Ike pats my leg. "Come inside. Eat, drink, give your dad a kiss. We can play a game tonight. Something goofy. And it will be fun. Even a little bit normal."

"There is no normal thing about the world right now, especially the world in this house."

"I know." He squeezes my knee. "But we can play Cards Against Humanity, and we can watch your dad laugh at the extra-gross ones. We can live the everyday moments until they run out." One last squeeze, and he goes back inside.

Watching my dad laugh is the best thing ever.

And I'm hungry.

I see a shadow come across the lake, from very far away. So small and dark. It pauses in front of me.

It's my heart.

No substance. Just a smudge.

Go ahead.

I close my eyes as the shadow settles itself where my heart belongs. Suddenly my chest aches, and I can't breathe.

I cry for fifteen minutes before I can go inside and eat lunch.

But I go in. I eat.

I watch my dad sleep while I make a slideshow of photos from his party. I see a frame around him, one that says *f a d i n g f a d i n g f a d i n g* in a loopy gray script.

When he wakes up, I kiss him on the cheek and show him what I made.

We have steak for supper, though my dad's has to be pulverized in the blender.

We play Cards Against Humanity.

My dad laughs.

I smile and cry at the same time, watching him.

Ike notices, but my dad doesn't,

and that's perfect.

Dad's Big Book of Advice #~~22~~
Work hard and be nice to people.

AUGUST 22

My dad's sleeping upright in his wheelchair, on the dunes. Ike must have moved him down there at some point. The early-morning light is kissing his face through clouds scattered on the horizon. It's maybe six o'clock, and the sun's just up. I've been up since three. Given that I went to bed at midnight, it's going to be a long day.

I soak him in: a slumped shape in the chair, messy hair, face full of stubble, legs that are way too skinny, everything wrapped in a blanket. It's an average, ordinary morning in Duluth, tourist capital of northern Minnesota, and thousands of people will be waking up to spend another day on vacation, if they're not already up to watch the sunrise. Then they'll come into Zenith City Treasure Box and walk along the lakeshore and find tiny agates and smooth pebbles of

238

shale. It will be a good day for them. And less than two miles away, Stephen Tobin Oliver's heart will stop.

I grab my camera off the back steps and take the only photos I'm taking in the next twenty-four hours: him, asleep in the sun as it rises over the water. First, I stay behind him and click off a couple shots, to see if I like the shadows, then I shift in front of him and try a couple different angles. The light is so delicate. New and precious. He almost looks healthy.

In some other dimension, he'll be able to run and work and goof off and all the things he hasn't been able to do for six months.

I cannot be happy about it. But I can be calm.

I can try, anyway.

My dad's eyes flutter open. He smiles, very faintly. "Voyageur. You weren't . . . supposed to find me here . . . what time is it?"

I check my phone. "6:01." His breathing makes talking so hard.

"Ike should . . . be down . . . anytime."

"Why so early?"

"Today we need . . . every single minute . . . both going to get . . . a workout . . . Are you . . . strong enough . . . to push me . . . closer . . . to the wet sand?"

"I'm not a weakling. And you're not that heavy." We get rolling across the dune grass, though it's tough. And I can't push him far on the beach. But he's closer to the water.

I wish for a sweatshirt, standing next to him as he's looking out over the water.

"Are you shaking?" He studies me.

"No."

He can clearly see I am. "Take it." He fumbles his blanket toward me.

"You need it."

"Not going to live . . . long enough . . . to get sick." And he laughs a real, honest-to-goodness Steve Oliver laugh, very quiet and wheezy but unmistakably his. "Take it."

I grab the blanket and pull it over my head.

"You'll miss . . . pretty colors . . . if you stay like that." His voice is so weak. So much weaker than even last week.

"I'm cold."

"I know you're . . . crying . . . Me too." A fumbling, feeble clawing comes at the blanket, not moving it, but trying to. "Honesty's . . . all we have."

I pull it off my head with the full intention to put it back over my face again, but his face stops me cold. He's so sad it takes my breath away.

"We can't both lose our shit at the same time." I reach and wipe the tears off his face, and he does the same to me, but it's more like a gentle punch, and I laugh, and he laughs, and then we can look at the sunrise.

"STEVE?!" The yell comes from behind us.

"Out here, Ike." I yell back over my shoulder.

My dad breaks out in song, quiet and wheezy, saying every third word or so. It takes me a while to realize he's singing "The Wreck of the Edmund Fitzgerald." Of course.

I start singing it with him, and it's amazing how many words I know.

Ike comes over the dune, and he sings right along with us once he hears us. "The lake, it is said, never gives up her dead when the skies of November turn gloomeeeee."

We finish the song together—Ike's strong baritone, my passable alto, and Dad's wheeze. It takes a bit, because it's a long song.

When we're done, Ike pats Dad on the shoulder. "Seriously, Steve, stop it right now. Today's not a day to be cold." Somehow that song makes you feel cold, even in August.

"Today I get ... to do ... what I want."

"Fair enough." He turns to me. "How you holding up, Tobin?"

"Dancing on the ceiling."

The smile he gives me is tender, under his own tears. "Same here."

"Enough crying ... for now ... We've got ... living ... to get done." Dad pokes at his face and tears with his uncooperative hand. "Doesn't this sunrise ... grab you?"

The wispy clouds keep the sun outlined, but the fierceness of the day is already streaming around them, getting ready to douse us with brightness. The lake is just itself, and the sand is just the sand. Squishy under my flip-flops.

Eventually Dad speaks. "Push me back ... time for breakfast."

Once Ike carries Dad up the back steps, he and I cook an enormous breakfast: pancakes, eggs over easy, and so much bacon. Ike feeds Dad more than I've seen him eat in a month: half a pancake, half an egg, and at least three strips of bacon. And we laugh. About Monty Python, the fish in Hawaii, my dad's first marathon where he got serious diarrhea that went down his leg—anything and everything he wants to talk about.

Dad falls asleep while Ike and I clean up, and we just let him rest there in the kitchen, maneuvering carefully around him so we don't bump his chair.

"Ready for this?" Ike is drying dishes while I wash. His voice is low.

I drop a glass and it shatters. I feel confident I've broken at least one glass a month for the last seven months.

"Are you cut?" He glances at Dad. No reaction. He's sacked. He's already used up so much energy today.

"No."

Ike drains the sink to clean up the glass. "All I'm doing is calling Rich, when it's time. That's it." His voice is a little louder than it has been.

"We both know that." Everything blurs in front of me.

"I'll sit with you both, once he's . . . taken it." He pats my back.

"Understood." I dry my hands on the other dish towel while Ike wipes the last few pans. Then I push Dad into the living room, so he can rest in the sun.

"Where's the stuff?" Ike follows me.

"He asked me to take it upstairs. All we need is a glass and some water for after. And the Zofran for before."

"My dad brought the Zofran last night." Ike gestures to the coffee table, at an envelope. Then he sits on the couch and closes his eyes.

I sit in the recliner. We wait for Dad to wake up. It's his day.

I drift off. But then I hear, "Tobin! . . . Up and . . . at 'em!"

Dad's smiling at me from his chair. "Where's Ike? . . . Visiting to do!"

I sit up, rubbing my eyes. "Visiting? Ike's right there." I point at Ike, asleep on the couch.

"Yes, ma'am . . . going downtown." He seems stronger, though that's not possible, strong and confident.

"We are?"

"IKE!" He hollers, like he would if Ike were in Wisconsin rather than three feet away, but he's still barely audible.

"Right here, boss. What do you need?" Ike snaps to attention like he wasn't asleep at all.

"A shower . . . then visiting . . . One last . . . constitutional. . . . Want to wear . . . my running shoes." His eyes are actually sparkling, like there's another twenty-five years to live behind them. Or fifty.

"My wish is your command." Ike wheels Dad to the bottom of the stairs, scoops him up, and heads upstairs to the bathroom.

Once Ike is done with Dad's shower, he gets Dad dressed in his boxers. Then I dress Dad the rest of the way while Ike showers. While Ike and Dad wait on the back deck, I get ready. Three of us will walk west, enjoying the sun and the day. Three of us will walk back. And then there will be two. And then, when Ike goes home, it will be me.

Dad talks about everything. And I mean everything. In breathy bursts.

"A car is . . . marvelous . . . magnificent invention . . . Or sunlight . . . Marvelous . . . Shadows . . . Breathtaking . . . And look . . . Wisconsin . . . We can see . . . another state . . . from here . . . Trees . . . squirrels . . . nature is . . . breathtaking . . . isn't it?" It's all wheezy and quiet, but it's nonstop babble. And I want to listen for a million years.

We go door to door, and store to store, wherever Dad knows somebody. He acts like he's on a grand tour, in and out of kitchens, distilleries, showrooms, and everything in between. People are happy to see him and ask him how he's been. He says the disease isn't going to win. The pity in their eyes is intense, since they know that's false, of course. I want to scream *YOU DUMBSHITS HE'S GOING TO DIE TODAY SO OF COURSE THE DISEASE ISN'T GOING TO WIN BUT HE'LL STILL BE DEAD.* But I stay quiet and try to smile.

Eventually we go by Sid, outside of Rocky Mountain Chocolate Factory, and we stop and listen for a bit, in the back of the crowd. Sid knows we're there, because I see him smiling bigger than normal. When we leave, I see Dad motion to Ike, who leans down to listen, then lifts Dad's wallet out of Dad's back pocket. A fifty drifts into Sid's violin case, and Sid's eyes get wide, but he winks at me, and I wink back.

We walk by Trash Box, but Dad doesn't want to go in. Allison sees us from behind the counter, through the window, and she waves like her hand is made of lead. She looks so sad. Dad waves back in his Muppet way, with his whole arm, and that makes her laugh, which makes Dad laugh, and then we're just having a constitutional again.

Dad's talking a mile a breathy minute about how this or that store was a titty bar when he was a kid, and who knew Canal Park would become a respectable tourist destination? I text Paul while we're window-shopping at the store next to Trash Box: *Want to come eat lunch with us? We're in front of the old titty bar (?).*

Maybe thirty seconds later, Paul is there. He doesn't say a word, just joins us.

Dad decides he wants to get takeout pizza and go out to the lighthouse, so we can watch the lake. By this time, Dad has noticed that Paul's with us, and he and Paul talk a lot about how seedy Canal Park was, and how long ago the Oliviers came to this part of the world, and every historical thing my dad's brain lands on. We grab a pepperoni pizza and some drinks, then wheel our way out toward the lighthouse, which juts out on a long cement walkway to form one part of the channel to the shipping bay. The other side of the channel is formed by Park Point and another lighthouse.

He seems so strong today. So with it.

Maybe today is too soon.

By the time we get out there, it's past lunchtime and into naptime for children and tired parents, so it's not horribly crowded. The pizza's still a bit warm, so I eat a slice. But it sits in my stomach like a ball of cement.

"Look!" Dad's trying to point out into the lake, but his hand isn't cooperating. Paul and Ike have been talking about why anyone would surf in Lake Superior when the only time there are waves are dangerous storms.

"What?" I turn. I've been staring at a family who's trying to get their pedal cart working—you can rent a covered bicycle-cart thing for four, and pedal it all up and down the lakefront—and all they've succeeded in doing is going backward.

A huge ore ship is steaming toward us. I hear the lift bridge start clicking. The ship toots, and then the bridge toots its long-short-long-short pattern, each greeting the other. The roadway creaks and groans its 125 feet up in the air.

This isn't the first ship through here today, and it won't be the last, but Dad watches like they planned it just for him. Ike hands me a Kleenex, and I wipe my eyes while he's wiping his. Paul pulls out his hanky and gives a big snort into it. The pizza is forgotten.

Then the ship turns the corner into the bay, to unload or load or whatever it's going to do, and it's gone. Dad looks disappointed. "I think . . . want to go home now."

"No more places to visit?" Ike wants to make sure.

"Nope."

"But what about ice cream?" He grins at Dad.

"Oh yeah! . . . Can't forget . . . about that." He's tired, that's clear, but there's more adventuring to be had.

"Coming right up."

It takes a while to walk over to PortLand Malt Shoppe, because it's on the other side of the highway, west of Canal Park and a bit north. It might be a twenty-block hike, but Dad dozes while Ike pushes. Paul and I just walk. Nobody talks. Once we're there, Dad wakes up and asks for an enormous chocolate malt. Ike gets chocolate mint in a cone, I get strawberry in a cup, and Paul gets nothing. I take two bites of mine, then hand it to Paul. Gag. He takes a bite and throws it in the garbage.

Dad smiles and sips at his malt on our long walk back, saying hello to people as they pass him while Ike pushes with one hand and eats his cone with the other.

As we get close to the back door of Trash Box, Paul steps in front of Dad and holds up his hand to stop Ike. "Let me go get Allison."

Dad sighs.

Paul is stern. "She's your sister."

Dad actually rolls his eyes. Ike and I share a glance, but I keep quiet.

Not thirty seconds after Paul goes inside, he's back out, with Allison at his heels. She's already started sobbing.

"You can't do this, Steve." She kneels in front of him, bare knees on the gravel in the alley. "You just can't."

"You have . . . no idea." His face is soft, amazingly, and he's looking at her with love instead of the annoyance I expected. Maybe her tears changed him.

"Think about Tobin." She glances over his head at me. I look back.

"Tobin knows ... I'm a mess."

She lays her head on his knees and sobs. He pats her hair. Paul's feelings are streaming down his face. Ike's too.

Finally, she raises her head, stands up, and brushes the gravel off her skin. "Thanks for being a good little brother. You were a jerk sometimes, but I love you."

"Love you, too ... Allison." His awkward hands reach toward her, and she bends down and hugs him so hard I think he'll shatter. When she lets him go, she backs toward the store, not taking her eyes off him. No sobs. Just tears. Then she turns and goes in, banging the door against the wall, taking out her anger and sadness on something that can't hurt her.

"I'll never see you again." Paul looks directly at Dad, straight into his eyes.

"I'll come back ... as a butterfly ... or an ore ship."

Paul chuckles, just a tiny bit, and bends down to hug my dad. "Godspeed, nephew. I'll miss you." He doesn't hug anyone else, just disappears into the back door of Trash Box, shoulders shaking as he goes.

Dad watches Paul disappear, then he starts to sob. I walk next to him to hold his hand. We're ten steps from the lift bridge when the horn starts to blow. And my dad starts muttering instead of weeping.

"Goddamn ships ... goddamn people ... driving goddam ships ... Fuckers ... people are waiting ... goddamn body." He tries to stand, even though he has no strength, and Ike gently pushes down on his shoulders. It takes nothing to stop him, even though he continues to try and get up.

"Hate people ... hate ships ... hate Duluth ... and you, Tobin ... everything ... Even you, Ike! ...Whole world! ... My body!" He's not loud anymore, but he's obviously unhappy. People notice his agitation.

"Just sit tight, Dad." I try holding his hand, but he yanks it away in slow motion.

"Have to ... get out of this chair ... Stop touching me ... Ike!"

Ike's got his hands on Dad's shoulders, and he's holding him in place.

"It's okay, Dad. Give it a minute."

Ike's eyes are leaking, too, so then we're two crying people waiting for the ship to pass under the lift bridge, with probably twenty tourists standing around us and the angry man in the wheelchair. Ike sings the Spanish lullaby, hands on his shoulders, and I rub his arm.

Once the bridge starts coming down, he settles. At this point, the twenty tourists have moved to the south side of the bridge. We're the only ones left on the north walkway.

"Look at ... shadows ... patterns ... waves ... how pretty ... the sun is ... Just look ... Tobin." He continues to talk as we go across the bridge, acting like nothing happened. The tourists on the south just stare at him while they walk across. Ike and I ignore them while Ike pushes him faster.

But once we get across the bridge and clear of the tourists, who never walk very far on to Park Point, we slow down. Way down. Ike wants to linger, too. He could be crawling and pushing my dad's chair, and it would be too fast.

Even though I want it to take a year, we make it home in half an hour. Ike carries Dad into the house and deposits him on the couch while I push his chair up the hill and put it next to the front steps.

"What now, sir? Anything we can do for you?"

Dad thinks. "Out of . . . wishes."

Silence. Nobody moves.

Finally, Ike speaks. "What does that mean?"

"It's time." Dad's voice is even more quiet than normal.

I am so cold.

Ike is solemn. "Would you like to go up to your bed?"

Dad nods toward the back door. "Probably shouldn't . . . do it outside . . . should we?"

"Probably not, just in case someone comes by."

"Move my bed . . . so I can see . . . out the window?"

"That I can do." Ike heads up the stairs.

"Tobin . . . come here." He pats the couch next to him, and I sit. Then I'm sobbing in his lap.

"Please don't do this, Dad. Please."

"Tobin." He tries to stroke my hair. "Oh . . . sweet Tobin."

"Please don't. I need you."

"Need you, too . . . And legs . . . a quiet brain . . . not me anymore."

I just clutch him and cry.

"Couldn't have asked . . . for a better . . . daughter . . . Remember that . . . okay?"

"Daddy, please." And then I can't talk, and neither can he. I feel the tears on my ear that's turned toward his face.

We stay like that for a long time. When his hand stops moving, I realize he's fallen asleep, so I sit up as carefully as I can.

Ike's in the recliner across the room, just watching us. "His bed is ready."

"Should we wake him up?" I stand and try and unkink my back.

"No." Ike yawns.

"What time is it?" I yawn, too.

"5:00."

"Maybe he'll wake up tomorrow. That'd be great."

Ike and I go into the kitchen, and I pour myself a glass of water. Ike takes a beer from my dad's stash. We sit at the table and wait. I put my head down and drift off.

A shriek makes me bolt upright. "IKE! . . . TOBIN!"

"Right here, Dad. Right here." We race into the living room like we're on fire, or Dad is.

His eyes are scared. "Devils . . . chasing me . . . in my dream . . . Won't happen . . . right? . . . Should go . . . to heaven?" He's a frightened five-year-old.

"Of course you will." Ike leans down to give him a hug, and then I do. "You're the best man I've ever known, aside from my dad."

I nod, because I can't talk.

"What can we get you, Steve? What would you like now?"

He closes his eyes and sighs. "Ready to go . . . upstairs."

"First, let's take this. So you don't throw up the drugs." He hands Dad the Zofran, then goes to get a glass of water. Dad manages to get the pill to his lips, but the glass is too heavy. Ike helps him with it, not looking at me. Then he scoops up my dad and walks by me, carrying him upstairs.

I try and slow my heart down, but it doesn't work.

Then I follow them.

Ike's rearranged Dad's room so the bed is right next to the north window. He gently sets Dad down in the bed, takes off his running shoes, then covers him up with the sheet. The late afternoon sun is gushing through the west window.

"What can I get you, Steve?"

"Glass of water ... glass ... orange juice ... for meds." Even weak and wheezy, he sounds in charge, which is a relief. "Scissors ... to get ... the box open."

"The lightest glasses we have, okay, Ike? The absolute lightest."

"I'm on it." Ike leaves.

Dad looks at me. "When you're ... an EMT ... have to be careful ... with your words. Meeting people ... on the worst days... of their lives ... Can't be rude ... or uncaring." It sounds like someone's squeezing his lungs. "Have to find ... the right words ... to help them ... with their fear ... or grief."

His face tells me he's failed me.

"I have ... no words ... for my own family ... I hate ... irony." He smiles, and tears run down his cheeks. "Love you ... Tobin ... only words ... I have." His lips are slightly blue from lack of oxygen.

"I love you, too, Dad."

Ike comes back into the room, carrying plastic glasses of water and orange juice, with scissors looped over one finger.

"There." Dad tries to point toward the bedside table, which Ike has shoved against the side of the bed. Ike sets the glasses down. "Hand me ... box." Ike does. "And scissors." Ike does.

"I'm going downstairs now, Steve." He bends and hugs my dad for a long, long time. "Please be with me when I'm working on my rig. I'll need you to watch over me."

"Will do ... son ... love you ... Isaac Richard ... Navarro."

"I love you, too." And Ike leaves, face wet, not looking at me or my dad.

Dad's face is wet, too, but he's resolute. "If I can't . . . you'll still . . ." He's breathing hard. ". . . help me?"

That question sails out the window, but the lake says nothing. She just swallows it whole, into her icy belly.

"I promised I would."

He relaxes into the pillows Ike has stacked behind his back. "No way . . . to thank you."

"Haunt the Colorado School of Visual Arts and take all my tests for me?"

"Deal." His smile is faint. "Prop me up?" I do my best with all the pillows he has. He's ready to concentrate on the box.

But he can't get it open. He works for a long time, with and without the scissors, and I see his patience fray with every move. After twenty minutes, he lies back on the pillow.

"Want me to try?"

His eyes are closed, but he nods. Just barely.

I zip the tape open. Inside, in a lot of padding, there are two small bottles. They seem too little to matter.

"Why two?"

"Had to . . . make sure . . . dose . . . high enough . . . No coma."

Oh my god. I hadn't thought of that.

I peel back the foil from the bottles, take out the corks with the scissors point, then pour the bottles into the orange juice. The bottles are half the size of those liquor servings you get on airplanes.

"Tobin."

"Yes?"

"Thanks for . . . being . . . mine." He can barely speak now, and his breathing is ragged.

"You're the best dad a girl could ask for." The tears are dripping onto my shirt.

Somehow my hand moves the glass to his mouth and tips it forward. He drinks the orange juice while my hand lifts the glass slowly, and he grimaces.

Then I pick up the glass of water. "Just to get it all down." I help him again.

When he's done with the water, he leans back on the pillows and looks out the window.

"Can you see her?" I crawl into bed next to him, and he puts an arm around me. Like we did until I was thirteen.

"See her... just fine... gorgeous... dangerous... all ours."

And we stay like that. He closes his eyes.

"Dad?"

No answer.

I sit up and look. He's unconscious. His head nods to the side.

I get out of bed and go to the top of the stairs. "Come on up, Ike."

And he does. I sit on the bed next to Dad, and Ike sits at the foot. I hold Dad's hand. We look out the window at the lake. It's 6:25.

We sit for a long time, and no time, in silence.

I will never feel like a criminal. Ever.

Closer to sunset, his breath starts to sound weird. Scary. Hitchy. Gaspy. A deep chesty rattle. There are longer and longer pauses between rattles.

Ike can see it freaks me out, and he one-arm hugs me. "It's part of the process."

The rattles keep going. My skin crawls. But I hold his hand.

Dusk comes across the lake. There's a pause. Then Dad takes a breath. His chest settles.

And doesn't rise again.

It's 8:01 p.m. The sun sets tonight at 8:06. I checked this morning.

If my dad knew he died almost exactly at sunset, he'd be laughing his ass off. He'd say it was a bad dad joke.

I look at my dad's face, expecting him to be smiling at the joke, and he's not there.

There's a body that looks like him—sort of—but he is literally not there. It's a husk. It's a meat sack. It's a thing, not a man, not my dad. It's a total cliché. But it's true.

My dad is free.

Ike stands up. "Time to call Rich."

"Is there anything I should do?"

"No. You said goodbye. Your dad's just fine. And my dad will be here in a little bit, to take care of what's left behind." He envelops me in a bear hug, then bends down to kiss my dad's body on the forehead. "Rest easy, Stephen Tobin Oliver."

I kiss Dad, too. One last time. And we go downstairs as the light fades in the window.

After Rich and Lexi have left with Dad's body, Ike hands me a note. "He wrote this for you last night."

"I don't know if I have any more tears in me."

Ike smiles a weary smile. "You still want to read it."

It looks like a pencil has attacked the paper, then self-destructed. But slowly the marks start to coalesce into words.

Dear Tobin, my sweetest girl, the most awesome person on the planet:

Death is just a change of address. I'm moving from where you can see me to where you can't. But I'm still here. Me and the lake. We'll always be here for you.

One last dad joke. What do you call a boomerang that doesn't come back? A stick!

My love is with you on your travels, Voyageur.

Dad

I fold it up, give Ike a hug, leave the note on the table, and go to bed.

There's nothing else left to do.

Dad's Big Book of Advice #23
Never give away my stethoscope.
Keep it and listen to your heart when you miss me.
I'm always there.

AFTER
AUGUST 27

It's two days after the memorial.

Allison is here with me.

I hate it.

It was bigger than Dad's birthday party. At least three hundred people. But no Mama Duck.

He wanted his service at the Beach House, so we had it on the sand, and everyone who wanted to stood up and talked about him. Then all the families of the people who work for Dad's ambulance service put on a big spread inside. My voice gave out from trying to thank people.

After everyone was gone, Allison, Paul, Ike, Rich, and I took a boat about ten miles out and scattered his ashes. Mark, the guy who owns the boat, was one of the guys who worked for their ambulance service. When we were on our way out, he told us all about the time Dad decided he was going to climb Split Rock Lighthouse and got arrested by the state park rangers. He was twenty, Mark said, and he had to go to court. Allison didn't even know about it.

Dad's ashes floated for a long time. I threw in flowers from the memorial service, too. We watched for a while, then we went back, and Ike took me home. Then everything went on.

What's not the same?

Nothing looks the same.

Or tastes the same.

Or sounds the same.

Or feels the same.

Or is the same.

But I think he's the same. He's somewhere else, but he's still the same dude. Still funny and happy. Still running and laughing and having a good time.

Gracie and Sid must have worked out a texting schedule between them. Every few hours, one of them pings me with some version of these messages: *Doing ok? Can I get you anything? Do you want me to come over?* I text each of them the same thing: *Doing OK. I don't need anything. Come over anytime, but I don't have anything to say right now.*

I'm sitting out on our beach, looking north. School starts September 4. I have no idea how to be a senior. I have no idea how to be an orphan. I have no idea how to pack my dad into boxes. So I stare at the lake.

I spend most of my time outside or in my room because I can't stand to see Dad's stuff in the house, and I won't let Allison clean it out.

I'll be eighteen at the end of September. Then she'll go home.

And it won't be soon enough.

"Tobin?" Allison is calling for me.

"Down here." Not that I want her to find me, but if she doesn't know where I am, she'll send out the cavalry.

She comes and sits next to me on the beach. "Ready for school?"

"Nope."

"Should we go shopping? Don't all senior girls need new clothes?" She smiles. "We should book your senior photos soon."

"No clothes. No photos. I'm good."

She studies me. "I know this is hard."

"I can't imagine you do but thank you."

She sighs. "I have something for you." She hands me a journal-sized book covered in black cloth. "It's from your mom. I don't know how many she sent. Rich has one, I know." She stands up. "There's a letter in the front for you. Come inside when you get hungry again." And she walks back over the dunes toward the house.

I open the book and read the note.

Dear Tobin:

In small towns in France (and sometimes in big cities), they place black funeral books on the doors of houses where people have died. People come by and write condolences in the books. When Paul told me your dad had ALS, I decided to do something similar for you. I sent a book to Allison, a book to Paul, and a book to Rich. I might send a couple others, but I'm not sure. I want you to have as many memories of your dad as possible.

Please don't be mad at Paul for telling me. He was right to do so.

I know my mothering skills are awful. Boxes of objects don't make up for anything, especially not now.

I'm going to be in the States in October. Can I come and see you? I understand if you don't want me to. But I hope you'll let me. Even though it feels like it right now, you're not really an orphan.

I love you. I hope you believe me.
Mom

Her monthly box came a day ago. I took everything in it—a French fashion magazine, some chocolate, some really expensive lip liner, judging from the package, and a T-shirt—and I buried it all right at the shore. With a shovel. Then I jumped on the spot and splashed and yelled and generally acted like I'd lost it.

Because I had.

I flip through the book, and Allison's filled it full of things I don't know. When he was a kid, when their parents were

259

alive, when she visited him in New York, when he came back to Duluth, when he married my mom, when I was born. It's all there.

"Tobin?" Another voice, but one I like.

"Down here."

Ike comes over and plops into the sand. He's got a black book in his hand, too.

"How did you know Allison just gave me hers?"

He raises an eyebrow at me. "Rich thought he was special."

"Of course he is. He's just not the only one with a funeral book."

He hands it to me. "I was there when Rich and a bunch of guys were writing in it. They were laughing their asses off."

"Perfect."

"What did insurance say?" He knows I had to meet with them. Two different insurance guys, actually, with two different kinds of policies.

"There are funds I don't get until I'm twenty-five, but I get some cash when I turn eighteen. Which is in about a month. Then Allison will go home, and I can live here by myself, and then I can go to college and have it all paid for. With maybe a little left over to live."

Ike gives me a sad face. "You know I can't live here, right?" He's been at Rich's house since Dad died. "It would look really bad. Rich would kill me."

"So get yourself a girlfriend, and then the two of you can move in. You can pay rent."

Ike chuckles. "Like he'd like that any better. And who's got time for a girlfriend? Work and school is enough."

"School?"

"Lake Superior Community College." He points in the direction of the campus. "Next semester full-time, but I'm taking an online class right now, just to get warmed up. The semester started the day your dad died, ironically."

I attack him with a hug. "Good job, dork. But seriously do find a girlfriend. I could use a sister. Just make sure she's nice."

That makes him laugh long and loud as he stands, brushing the sand off his butt. "For now, read the book. And remember what I told you. No wrong way to grieve. You just have to do it."

"Yes, sir."

"I love you, Tobin."

"Love you, too, brother."

He thumps me on the head and walks over the dunes.

I stare north into the lake.

I think about what I'll do if anyone finds out what I did. Tell the truth, I guess.

What other choice was there? He needed to be free. There was no question.

I think about how cold the lake is. It's the coldest Great Lake.

I think about being a senior. And about the Colorado School of Visual Arts, and what it's like in Colorado. I wonder where my dad is now.

It takes a bit to get his wheelchair down to the water's edge. Even empty, it's still a bitch to push through sand. It takes me a while to get the photo set up in a way that satisfies me.

I tip his chair over, headfirst, into the shallows. Like he's fallen out and drifted away. I float the action figures next to his chair: Lando, Rey, Mystique, Professor X, and next to the crowd is a tiny Mama Duck replica Chip brought for Dad.

It is surreal and weird and kind of perfect.

I get shots from several angles. Then I go up to the house, have lunch, read my funeral books, and wait for my friends to come over. Or my brother to come back. I think about how to thaw out.

I only had seventeen years with my dad, but maybe that was enough. He was kind of like a slingshot—he taught me all he could, then he launched me out into the world. Now I'm sailing over everyone's heads, with no idea where I'll land.

Maybe that's all right. He'll still be there.

Dad's Big Book of Advice #24

According to energy conservation laws,
nobody ever leaves.
We just get less orderly and more spread out.

September 15

Two pounds of paper and images are flying, trucking, delivering their way to Colorado. Dad-plus the Star Wars X-Men Fam-is all over it. Healthy dad, sick dad, laughing dad, staring dad with giant glowing duck. Not a perfect thing, but a good thing, a thing with heart, soul, and image. They can see him. Witness him. He'll get to Colorado a year before I will.

A tiny sliver of my old heart drifts on the bottom of the lake. Such a miniscule chunk of blackness, no bigger than the tiny stones scattered along the shore, dark and cold. There's a new one inside me, pieced together from shared bits of others: Ike and Paul and Sid and Rich. Some Gracie. Tiny bit of Allison. Maybe even some Meredith, plus a big yellow chunk of Mama Duck heart. It's still not sure how to beat. But it's there. In time, it will start. It will remember.

NOVEMBER 10

I make the rock cairn at the edge of the water. I picked them specially—flat, stackable—from farther up the shore. These rocks don't exist in my backyard. Here it's just sand.

Today is the anniversary of the wreck of the *Edmund Fitzgerald*, an iron ore freighter that left from here and sank a day later, killing all twenty-nine people on board. Dad would have remembered it like he always did, by playing the famous Gordon Lightfoot song once for as many times as I am old—eighteen this year. I don't know if other people in Duluth, or other people who live along Lake Superior, remember this day. But he always did.

So I'm remembering him remembering his favorite ship as he played his favorite song.

The cairn shifts a little as I place the top rock, but it holds. Five in the stack. One for him, one for me, one for Ike. One for the future. One for the past.

I had no idea that pieces of my memories would just . . . drift away. Like the ashes he became. They float off, and you know you'll never get them back.

Silly little things. Which side of the door he left his running shoes on. Which days he wanted peanut butter on his toast, and which days he wanted rhubarb jam. Stuff I didn't pay much attention to in the first place—but I should have.

Those things drift out from the shore, and all that's left is the big stuff. The color of his hair (blondie-brown, a bit of white by the end). The color of his eyes (gorgeous blue, the same shade his lake sometimes is). How he looked when he bounced out the door, on his way to save people. How tired he was when he came home. How he smiled when I told him about my day.

I have the important parts. But the ashes—the daily details—wash away.

It hurts.

He got to decide. It was his life.

But other people can be angry with his choice.

Or lonely afterward, and sad.

I'm so grateful he was my dad. Is my dad. Somewhere, he's still my dad.

My love for him is the size of this lake.

If it had been me, he would have let me choose.

The water ripples a tiny bit around the cairn, but the rocks hang on. The lake is still today. And freezing, of course.

It's only going to get colder.

But spring will return.

Even if it seems like a million years until it arrives.

ACKNOWLEDGMENTS

I like to write books that are villages. This one is no different.

Many thanks to Paul Dobratz for telling me stories about your dad, and about your dad's struggle with ALS. What a man, and what a son that man raised. You are so kind to share him with me.

Many thanks to Lisa Kronk, who I'm convinced my dad sent specially to me, for all of her expert ALS knowledge *and* her excellent proofreading skills! Thank you for helping me make Steve a living, breathing human struggling with a horrific disease.

Many thanks to SMSgt Filiverto G. Rodriguez, USAF (retired), who helped me understand Ike and where he comes from, on many different levels. Thank you to his daughter, illustrator Christina Rodriguez, for introducing me to your awesome dad. Thank you both for helping Ike and Rich become well-rounded humans, and thank you for being a living embodiment of why father–daughter relationships matter.

Many thanks to Craig Samborski, for teaching me how Mama Duck works, and for having such a cool job. Mama Duck spreads joy wherever she goes.

Many thanks to Darlene Daniels, Anishnew, Garden Hill First Nation, for her thoughts about how the Ojibwe around Duluth would have received Mariette. I hope I got it close to right.

Many thanks to Dillon Navarro, for letting me borrow his last name; to Alexa Zarn, for helping me understand a little about paramedics; to Chelsea Marie Hanson for sharing the Spanish lullaby; and to Austin Oropeza, who educated me about what Rich would bring to a birthday party.

Many thanks to to Minnesota Public Radio and Dan Kraker for reporting on Lady Superior's return of Paul Kellner's canoe.

Many thanks to the Mankato runners on Steve's Grandma's Marathon committee (especially the ones who were volunteered by their spouses): Kerri Ambrose, Ken Ambrose, Rachael Hanel, David Hanel, Kevin Langton, and Layla Pappas. Appreciation and love to Kerri for being as kind and generous in real life as Book Kerri is to Steve.

Enormous thanks to the people who got this book's journey started (Amy and Kat) and to the people who finished it (Michael and Nicole). Without the four of you, Tobin, Steve, and Ike would be nowhere. Thank you to Stacey Barney for the seed of the idea for this book. Thank you to all the folks at Skyhorse who helped make this book a physical reality.

Heaps of thanks to the Lobitz family for introducing my family to Lake Superior and including us in trips to your favorite place. Thanks to the city of Duluth and the North Shore for being you. Thanks to Lake Superior for all her treasures, both tangible (rocks!) and inscrutable. Thanks to Park Point for being the perfect place to set a book (I realize there isn't a dock at the Beach House, but please allow me some creative liberty), and thanks to Gordon Lightfoot for "The Wreck of the Edmund Fitzgerald."

As always, my heart belongs to Dan and Shae, for so many reasons, but especially for putting up with someone who writes books. You are always and forever my loves.

And, as always, many thanks to my Siblings in Ink, for your expertise in helping me get and keep my shit together. Thank you for your brilliance, and for fifteen years of writing books together.

If I have forgotten anyone, or made any mistakes, I humbly apologize.